There was something here that
Lavasseur simply could not understand.

In France, this girl would
be courted and flirted with
as naturally as breathing.

Gaiety and laughter were in her;
he was sure of that.

But she was stifled
in some way, held down.

Somewhere
beneath that docile exterior,
there were banked fires waiting.

With a touch of illogical recklessness,
he wished that his
might be the hand
to stir the sleeping embers,
and he knew
in a moment of real regret
that this could never be.

Her Contrary Heart

Lois T. Henderson

LIVING BOOKS
Tyndale House Publishers, Inc.
Wheaton, Illinois

First printing, Living Books edition, November 1984

Library of Congress Catalog Card Number 84-51320
ISBN 0-8423-1401-6, paper
Copyright © 1974 by Lois T. Henderson
Printed in the United States of America

In loving tribute to the memory of
Lois T. Henderson,
beloved wife of Albert J. Henderson

Foreword

This is a captivating account of a real girl whose life spanned the three most important periods in the history of the Harmony Society.

Though fictionalized, the narrative follows historic events very closely and successfully captures the essence of Harmonist life and thought.

By careful use of existing documents, Lois Henderson has not only recreated the Harmonist spirit, but she has skillfully depicted a beautiful, innocently seductive, impulsive, and warm human being in the person of the lovely Harmonist, Hildegarde Mutschler.

The reader (even one such as I who has worked extensively with the local documents) is caught up immediately in the absorbing story of a sweet and poignant romance, and puts it aside reluctantly at its conclusion.

Josephine M. Elliott
Archivist, Indiana State University

Preface

In 1803, Johannes Georg Rapp left Germany to seek religious asylum in the United States. Long dissatisfied with the coldness of the state church and plagued by official persecution when he tried to worship in his own way, Father Rapp, as he was known by his followers, felt that he might find peace in America. He found more than peace; he established one of the most successful communitarian societies of the nineteenth century. In less than fifty years, he built three towns in Pennsylvania and Indiana, led his society in the development of successful manufacturing, agriculture, and trade, and never wavered for a minute from his conviction that Christ would return to rule upon this earth. The Harmonists, Father Rapp's followers, lived and worked and prayed, trying to purify their lives that they might be fit to be the "bride of Christ" when he returned for his earthly reign.

Among his followers, there was a family named Mutschler. Hildegarde Mutschler, beautiful and spirited, did not live to be old, but her influence, whether for good or ill, was great. She and the others who shape this story were not created from imagination. With a few minor exceptions, they were all real people, but their lives bear the mark of fiction. I have tried to tell their story honestly and with understanding.

Note: Several minor incidents and one major event (the attempted elopement of Gertrude Rapp) are based on the author's imagination and/or the faded remnants of old rumors. Almost all other events in the story are based on fact.

Introduction

MARCH 1825

For a decade, for ten holy years, the village of New Harmony on the Wabash River in southern Indiana had grown and prospered. Its nearest neighbors, whether or not they approved of its inhabitants, were forced to admit that here was a vigor and power seldom seen in America in the early nineteenth century. The vine had grown, sturdy and strong, putting forth leaf and fruit, and the resulting wine, purple and sweet, had sold downriver for much good silver. The textile factories had buzzed with incredible industry, the brick kilns had poured forth building material for the rosy houses, all built alike, and the gardens had produced such excellent produce that the central store could sell it to neighboring communities, because even rural people recognized superior quality when they saw it.

Now a change had taken place. The factories were silent, many of the vines had been uprooted for transport, and most of the houses wore a silent, shuttered look. Gossip had it that the town had been sold lock, stock, and barrel, and the people were moving back to Pennsylvania. But although one found it hard to believe that a town could be sold, evidence seemed to indicate that the gossip was true. A strange assortment of men and women under the direction of some young English visionary— did they say his name was Robert Owen?—had come in, and the sober, reserved, quiet people who had built the village were slowly disappearing. Several boatloads of them had gone in the fall and early winter, and now, on this day of thin March sunshine, another steamship had pulled up to the wharf, and the people—women and girls mostly with only a few men—were carrying everything that wasn't fastened down into the interior of the boat. It was like an exodus, if one wanted to be biblical. And if one were to judge from the hymns that rang out from the church on Sundays and Wednesdays, there was much here to be biblical about.

But an exodus? In this day and age? The neighbors shook their heads and clucked their tongues. Of course, it would be no great loss if they left, these Harmonists. Unsociable they were, quiet and unfriendly and pulled into themselves. Hardly ever spoke to a man, even when they passed him on the road. What's more, none of them spoke English. They'd been in this country for twenty years, or so some people said, and they still spoke only German—and some sort of a dialect at that.

Seems they could at least learn to say "Good morning" like civilized people, so the neighbors said tartly to each other and then went on about their own business. There was more to do on a March morning in rural communities than to speculate about a people who remained strangers even though they had lived for a decade in this land.

But how could they know the truth, these simple people of Indiana who judged from exteriors? What could they know of the Harmonists, the chosen people, who had heard the word of God louder and more plainly than they had ever heard a temporal sound?

No one could know, of course. No one except the few who listened and understood and followed, without question, the ordinances of God's newest prophet, Father Rapp. To ordinary men, George Rapp might be only a vinedresser and a sort of mayor, perhaps, who was an acknowledged leader of his people. But to the knowing, to those who had been touched with the flame of truth, he was a prophet who had been chosen to lead his people to a promised land. New Harmony was the third place these people had gathered together, but even here, the journey was not finished.

Walking alone in the maze that twisted through the gardens, Father Rapp listened for instruction. And finally God spoke to him, told him that this was not the place to wait for the second coming of Christ. As God had told him in

Germany and again in the first village of Harmony that he must lead his people forth, so now he spoke again, and the heart of the old man quivered within his breast.

"Thus saith the Lord," Father Rapp thundered to his people, his strong, old face kindled to a beauty by the intensity of his vision. And no man among them questioned God's word. If there were women who looked at their neat yards and tidy houses with eyes that blurred with tears, they let no one see. And earnest prayer soon dried their tears.

If the men were driven by duty and the women by the strength of prayer, the young people were spurred by a fervor that burned hotly in them. And perhaps there was none more fervent, nor more the victim of her fervor than Hildegarde Mutschler. The daughter of Gerhard and Christina Mutschler, she had been born into the Society, had never known any life outside of it. She was eighteen, slender, and lovely with fair skin and honey-gold hair that twisted into small curls when it could escape the tight braids; she had neat, regular features (except for a mouth that was a trifle too wide) and eyes so blue there was always summer in her glance. She was quick and eager, warm and giving, but her fervor made her feel that her gaiety was wrong, and she struggled to be a model Harmonist. When she failed, it was with the utter, total feeling of calamity; when she walked in grace, she heard the angels singing around her head.

No one among the Harmonists went to his

knees more willingly than Hildegarde. But no one else laughed with such delight over the playfulness of new kittens or the discovery of the first white trillium in the spring or the antics of long-legged, awkward calves. And those who loved her watched and held their breath, not quite sure how she would be blown by the winds which buffeted her with such contrary forces.

Chapter 1

On the March day that the steamship arrived in New Harmony, Hildegarde was everywhere at once. She was not nearly as concerned about her clothing or the furniture as she was about the seedlings and plants which were her particular responsibility. She had acquired a fair amount of botanical knowledge, and her hands possessed that peculiar magic which could take the weakest seedling and make it put forth new roots and grow toward lusty maturity. For nearly a year, she had held the position of chief gardener for the central gardens, and it was a position she loved and performed with zeal.

More than once she stumbled over the piles of articles on the floor as she made her way from the sunny riverbank into the dark interior of the cargo deck. But nothing dampened her eagerness, and her laughter spilled over into the air.

"You seem unduly happy, Sister Hildegarde," a dour-looking man said to her finally. "We're working for a holy cause, you know. I'm not sure that such levity is seemly."

Hildegarde clapped her hand over her mouth. This was a voice of authority. Romelius Baker, storekeeper and scribe, was a man to be respected.

"I'm sorry, Brother Romelius," she said. "I know I ought to be quieter, but I'm just so glad that this day is finally here, I guess. The winter has been long—just waiting."

Romelius Baker cleared his throat, and a younger man standing in the doorway spoke up.

"Never mind, Brother Romelius," he said. "One can hardly expect kittens or new chicks or children to be properly silent."

Hildegarde felt a quick blaze of anger. "I'm not a child," she said hotly, unable to keep the quick words from pouring out. "I beg your pardon, Brother Conrad, but I'm not a child!"

Conrad Feucht only smiled in a calm, superior way that incensed her further.

But before Hildegarde could say more, Romelius spoke sharply. "Enough of this," he said. "You aren't helping matters, Brother Conrad. We won't discuss it anymore."

Hildegarde felt the quick choking of tears in her throat. It had happened again—the familiar temper blurring the noble resolve she made each morning on her knees: to be as calm, as steady, as devout as Father Rapp. She pulled her skirt close and turned to leave the boat, averting her face and blinking hard to keep back the tears.

Brother Conrad spoke lightly. "Don't cry, Sister. I was only teasing. I'm just as glad as you are that today has finally arrived."

She stopped, startled. Although he was young, Brother Conrad already had a prominent position in the Society. She couldn't believe that he had spoken almost as though he were begging her pardon.

Conrad turned away from her. "Forgive us, Brother," he said to Romelius. "We aren't as wise as we ought to be."

Conrad did not turn toward Hildegarde again, and she felt that his back to her was a deliberate kindness, presenting her with the opportunity to escape an awkward situation. She ran swiftly down the gangplank and started up the long, narrow street that led to her house. The garden stuff was all packed and safe now, so she could go home to see if her mother needed anything. As she walked along the street, her eyes saw the early signs of spring—the swollen buds on the trees, the rank green in the fence corners—but her mind kept darting back to the boat. The memory of Conrad's last statement to Romelius Baker kept repeating itself in her memory. "Forgive us," he had said, as though they were friends, as though he were merely one of the boys who worked under her direction in the gardens, as though he were not a doctor, second only to Dr. Mueller who was nearly as great as Father Rapp.

Her steps slowed as she tried to comprehend it all. She wondered if possibly, just possibly, Conrad was remembering his own youth, when he was only eighteen and life had bubbled sweetly and irrepressibly in his veins. Or had it? Hadn't he always been biddable and wise?

Memory came suddenly to Hildegarde. How many years ago had it been when she had been witness to the act that had changed Conrad's life? Six years at least. She had been only about twelve, a thin little girl with long braids and boundless energy. Her companion that day, as on so many days, was Gertrude Rapp, a sturdy, round-faced little girl, sweet and sensible, granddaughter of Father Rapp, two years younger than Hildegarde. They had finished their lessons and were sitting on the grass under the elm trees, weaving daisies into chains. They talked as they twisted the long green stems together, paying no attention to the young man who was working in the garden near them.

Then suddenly men's voices filled the air, and the little girls looked up to see Father Rapp and Dr. Mueller coming across the grass. Hildegarde stared with admiration at the two men. How straight they were, how wise. Dr. Mueller was the shorter, and his brown hair and beard shone with a hint of red in the bright sun. He was gesturing with his hands and talking earnestly to the old man who walked beside him. Father Rapp's hair was almost totally white, even then, and it hung to his neck and curled around his ears, growing down his cheeks to mingle with the luxuriant white beard which was long enough to touch his breast. He walked as he always did, hands clasped behind him, head bent a little. When he walked like that, meditating, thinking who knew what, it behooved a child to get out of the way without delay if she did not want to be stepped on. Hildegarde and Gertrude watched as the two men came up to the boy in the garden.

"Is this the one?" Father Rapp asked.

"Yes, Brother." Only the doctor and a few other men called him "Brother." It would have been disrespect or worse for a younger person to use any title but "Father." "This is the boy. Conrad Feucht. A bright lad. Steady and dependable."

While the two men talked, the young boy looked up at them from his kneeling position on the ground, and from where she sat, Hildegarde could see the hard pulse that beat in his temple as his eyes swung from one man to the other.

"How old are you, Brother Conrad?" Father Rapp asked.

"Eighteen, Father." Still the boy knelt as if he had forgotten how to stand. His eyes, very blue in the sunshine, looked a little scared, Hildegarde thought, which was foolish. Father Rapp was no one to be afraid of, she reflected; he was kind and loving if you were good, but maybe this Conrad Feucht hadn't been good. Maybe he had taken more than his share from the common storehouse. She listened with curiosity.

The old man stared at the boy for a minute and then spoke decisively. "We've chosen you to go into the world, Brother Conrad. You'll be Brother Christoph's assistant, which means you'll have to learn English, and travel, if necessary, to buy medicines—or do whatever else Brother Christoph wants you to do. Do you understand?"

The boy got to his feet, and Hildegarde saw his big hands clench and unclench. There was neither excitement nor regret on the narrow, clever face.

"Yes, Father. I understand. I'll do my best."

The old man smiled, and his face was suddenly almost beautiful. "I'm sure you'll do very well indeed, with God's help. Brother Christoph, train him as you please." He turned on his heel and headed across the garden, nearly running over the two little girls and never even seeing them surrounded by their daisy chains.

"We'll talk about this later," Dr. Mueller said to the boy. "When you've finished your work in this end of the garden, come over to the apothecary room."

Hildegarde saw the doctor's hand drop with an affectionate squeeze onto the boy's shoulder and then he, too, turned and left the garden. Hildegarde watched the boy very closely, her hands resting quietly on the blossoms. He was standing motionless, his eyes staring sightlessly in front of him, the pulse hammering in his temple. Young as she was, Hildegarde knew that his life had been completely altered in that brief exchange of words. Was he scared? Hildegarde wondered. Would he rather stay in his garden where he always seemed to work with such joy?

But he had made no protest, she realized. He had merely looked at the old man standing before him and had agreed. Hildegarde abruptly turned her eyes away from the boy, feeling as though she had no right to look at him. She remembered with a terrible feeling of guilt all the times she had questioned the orders her mother gave her, even rebelling against the hours she had to spend doing tasks, regardless of how light or simple they might be. How many times had she stolen away to climb trees or get disgracefully muddy and wet playing along the river edge?

She looked at Gertrude through her lashes, but Gertrude was busy with the daisy chains, her face as serene as ever. Gertrude would never argue or rebel; Gertrude would see nothing brave or wonderful in Conrad Feucht's complete obedience. *It's only me,* Hildegarde thought miserably, *I'm the only one who is ever bad.* Out of the corner of her eye, she looked again at the boy who stood in the garden. As she watched, he turned his head and saw her. Amazingly, he grinned at her—a wide, happy grin that made him look very young—and then he dropped to his knees and began again to do the task which had been interrupted by the coming of the men. . . .

In the cold March sunshine, Hildegarde stood completely still, remembering that day. How awful of her to get angry on the boat just now, to have forgotten what Conrad was like. He wasn't thinking of himself when he used the pronoun "we," she realized. He was only being kind, taking attention away from her, sharing her guilt.

I'll never get angry again, she vowed, terribly solemn—*never, never*—and knew, even as she vowed it, that she was a creature of impulse, and that this was her gravest sin.

Next morning in the Mutschler home, bare now of furniture, Hildegarde and her mother woke to the first faint sound of birds. From their pallets on the floor, they looked at each other in the hesitant light of dawn.

"It has really come," Frau Mutschler said heavily. Part of her yearned to be reunited with her husband and son who had gone to Economy many months before, but part of her clung to the familiar house.

Hildegarde sat up swiftly, hugging her arms around her knees. "Oh but, Mutter, I'm so happy. Aren't you happy, too?"

"This has been a good home," the woman said slowly, hesitating to voice her reluctance even to her child.

Hildegarde flipped her hand in a casual gesture. "Of course, it's been a good home," she said impatiently. "A perfectly lovely one. But don't you think the houses in Economy will be as nice? Maybe even nicer. There are hills there, you know. Not flat and plain like here."

Frau Mutschler struggled to her feet. Her body was thickened by good food and hard work, but her wide, calm face bore the memory of beauty. "You're young," she observed. "You don't even know what you're talking about. But it's good to be young, I suppose." Then her voice grew stern. "Braid your hair," she said. "We have to hurry. You know they want to leave at the first possible minute. So don't dawdle."

"Yah," Hildegarde said and lowered her lids so that her mother might not see the excitement which she knew was dancing in her eyes.

As they all hurried from the dormitory where breakfast had been eaten, Hildegarde paused in the entry. Under the stairwell, one of the members had scrawled in chalk ten months before, "On the twenty-fourth of May 1824, we have departed. Lord, with thy great help and goodness, in body and soul protect us." Her fingers touched the chalked words, careful not to smear them, and her lips moved, saying the words.

Her mother came to stand beside her. "The Lord will *have* to be with us," Frau Mutschler said. "It's a long way, and the river is high and wild this time of year."

But it was impossible for Hildegarde to feel any reluctance or fear about the trip. The journey's end was the only thing she cared about.

At the river's edge, all of the members of the Society who were still in Indiana gathered together, and Hildegarde felt the warmth of love fill her heart. She wanted to gather them all in—the old men, the quiet, red-cheeked women, the few children—and tell them that she loved them, but she kept silent, letting the love have its way with her rapidly beating heart while trying to keep as much of it as possible out of her face.

Brother Frederick, Father Rapp's adopted son, stepped before the people. He was a tall, handsome man about forty years old. All her life, Hildegarde had heard of Frederick's honesty, his skill, his wisdom. And yet she did not love Frederick the way she loved Father Rapp. She respected him with all her heart, but she was a little afraid of him. His dark eyes had a way of seeming to look directly through her, and she had the uncomfortable feeling that he could see any flaws in her nature which might successfully be hidden from others.

He began to pray, and the heads of the people bowed in earnest supplication. Then Frederick started to sing, and all of the voices joined in, strong and true.

> *Harmony du Bruder Stedt, Friede soll*
> *rich decken*
> *Gott sei mir dir frue und spat, Kein*
> *Feind darf dich schrecken;*
> *Denn die Zeit ist numehr da, wo du*
> *kanst bestchen;*
> *Gott ist seinem volke nah, er vird dich*
> *erhohen.**

And then they were on the boat, and the wheels were beginning to turn, slowly at first,

---

*Harmony, thou brother state, peace unto thee ever.
God be with thee soon and late, foes affright thee never.
For it doth now appear, Thou are steadfast, Holy.
God unto his flock is near, and he will extol thee.

spilling water like jewels in the morning air. Standing on the deck, Hildegarde found herself clutching her hands tightly together. But it wasn't fear; it was necessity. If she didn't squeeze her hands together, they would clap at the joy which filled her, at the journey which was about to begin, and at the new life which waited at the other end of it.

Chapter 2

The first day on the river was unseasonably warm for the end of March. The sky was softly blue with only a few traces of cloud, and the sun touched the skin with tender warmth. Spring seemed to be crowding into the Wabash valley with a rush, turning the willows green, thrusting daffodils above the dark earth, blurring the maple branches with pink buds. Clear and dark, boiling past the sides of the *Bolivar*, the river splashed away from the huge wheel with a cheerful sound. Hildegarde was enchanted with the boat and the weather. After she had explored all decks of the boat, being awed and impressed by the chandeliers, carved woodwork and plush seats in the central lounge on the passenger deck, she spent as much time as possible on the walkway outside the women's cabins, basking in the sunlight like a contented cat, delighting in the hours that had no specific tasks to fill them.

But the brief gold-tinted journey on the Wabash was only a deceptive prelude to the struggle up the Ohio River. Once the turn had been made and the laboring journey against the Ohio's wild, spring current had begun, everything changed. The weather decided to be honest and act like the last few days in March should act, and the skies, smeared with dark, ragged clouds, seemed to drop almost to earth. Even the members of the Harmonist band who were on the boat found little inspiration for their evening concerts, and the tunes they played were somber and depressing.

One dark day after a week or more of the dismal cold, Hildegarde found her way down into the cargo deck to check on the tiny sprouts of fruit trees and the Golden Rain trees which she had brought wrapped in burlap. Crisply, efficiently, she saw to it that the moisture was maintained, and she made careful notes in her small book. Ducking her head, she came out of the dim interior to the cleared deck space which surrounded the cargo hold. She grasped the railing and faced into the wind, feeling an exhilaration at being so close to the wild motion of the river.

A strange voice spoke at her shoulder.

"Ain't it a little cold to be out on the open deck? A young girl like you?"

Hildegarde smiled at the pilot's mate who stood facing her. "I am not understand," she said carefully in English. "I speak German."

Actually, she could understand a small amount of English, because she and Gertrude and Pauline Speidel had studied it for awhile, but she felt awkward and inept in it.

The man shrugged. "I been hauling you Harmonists up and down this river for months now," he said just as though she could understand every word. "But I sure don't understand you. Talking German like you was still in Germany, all dressed alike, with nothing different about any of you. Like you was cut off a pattern."

She smiled politely but helplessly. His pronounciation was completely incomprehensible to her.

The man smiled back, her inability to speak English in no way deleting from the fact that she was a pretty girl and it had been a dull morning.

"Current's getting mighty strong," he said, leaning over the rail.

Hildegarde looked obediently at the water, wondering if he had said it was pretty or dangerous or shallow.

"Pilot's cutting over toward the shore," he said. "Sometimes its safer that way, but I think he's making a mistake today."

She nodded her wind-mussed head, and the man admired the curly wisps of hair that had escaped her braids. He wished she could speak English; he had a hundred questions he'd like to ask about these Harmonists and their queer ways. But they all shut up when you asked them anything. Pretended they couldn't speak English or looked dark as a thundercloud when you asked about the personal things, like was it true they owned everything in common? Or far more unbelievable, was it possible that a man lived with his wife as though they were brother and sister instead of man and wife? Probably a crazy rumor. A man was a man even if he did wear odd hats and put all his grain into a common warehouse. But not to sleep with the woman he married! What would make a man do a thing like that? Especially if they had girls in their society that looked like this one.

There was a sudden hard jolt; Hildegarde lost her balance and struggled to keep from falling. The mate caught her in his arms, bracing his body against the lurch of the boat, sharply aware of the soft warmth of her body.

She looked at him with the naive gratitude of a child. There was no coquetry in her glance, no awareness of his masculinity.

"Thank you," she said in breathless, pretty English. "What is?"

"We've run aground on a mud bank," he said, setting her free. There was no excitement in holding a woman who didn't even know she was being held. "I knew it wasn't the place to try to go near shore. I'll go up and see what's to be done."

The boat seemed to tremble, and although Hildegarde had not understood all that the man said, she grasped the idea that the boat had run aground. She supposed she ought to go up to be with the women, but stubbornly she remained where she was, feeling a quickening of her heart at the possibility of danger.

There were shouts from the pilot's cabin and

dark-skinned men ran out from the furnace room to look at the situation, to gaze aloft for instruction.

"We'll back 'er up and try again," shouted the pilot. "Give 'er full steam when I give the word."

The large paddle wheel in the back reversed itself and dug into the water, but the boat did not move. The Harmonist men began to come down from the passenger deck and gather near the rail. For a few minutes Hildegarde was ignored, and then Romelius Baker approached her.

"Sister Hildegarde, what are you doing down here alone?"

She knew what her reaction ought to be. She was fully aware of the proper reply, compliant and gentle, but she looked up into the somber face of Romelius and allowed stubborness to have its way with her.

"I was checking on my trees," she said, "and I decided it was more exciting down here than up above. Especially when we got stuck."

He looked as though there was a quick answer in his mouth, but he swallowed it and turned away. "Do as you please," he said. "You know your duty."

Yes, she knew her duty—even when she didn't like it. With only a backward glance, she mounted the steps and entered the cabin.

Frau Mutschler looked up from her knitting. *How could they remain so calm,* Hildegarde thought, *with the boat lurching and struggling beneath them?*

"Are the little trees all right?" Frau Mutschler asked.

"They needed more water. I don't want the roots to dry out. Do you know we're stuck on a mud bank?"

Her mother looked so frightened that Hildegarde instantly regretted her quick words.

"Stuck?" Frau Mutschler gasped. "Will we blow up and sink?"

"I'm sure not," Hildegarde said. "But I think the men are going to have to get out and pull."

"We can pull too," the mother said. She gathered her knitting resolutely into a ball and got to her feet. "We'll go down and see," she added.

Most of the women in the cabin followed Frau Mutschler's lead and put away their handiwork to go to the deck below. Hildegarde followed, glad that there was now a reason for her to go back out into the cold air. She saw the mate hurrying down from the pilothouse, his face tight with concern.

"She'll have to be pulled off," he announced to the men. "Think there's enough of you to do it?"

Brother Romelius stepped forward, and his English was heavily accented but completely adequate. "Yah, there is plenty of us. The womans can help, too."

The man looked doubtful. "Women? It's hard work."

"They do haying and farming," Romelius said. "Strong enough they are."

There was still doubt on the mate's face, but he began to rap out orders which were immediately translated into German by Romelius. In an amazingly brief time a cable was thrown out, and the Harmonists were rowed ashore to take their positions along its length, preparing to haul the boat from its mud prison.

Hildegarde, like the other women, was placed between two of the men and when the cry of the pilot, "Haul away!" rang across the water, she felt a sudden exhilaration at the taut power of the cable in her hands. She braced her feet against the wet earth, concentrated on the black-jacketed man in front of her, and tugged with all her strength. At first they were unsuccessful, and they stopped to rest. Then the call came again and the mighty, joint effort exerted a pull that tightened the cable until drops of water flicked off it like small frightened transparent bugs. Still the boat remained stationary.

Someone started a rousing hymn of praise. By straining, Hildegarde could see that it was young Conrad Feucht, who had spent this entire trip studying his books. Now his voice rang out clearly, bringing the other voices in with it, and the unified strength of the people seemed to pour out with the music. And the boat moved. There was a shudder and a wrench and then it was floating free.

"I daren't wait to pick you up here. There's a dock up the river about half a mile. Can you walk it?" The pilot's words swept in on the chill wind, and Romelius translated.

"First we pull his boat, then we have to walk part of the way," said Hildegarde tartly.

The man in front of her turned and smiled

dourly. "Just be grateful you don't have to walk *all* the way," he said. "Or ride a flat boat out in this kind of weather."

Hildegarde lifted her chin, prepared to answer sharply but she caught a warning look from her mother. With obvious reluctance she swallowed the retort. Then to her astonishment, she found that Conrad Feucht was looking at her with an expression that could almost be interpreted as approval.

"She's right," he said. "I'm not sure our contract calls for full payment if we're put to such trouble."

"Brother Frederick will know," one of the men said comfortably. "He can't be hoodwinked by anybody. No one pulls anything over on *him*."

Everyone nodded in agreement and turned resolutely to walk along the riverbank. Hildegarde shrugged, thinking how typical it was that her opinions would be regarded as impertinence but Brother Frederick's opinions would be honorable and worthy. She wavered for a second between anger and amusement and then decided it wasn't worth her concern.

The hike along the wet, marshy riverbank was anything but pleasant, and a fine chill rain started to fall which only added to the discomfort. Hildegarde felt her dress sticking to the back of her neck and a quick shiver passed over her body.

"Are you cold?" her mother asked with some anxiety. "You mustn't get chilled, or you'll get the lung fever again." She pulled her own shawl from her shoulders and placed it about the nar-

along the shore, and there was the excited sound of people running down to the bank to stare across the water toward the *Bolivar* with its cargo of humanity and song.

Shouts rang across the water—questions and a name repeated over and over. Straining to hear, to understand, Hildegarde finally caught the name.

"It's Lafayette," she explained to her mother and the women beside her. "They're calling for Lafayette. Do you suppose they think he's on board? Is he around here?" She heard Brother Romelius call a question in English up toward the pilot deck.

The pilot's mate leaned precariously over the railing of the pilot deck, far above their heads. "They think Lafayette is on board," he shouted down. "He's due to come up the river any day now on his way to Pittsburgh. They think the band is playing because he's on board."

Romelius translated, and the soft sound of mirth drifted among the Harmonists. What a ridiculous idea! A great general like Lafayette associating with the likes of them.

Brother Conrad, who was acting as band leader since Dr. Mueller was not on board, whispered quickly to the man nearest him, and the whisper traveled among all the musicians. With a quick sweep of his hands, Brother Conrad marked the downbeat, and the rousing strains of the "Marseillaise" rang across the water. The cries of the people on shore got fainter and fainter, but it was clear to Hildegarde what they were saying. Hooray for Lafayette! Vive le Lafayette!

She giggled. It was something the Harmonists did not usually do—deliberately make a joke. But, oh, what a delicious one! Probably years from now, some of these folks would be telling their grandchildren that they had seen the boat on which the famous old general made his way to Pittsburgh. *I wish it were real*, Hildegarde thought. *I wish I could really see him. I wish I could meet him and talk to him and*—and her thoughts drifted into the daydreams of the young, peopling her world with the great and the famous, the elegant and the beautiful.

The fair weather lasted for the rest of the journey, and Hildegarde endured the passing hours with steadily mounting excitement. When the word spread through the people that they had reached Pennsylvania, and that the next day would find them at Economy, she felt so happy that she wanted to run with the wind in her face or stand on a high hill and laugh at the sky. But there was no place to run, and the hills which leaned against the sky were quite inaccessible to her on the slowly moving boat.

She stood outside the women's cabin and gazed at the hills which lined the river. She had almost forgotten what they were like. After all, she had been only eight years old when they went to Indiana, and so it seemed as though she had lived all her life on the flat land by the Wabash. But now, with the hills around her again, climbing darkly into the sky, she felt the stirring of old memories. She remembered the times she had climbed the rounded slopes behind the first village of Harmony in Pennsylvania and had stood above her known world, like a queen, like a magic child. And, oh, how close she had been to God.

Now the hills were bringing it all back, and she knew that she was going to be happy here. This would be a land of enchantment to her—lovelier than anything she had known before because these hills were higher and darker than the ones she had climbed as a child.

During the morning of the last day, they passed a small town, and the mate cried down from the pilothouse. "Beaver. That's Beaver. Won't be long now. We'll shoot a warning. Let 'em know we're coming."

Romelius was not there to translate, so the loud boom of the cannon brought a cry of terror from many of the women and caused Hildegarde's heart to pound hard enough to jar her body. But she realized at once what had happened, and joy filled her. They must be almost home!

The next time the mate shouted over the rail, they were prepared for the cannon shot even though they could not understand the words.

"Next town Economy!" shouted the mate, and they all recognized the word and gathered at the rail. The minutes passed slowly, and Hildegarde scanned the wooded shore that sloped down to the river. The boat steamed around a slight bend, and there on the left side of the river was a crowd of people waving their arms and shouting greetings. They had heard the cannon's warning and had come to greet the *Bolivar*.

Hildegarde saw the familiar flat-crowned black hats of the men, the long, full-skirted blue dresses of the women; she heard the voices calling in the Swabian dialect, and she found herself waving with great excitement, straining to see faces clearly. It seemed as though she ought to jump out of the boat and start swimming, just to get there faster.

Finally, the *Bolivar* was close enough to shore that individuals could be recognized. There was Hildegarde's father waving and smiling, his blue eyes touching Hildegarde's face warmly and then searching among the other faces until they found Frau Mutschler. His lips moved, saying her name, and then he looked away until he no longer felt the warmth of his blood in his cheeks. There was Gertrude, pink-cheeked and eager, and Maria waving excitedly. There were the others—the well-known, beloved family— but where was Father Rapp?

The sun started to slip behind the hills across the river, and the apricot glow it cast seemed to color the Harmonists with its beauty. Just as the boat bumped softly against the shore and three agile men leaped out to moor the lines in the bollards, Hildegarde saw him. He had evidently been working until the last minute and had hurried down the long slope to meet the boat, running like a young man in spite of the fact that he was seventy-two years old.

His face looked strong and glad and filled

with welcome, and the light of the setting sun shone around him with a glory. Hildegarde stood motionless at the rail.

"I'm scared," she confided to her mother. "I don't feel—worthy."

"Nonsense!" Frau Mutschler said, but her voice trembled. "You're being silly."

"Not silly, Mutter. Just—well, it's like looking at heaven."

But her mother was no longer listening, and Hildegarde was caught in the crush of the eager family crowding toward the shore.

Chapter 3

All the rest of her life, in trying to recapture her first impressions of Economy, Hildegarde found herself unable to sort out individual, distinct sights and sounds. Her blurred memory sharpened into focus, however, at the moment that she first stepped into the brick house which was to be her home. Built like the others, it still managed to give out an air of warmth and simple dignity and charm. The brick, made in their own kilns which were already operating, was a clear, soft red. Inside, the square entry hall with its stairway angling to the upstairs, the small kitchen, the large family room and the bedrooms were all plastered with clean white plaster, and the windows which let in the last of the daylight were recessed above the deep sills.

Hildegarde walked from room to room, enchanted with all that she saw, not concerned at all with the exterior town, its factories or inn, or even the gardens behind the Great House which would be her working site. Now, for this minute, it was enough to be inside these doors, home at last.

But there was no time for leisure or dreamy gazing out of windows. The boat had to be unloaded before the darkness settled. Regardless of weariness or the excitement of homecoming, Hildegarde and the other Harmonists had to begin bringing up their possessions from the *Bolivar*. She worked hard, but the final loads had to be carried in with the aid of torchlight, and more than once she stumbled wearily on the unfamiliar ground. The task was accomplished at last and the *Bolivar* steamed on toward Pittsburgh.

Then, in spite of the general fatigue, there was a call for a meeting on the large plot of ground between the river and the Great House. They sat on benches—women on one side, the men on the other.

Hildegarde found herself suddenly and overwhelmingly sleepy, and only the sternest self-discipline kept her awake. She was roused a little by the singing of a hymn of praise, but when Father Rapp stood to speak, she had to fight to keep her eyes open. The old man's face, ruddy in the torchlight, was both loving and stern. Hildegarde listened to his expression of gratitude to God that a part of the family had arrived safely, but she was really too tired to grasp the stern injunction which followed.

"Withdraw from the temptations of the enemy and the world, that you may keep your inheritance among the true Israelites," he said with intensity.

The words, or words like them, were so familiar to Hildegarde that she felt no real reaction at all. It never occurred to her that the old man might be preaching directly to men and women like her parents who were newly reunited and who might find the first hours difficult in spite of their piety and obedience. She only hoped, a little fuzzily, that the talk would be brief.

Mercifully, feeling the exhaustion of his flock, Father Rapp cut short his sermon, sending the people to their homes with a benediction. Hildegarde stumbled through the dark streets holding her father's arm, grateful at last to reach the new house, to mumble sleepy goodnights and to mount the steps, too tired to even say her prayers before she fell asleep.

She could not know that her parents stood for long minutes at the foot of the steps, allowing themselves the touch of hands, but nothing more. They prayed together, asking for the strength that would allow them to go to their separate beds rejoicing. To have parted with regret, with bitterness, would have been a denial of all they had been taught, of all they believed. For awhile, their hands clung together, and then slowly, the prayer brought a peace, a loosening of fingers, and when they said good-night, they were able to smile.

Spring came more slowly to this place on the Ohio River than it used to come in Indiana. Hildegarde, eager to get at her planting, was dismayed by the sudden snow squalls that usually melted by afternoon and by the days of dark rain which slowed down the preparation of the ground. But there were sunny days, too, and then the people worked at their assigned tasks—some plowed and prepared the fields for the crops of rye and wheat and potatoes, some worked at the building of more houses in order that there might be housing for the final groups of Harmonists who would be arriving soon. The women, who could not be used in such heavy tasks as these, prepared individual vegetable gardens, worked in the textile mills, or did the lighter tasks in the tannery and kiln.

For the most part, Hildegarde was assigned to the task she loved most—planning, preparing, and planting the park and gardens which would lie between the proposed Great House and the river. This was her joy—to work with the earth, to try to develop stronger and sturdier strains of flowers or vegetables, to pamper exotic fruit trees, orange and lemon, which, though never intended for this climate, had been planted in huge pots so that they might be brought inside during the winter and had been persuaded to blossom and bear fruit.

Mornings, in the company of Gertrude, Pauline, and the other young people who showed enough mental agility to warrant keeping them in the schoolroom, were spent in study under the tutelage of Dr. Mueller. This Hildegarde loved, too, and she studied all the books of botany in the library, seeking always to know, to learn, to grow.

Hildegarde was delighted when Maria Baumann managed to be named her assistant. They worked together in the fragile April sunlight, talking with animation, exuberant over the fact that this was a young town, and they were young, and that April was the month for youthfulness.

One afternoon, when April was nearly over, Hildegarde and Maria, with several younger boys to help them, were setting out a garden of herbs. Hildegarde had talked long and earnestly to Dr. Mueller, and he had given her valuable advice on the growing of medicinal herbs. Producing them here in the village would save expense and inconvenience. The young people toiled over the dark, damp earth, setting out the slips of camomile, the small tender sassafras trees, and boneset plants.

Hildegarde sat on folded burlap, a book on botany on her knees, so intent on her studies and her intermittent orders to her helpers that she was completely unaware of the fact that Dr. Mueller, Father Rapp, and Romelius Baker were walking slowly across the park until the sharp sound of voices attracted her attention and she glanced up. Father Rapp looked dark and angry, and there was a deep gravity on the faces of the other two men.

"I was so sure there would be no enmity here," Father Rapp was saying. "Only a few months ago I wrote to Frederick of the friendliness of the neighbors, the openness I had encountered."

"I don't think it's enmity." Dr. Mueller spoke slowly, weighing his words. "It's jealousy. I think it's only jealousy."

"Jealousy!" Father Rapp's voice snapped with impatience. "Jealous of what? That we work harder than anyone else? That we started with less? That we are content with bread?"

Romelius Baker's face wore its usual somber look. Hildegarde wondered sometimes if she would recognize him if he ever really smiled. "Jealous of our success, Brother George. Jealous that we've already started manufacturing and that our fields are ready for crops. They're jealous that we have houses and streets where there was nothing a year ago."

"God gave them minds and backs and hands the same as he gave us," Father Rapp said. "Just because we use ours doesn't mean that we should be objects of jealousy."

"They're saying that we'll monopolize the industry in this valley," Dr. Mueller said.

"Their own wickedness condemns them." Father Rapp spoke with even greater harshness. "Man was born to pray, to work, and to prepare himself for a time of judgment. It's nothing to me—I tell you, nothing—that these ignorant louts speak against us. Besides, what industry is there?"

"They even tell lies," Brother Romelius said. "They accuse us of unspeakable things."

"Let them accuse!" The old man's face wore a fierceness which brought a trembling to Hildegarde. She, who had been a recipient of his gentleness, knew that she would want to die if this cold anger were ever directed against her. "I've been accused before—accused in Philadelphia of whoring in the streets, and God let me justify myself. I don't have the time or the patience to listen to tales of stupidity. I have to build a town—I'm trying to write a book—I have a kingdom to prepare! Carry your tales to someone else. I won't listen anymore."

He turned from the two men who were his closest friends and strode rapidly and decisively away. Hildegarde discovered that she was holding her breath, and that her heart was knocking against her chest. She wondered if the two men, standing dejected in the new grass, were feeling any of the fright which she felt.

Dr. Mueller shrugged. "He's not easy to convince, Brother Romelius. I guess we'll just have to watch and wait. Perhaps when Frederick comes. . . ."

Romelius looked so doleful that a funeral pall seemed to settle on him. "I don't think even Frederick can make him understand. Besides, Frederick is as determined as the Father to make this community the perfect one. There won't be any compromise with our neighbors— any more than there has ever been before. We'll go on as we've always gone on—"

There seemed no further words for him to say. Hildegarde, staring at the two men, suddenly found Dr. Mueller looking at her. She blushed, embarrassed to be caught obviously listening, but the doctor smiled with encouragement.

"I see you're planting the herbs. Is it going well, do you think?"

"I've been studying, and we're being careful,

but this climate is still strange to me. We might be planting too early. Have you talked to any of the natives?" She stopped in quick embarrassment. Would he think she was being critical of Father Rapp's attitude toward his neighbors? Oh, but she could never be critical of Father Rapp. Never. She wanted to say so, but the stern face of Romelius Baker seemed to stop the words in her throat.

"Brother Romelius has been talking to one or two farmers," the doctor said kindly, seeming not to notice her blunder. "You might be early in getting some of this into the ground, so make sure you take precautions if frost seems likely."

"I will," she said, nodding her head fervently, and the two men turned to stroll away. They were heading toward the long building which housed the store and post office. Hildegarde had seen the mail post stop an hour or so before, but since personal letters were a rarity in the community, she gave no thought to the contents of the small mailbag which had been dropped off at the door of the post office.

"We need string," one of the boys discovered. "Shall I run over to the store and sign up for some?"

"No, let me," Hildegarde said. "I'm stiff from sitting here, and I'd like the run across the grounds. I'll be right back."

She stood up, gathered her skirts a bit above her ankles and ran lightly toward the long store building. She was not really a strong girl, but she loved to move fast, and if she were forced to sit still for any length of time, nervous energy built up in her until she felt like a young and skittish horse. The breeze in her face would make her feel alive and ready to work again.

Brother Romelius was behind the counter, and if there was any lightening or darkening of his face at the sight of her running when she should have been walking, she could not observe it. He patiently heard her request for string, entered the item in the large book which contained the list of goods which the members of the Society got when they were needed. There was no money used by the Harmonists in this store which held a large and ample supply of goods; only the nearby settlers who had learned that excellent merchandise could be obtained at Economy paid cash for their purchases.

Hildegarde took the string and turned to go when Brother Romelius's voice stopped her. "I have a letter here for Father Rapp. He's walking out beyond the Beaver Road. Would you like to try to find him?"

She was astonished. Was the letter really that important? But if so, it would be entrusted to a man or Brother Romelius might even close the store and carry it himself. Or was it a gesture of kindness—knowing her love of running, her passion for the outdoors? She looked at the storekeeper with some surprise, and he held out a heavy envelope with an official looking seal on it.

Brother Romelius almost smiled. "I think this

might be a happy letter. Perhaps the Father will be glad to have it brought to him by a happy messenger."

Hildegarde smiled with delight. Brother Romelius might look somber, but there was love and understanding in his heart—for both the old man who had stamped off in anger and for the unimportant young girl who just happened to suit this errand.

"I'll find him as quickly as I can. I'll give the string to the boys and then start right out," she said.

"He won't be far. I imagine he'll be walking in that eastern meadow. Try there first. It's quiet there and he likes it."

Hildegarde remembered the place in Harmony, Pennsylvania, where Father Rapp had a sort of seat in a rocky place far from the village where he could be alone for contemplation. Now here, where the great amount of hard work that had to be done kept even the old prophet busy, there still had to be a place of serenity for him, a place where he could speak to God.

She darted across the new grass to where the boys stood waiting for the string, and then announced that she had an errand to perform but would be back soon. She could tell from Maria's face that she longed to run along, and for a second Hildegarde was tempted. They could stop on the way back and pick some arbutus and who knows what other discovery might be made? But resolutely she put the temptation from her.

It didn't take her long to find Father Rapp. He

had evidently walked off his anger quickly, and now he paced meditatively through the sparse woods flanking the Beaver Road that angled southeast out of the village. His hands behind his back, his chin on his chest, he gave no indication that he even heard the girl until she shyly spoke to him.

"Father. Father, here's a letter. Brother Romelius sent it to you."

He looked up quickly. "What? What?"

"A letter." She thrust it toward him.

He took the envelope and scanned it. "From Colonel Ramsey in Pittsburgh," he muttered. "More complaints, I suppose, and it's imperative that I know it at once."

"I don't think so, " Hildegarde ventured cautiously. "Brother Romelius said he thought it might be happy news."

"Indeed?" The shaggy white eyebrows rose a little. "How could Colonel Ramsey's joy or sorrow possibly concern me?"

He slipped a finger under the heavy seal, and Hildegarde turned to go.

"Wait," he said. "You've run a long way. If it's happy news, you can take my reaction back to Brother Romelius. Only walk more slowly. You're not a boy, you know."

So he had seen her running. She blushed and dropped her eyes, so she did not see the gratified look which spread over his face as he read the letter.

"Well," he said in a satisfied tone. "We're not such an object of scorn or envy as my brothers would have me believe. We've been invited to attend a grand ball being given in honor of General Lafayette. The entire Rapp family and any other representative of the Society we'd like to send."

"General Lafayette?" She stared at him incredulously. "Oh, Father, you will go, won't you?"

He spoke slowly. "I don't have time for fancy balls—but I suppose I shouldn't miss an opportunity to prove we're not what people say we are. Yes, I think we'll go—Frau Rapp, Frederick, Gertrude, perhaps a few others. Sister Pauline, I should think. She's a perfect example of our virtuous young women."

Hildegarde felt a longing that was almost faintness pass over her. It was wrong to envy, wrong to desire something that was worldly, but it seemed to her in that moment that she would give almost anything she would ever own to go to the ball. But she knew that she was not a Rapp like Gertrude nor docile like Pauline. She was only willful, stubborn Hildegarde Mutschler, and of course she would not go.

"Ask Brother Romelius to start to draft a letter of acceptance," Father Rapp said. "Ask him to say that we'll send several men who will represent the Harmonist Society—and several young women as well as the Rapp family. Tell him I said Sister Pauline—and you, my child? Would you like to go?"

"Oh, Father." She knew it was wrong to let her longing show, but she could not make her face into the polite, blank, indifferent mask it ought to be. She felt her blood heating her cheeks, and she knew her lips were almost trembling.

The old man frowned. "I'm not interested in this as a pleasure episode. I'm interested only in proving to these people that we're dignified, respectable, worthy people. Do you understand that?"

"Yes, sir. I. . . ."

"Still," the old man said, "I don't want it to be said that we're stodgy. We might as well send our beauty along with our virtue. Tell Brother Romelius you'll be going, too."

For a second she could not speak, but she knew that he would not approve of an emotional response, so somehow she firmed her lips, said a prim and proper thank you, promised to deliver the message, and walked sedately away. It was only when she was out of his sight that she pulled her skirts to her knees and flew like a freed thing through the woods. She caught a tree in her hands and swung around it, feeling light enough to fly if she ever let go of this earthbound trunk. Oh, think of it—think of it! To go to Pittsburgh, to attend a ball, to see the elegant people who would be there—perhaps even to meet the old French general who had done so much for America. Oh, it would be all the excitement she would ever need or ever want!

One more dizzy whirl around the tree and finally she was subdued enough to head toward the village with her message which somehow, some way, she must deliver with the proper humility and self-effacement.

"Herr Gott," she prayed suddenly. "Make me less proud. Make me docile."

But even as she prayed, her chin was high and the smile remained curved on her tender young mouth.

Frederick Rapp and the last of the Harmonists arrived at Economy during the month of May, and the rejoicing over the final and complete reunion was sincere. True, there had been some apprehension over the meeting between Father Rapp and the beloved son—or at least, he *had* been the beloved son. But some of the influential men knew that in October there had been anger and resentment on the old man's part because Frederick had sent bank notes made out to Johannes Baker instead of to Father Rapp. There had been speculations as to what Frederick's reasons were, and most had agreed that it was to simplify the bookkeeping. Frederick was incapable of unkind or insulting action. But Father Rapp's temper had flared, and it was common knowledge that some sharp letters had been exchanged. So when the *William Penn*, the Society's own steamboat, anchored at Economy, there were anxious eyes surreptitiously watching for Frederick's reaction to his father.

If anyone feared a sign of enmity their fears were instantly allayed by the scene which took place on the riverbank. The old prophet had quite obviously forgotten his anger, and the younger man embraced him with his usual warmth and affection. A sigh of gentle relief swept through the knowing members of the group. The love which was preached daily was still true. Nothing, it seemed, could cause dissension between these two great men—each so strong in his own way.

Chapter 4

The Ramsey ball was to be given during the first week in June. The three girls chosen to go talked about it as much as they dared. It came under the heading of frivolous gossip, and they all knew this, but at the same time it was such a novel and exciting event that they could not bear to just ignore it. They had already been told that they must go dressed in the finest dresses the Society could provide, as Father Rapp had not weakened in his decision that the Society should not be shamed but that its representatives should be as elegant as anyone.

Very few women in the village had a silk gown, of course, but Frau Rapp and her daughter each had one and there were a few others which were made available to the three girls to take in or let out as needed in order to fit. The dresses were made alike: all of dark-blue lustrous fabric, high at the throat, the gathered sleeves reaching to the wrist, the bodice fitting smoothly to the waist and then the skirt falling in graceful, deep folds almost to the floor. Since the dresses belonged to older women, all of them had to be taken in, but Hildegarde's task was greatest since she was the most slender of the three. They were given several hours each afternoon to work on the gowns, and they used the time for talking as well as sewing.

"Someday every one of us will have such a gown," Gertrude promised. "We're going to start to make our own silk."

Pauline nodded, evidently already aware of such plans, but Hildegarde was astonished.

"Our own silk? You mean silkworms and all?" she cried.

"Of course. We talked about this several days ago in class. Hildegarde, don't you ever listen?" Gertrude's tone was not sharp or admonishing but only a little amused.

Hildegarde's cheeks flamed. "I was probably reading. I don't mean to get so deep in books, but I can't seem to help it."

Gertrude smiled. "Well, you'd better listen now. Because you'll be responsible for the mulberry trees when they're brought in."

"How many? Will they be seedlings or good-sized trees?"

"I'm not sure how many. I'm still studying to find out how many we'll need. But lots and lots of them, I should think. We can plant them along walks maybe or in special groves."

Hildegarde stitched for a minute, watching the needle moving in and out of the lovely material. "Silver would be beautiful with this blue, wouldn't it, Gertrude?"

Gertrude nodded. "But a little rich for a Harmonist, don't you think?"

Pauline spoke quickly. "We must guard against vanity. You know that, Hildegarde."

Hildegarde bit her thread in two with a sharp snap of her teeth. "I get a little tired of plain things. I'd like to wear something bright red once, or yellow. Underneath where it wouldn't show," she added quickly.

Gertrude only laughed, but Pauline had little or no sense of humor. "Hildegarde, you really must be crazy. Red or yellow. You'd look like a—like a. . . ." She stopped, fumbling for words.

"Peacock," Hildegarde supplied with satisfaction. "I know. I wish I could."

"There are some pretty shawls in the chest," Gertrude said, trying to placate both girls. "Some lovely ones in blue that you'd love, Pauline, and some with color. You can have your choice, Hildegarde."

"Would it be wrong if they were different?" Hildegarde said.

"Don't be silly. Grandpa wants us to look our very best. And besides," Gertrude added with practicality, "there aren't three made alike."

"I'd like one with red," Hildegarde dreamed. "Or pink anyhow. And I'd like to wear my hair in curls. Could I, Gertrude?"

Pauline glanced at Gertrude in surprise, but Gertrude didn't seem to notice. Her eyes were on Hildegarde's face, and it was impossible to tell from the gentle expression on her face whether or not there was any desire in her heart to be as pretty as the golden-headed Hildegarde who was concentrating on her sewing, her lip caught in her teeth.

"Curls might not be—*verboten* for that one night. I'll talk to Grandfather."

Hildegarde looked at Gertrude in gratitude. In spite of the fact that Gertrude was younger than Hildegarde, the Rapp authority sat naturally and sweetly on her shoulders.

"Oh, Gertrude," Hildegarde breathed. "It's going to be purely wonderful."

Gertrude only nodded demurely, but there was an odd little catch in her throat, too, a feeling for which she had no definition or explanation. Her serenity was so seldom troubled that she was really less equipped to handle her own emotions than she would have appeared to be.

The day of the ball, the three girls, Frau Rapp, and Rosina—Father Rapp's plain, shy daughter—rode to Pittsburgh with Father Rapp, Brother Frederick, and Brother Johannes Baker. Hildegarde rode in the carriage with Brother Johannes, Pauline, and Aunt Rosina, so there was no casual chatter. Brother Johannes, a gentle, quiet man, might ordinarily have talked seriously of life's duties, but Hildegarde felt that he was not really well—there was a tightness to the skin over his cheekbones and a dullness in his eyes which was not normal. She decided he was just nervous about this venture into a fragment of the world which she was sure he would never have chosen for himself. Father Rapp had undoubtedly decreed that he should help represent the Society, since he was one of the few who handled English very well, and Johannes would never question his orders. As for Aunt Rosina, she moved through life like a shadow, touching lives with a sort of cool and refreshing touch, but making no real impression, and Pauline always held her tongue in the presence of her elders.

So Hildegarde was free to let her mind wander, to gaze with growing delight at the valley through which they rode. The woods were freshly green, and blossoming trees spread their branches in the perfumed air. The road followed the river, and at times it came into view—broad and sparkling in the sun, like a liquid road leading to the ends of the earth.

The world was very beautiful, Hildegarde felt. She had been told repeatedly that material beauty was not all-important and that one must be concerned with the beauty of the soul. And yet she had been taught to create beauty with her hands and mind, and it was extremely difficult for her to reconcile the two seemingly divergent points of view. She found herself being glad that the Christ was coming back to this land, to this place—that they weren't going to be transported at the sound of a trumpet to a heavenly place where she would be a stranger, where the dogwood would not bloom in chaste loveliness beside the river.

When she thought things like this, she always felt a little guilty, a little frightened. She felt a vague sense of relief that it was gentle old Brother Johannes driving the horse and not Brother Frederick. Brother Frederick would probably be able to tell what she was thinking even if she never opened her mouth.

The drive to Pittsburgh took about four hours and it was mid-afternoon when they arrived at the Harmonist house which had been purchased for the sake of convenience when Harmonist members came to Pittsburgh for the transaction of business. It was the first time the girls had seen the house, of course, and they were fascinated with the way it was built, fronting on the street which led down to the river, with no yard, no white fence, no garden. It was a gray frame house, and the scroll work on the windows helped form a sharp contrast between this and the simple rosy brick dwellings which were being erected in Economy. They agreed unanimously that they liked the Economy homes better, but they also agreed that it was interesting ("exciting" was the word in Hildegarde's mind) to stay in a house that was different from any other house they had known.

"I'll hang up the dresses," Hildegarde offered.

"Then I'll get out the shawls," Pauline said. "I'm so glad mine is plain blue," she added looking at the one which Hildegarde had chosen. "This mixture of pink and gold and white would make me feel funny."

"Well, it won't make me feel funny," Hildegarde retorted. "I think it will be simply elegant."

"The gold will match your hair," Gertrude said generously, and her eyes were warm.

After supper, they began to get ready for the ball, dressing with great care. They coaxed curls into hair accustomed to braids, they settled the silken folds of the dresses to hang smoothly, and they placed the lovely shawls carefully about their shoulders.

"I've never gone anywhere in my life without a cap," Pauline said suddenly. "I feel—I feel naked."

Her eyes were frightened. Gertrude patted her arm, and even Hildegarde tried to be soothing.

"Your hair looks pretty," Hildegarde said. "So smooth and neat. It *does* feel strange without a bonnet—but nice. Don't you think?"

Pauline just hugged her shoulders nervously, but Gertrude answered in a taut little voice.

"Yes, it *does* feel nice. Airy and nice. Your hair is lovely, Hildegarde. I could never get mine to curl like that."

"Here," Hildegarde said, and she coaxed small curls about Gertrude's wide, serene forehead.

Ready at last, Hildegarde stood waiting for the others, suddenly afraid to go downstairs.

"Maybe Brother Frederick will think we're too fine," she said and a nervous little giggle escaped her. *That's how I'll know if we look nice*, Hildegarde decided—*if Brother Frederick looks worried when he sees us.*

Brother Frederick did indeed look worried, and Father Rapp, dressed in a plum velvet jacket lined with pale blue silk, had a stern look which filled Hildegarde with foreboding.

"Before we go to this place," he said in his

most somber voice, "I think we should all join in prayer. We need God's help to keep us from the temptations and idolatry of the world."

They stood obediently, heads bowed, while he prayed, and then they moved out into the dusk, climbed into their carriages, and drove toward Colonel Ramsey's hotel.

The Ramsey Hotel, at the corner of Wood and Third Street, not far from the river, was in the busiest part of Pittsburgh. When they got there, they found that the hotel was ablaze with light.

"I've never seen so many candles in all my life," Hildegarde gasped.

"Foolish waste," Father Rapp grumbled. "Night was never intended to look like day."

Their carriage pulled up by the porch, and for a few minutes they watched stiff men in odd uniforms help ladies step down from other carriages.

"Look," Pauline hissed. "They're *bowing!*"

"No man has to bow to another man," said Frederick.

"Or woman," Father Rapp added with a fierce look at the three girls.

Hildegarde tried to look meek, but in spite of herself, she felt her chin go up when it was her turn to be helped down from the carriage. She simply couldn't help it.

They first entered a corridor which ended in a short flight of steps leading down to the ballroom. At the top of the steps, a major domo, very grand in his formal attire, halted the little party to ask their names. Frederick, poised as always and at ease even with the difficult English, gave the man a list of the names which he had previously prepared.

The major domo ran his eyes down the list and then, evidently memorizing the names immediately, turned toward the ballroom and called out in an imperious voice, "Mr. and Mrs. John Rapp, Mr. Frederick Rapp, Miss Rosina Rapp, Miss Gertrude Rapp, Mr. John Baker, Miss Pauline Speidel, and Miss Hildegarde Mutschler."

With a flourish that gave the impression that he might be conjuring them out of the air, he presented the group to Colonel Ramsey and his wife who stood at the foot of the steps.

The colonel, in his high-collared military uniform with gold epaulets and braid draped across his left breast, was elegant and distinguished, and his wife seemed quite the loveliest thing Hildegarde had ever seen. Her dress was of ivory satin, cut very low in the front, and her arms were bare. There were jewels at her throat, and her full, heavy skirt hung in luxurious folds to the floor. There were just no words for Hildegarde to say, and she stared speechless at this apparition while all knowledge of English seemed to fly out of her head.

The introductions were made, and the colonel was warm and polite as he greeted each of the Harmonists. His bow to Father Rapp was as courteous as though he were greeting a statesman, and he bent over the hands of Frau Rapp and Sister Rosina with infinite grace. The three girls were presented by Brother Frederick, and Hildegarde was at a loss as to what to do. One did not bow or curtsy to another Harmonist; such humility was not seemly. But this was different, Hildegarde sensed. Here a bow meant only politeness. With a touch of recklessness, she imitated the women she had seen preceding her in line, and dipped her knee with a pretty gesture.

"What lovely girls," Mrs. Ramsey said, her smile divided among them evenly, but her eyes coming back to Hildegarde's face. "How sweet of you to come."

The colonel made some polite, meaningless remark, but his eyes were properly appreciative when he bent over Hildegarde's hand. Then he turned to introduce the group to General Lafayette who stood watching them with sharp eyes which glinted with a touch of humor. The old general, now very white of hair and lined of face, held himself with military straightness and acknowledged the introductions with Gallic charm. He had quite obviously heard of George Rapp, and he greeted the old prophet in German, a gesture which delighted him and brought the first smile of the evening to his face. They exchanged a few pleasantries, all that were permitted in the receiving line, but Hildegarde overheard the general say, "I will surely see you before I leave this place. I want to talk to you."

Then it was her turn to stand before the famous general, to look up into his eyes that held such a blend of aged wisdom and child-like candor. She curtsied slightly and stared at him, speechless with fright and wonder.

He kissed her hand, his beard tickling her skin but his lips as warm and ardent as a boy's. "Quelle une belle petite!" he murmured. "Like a rose in a garden of cactus."

The French and English both escaped her, but the look of admiration in his eyes brought hot blood to her cheeks. She wished she could think of a proper reply, but she could only smile shyly.

The greetings completed, the Harmonists made their way to gilt chairs that lined the walls, and there they sat—Brother Frederick and Brother Johannes a little stiff and reserved, Father Rapp amazingly relaxed and almost indifferent to his surroundings, and the women shy and quiet. Hildegarde looked and looked, unable to get her fill of the beauty which surrounded her on every side.

The women's dresses completely amazed and delighted her. She was fully aware of the fact that she would never have felt comfortable in the great majority of them—the wanton display of creamy bosom and rounded shoulder would embarrass and dismay her. But, oh, the color! The sheen and glitter of silk and metallic cloth! The drape of skirts that made them stand out from the body as though they were supported by something! She felt a little giddy just from looking at so much beauty, and she discovered to her astonishment that the lilting tunes which swept the couples about the floor made her feet, in their decent, sturdy shoes, tap a secret rhythm behind her concealing skirt.

Several times, young men came up to Father Rapp, bowed deferentially, and made what appeared to be an appealing gesture of the hand toward Hildegarde. Their request to be introduced to her so that they might ask for a dance was not lost on the old man in spite of his extremely limited English. His reply was an abrupt *Nein* and a look so fierce that the young men did not dare press their cause further.

But one young man, more brash, more daring, more emboldened by her beauty than his fellows, coaxed Colonel Ramsey to introduce him. The colonel seemed a little awkward and glanced somewhat apologetically at Father Rapp, but he performed the act of introduction. The boy, tall and handsome, bent low over her hand, and his eyes touched her face with an intimacy she had never encountered before.

In spite of her naiveté, however, something about the boy's bemused stare, the warmth of his fingers on hers brought a quickness to her breath, a new heat of blood to her face. She could not define the feeling which swept over her nor could she understand its implications. When the pilot's mate had caught her in his arms on the *Bolivar*, she had not been stirred at all. But now, surrounded by the bewildering sounds and sights of a glittering world, she was suddenly aware of unfamiliar currents of emotion which both frightened and intrigued her.

"May I have the honor of this dance?" the boy asked.

The music was so loud, the movement of the people so distracting that she had great difficulty in understanding him. Her confusion only seemed to add to her charm.

He repeated his words slowly and distinctly, and when she realized that he was asking her to join the kaleidoscope of color and music on the dance floor, she was filled with dismay and longing. She had never learned to dance, of course, and she was sure that she would stumble and be disastrously awkward. Besides, Father Rapp would surely frown on such a worldly activity; of that she was certain. Still, she hesitated for just a few seconds, savoring briefly the sweet knowledge of what it would be like to glide lightly, delicately across the floor, guided by the young man who was looking at her with such a strange and exciting intensity.

But her training did not desert her. She turned to Father Rapp for instruction, saw his disapproval plainly, and she knew what her answer must be.

"Thank you," she said softly so that he had to bend for the words, and she caught a scent of pomade which she did not recognize but found very pleasant. "I am not dance. I am not know to dance."

"I could teach you," he said eagerly.

"No. I am not." Her voice was soft but firm.

The young man apparently recognized finality when he saw it, and gracefully bowed again over her hand. This time his lips touched her fingers with a soft lingering touch that sent a strange prickle up her arm, and she pulled her hand away quickly. For reasons she could not even understand, she found herself almost afraid to look at Father Rapp, but after a minute, she slid her eyes toward the old prophet, half expecting a fierce frown. He was, however, watching her with a bland sort of approval. She was puzzled for a minute, and then she realized that he had seen only the negative shake of her head, the quick withdrawal of her hand. He had not known of the feeling that had shivered up her arm, or of the way her heart had jerked in her breast.

The evening wore on, and the light supper of oysters (an unknown delicacy to Hildegarde who stared at them suspiciously until she worked up the courage to swallow them as she saw others doing) and small pastries was a pleasant interlude. Then, before midnight, Father Rapp showed signs of restlessness, indicating his desire to leave. It's like being a poor peasant girl at a fairy ball, Hildegarde thought, remembering a tale of her early childhood—all the loveliness will disappear in a puff of smoke. *I don't want it to end,* she thought. *I want it to last and last.*

Just before Father Rapp stood up, General Lafayette left the distinguished people with whom he had been talking and moved toward the little group of Harmonists. Father Rapp, seeing him coming, stood to speak to him, and they talked together, speaking in German, talking earnestly and warmly.

"I would like to come to see how you live," the general said. "I've heard of your way of life and of your success and energy. I want to see it for myself."

Father Rapp bobbed his head affirmatively. "I'll send my son Frederick to fetch you. The inn is comfortable, the food good, and the wine excellent. It would be a privilege to have you visit us."

"One day then, before I leave this area," the general promised, smiling. His eyes moved over the little group and settled on Hildegarde. "I would like to have the honor of dancing with one of your girls. That golden-haired child—would she dance with an old man?"

"Dancing is of the world," Father Rapp said stiffly.

The general laughed easily. "I'm an old man with very little of the world left. She'd have no trouble following my slow steps. It might impress these Americans that the French and Germans are friendly. Don't you agree?"

Father Rapp hesitated. There was no danger of worldly contamination on the part of this old man, and although Hildegarde was a difficult child to train, this little act might make these influential people realize that the Harmonists were none of the things they were accused of being.

"A small dance," he conceded. He led the general to Hildegarde who got up from her chair hastily, overwhelmed by this thing that was happening to her. She was terrified lest she stumble, lest she bring humiliation to Father Rapp and the general. She sent a quick, longing glance toward Gertrude, who smiled encouragingly.

"I've never danced," Hildegarde confessed when the general had taken her hand and led her onto the polished floor.

"You know music?" he said.

"Oh, yes."

"Then just listen. Put your hand on my shoulder—so—let your feet move to the music. Smile."

To her amazement, she was not awkward. Her feet moved smoothly with his, her body felt and absorbed the music, and her dearest wish came true! She was dancing with one of the most famous men in the world. She wondered hazily if she might die from pure happiness.

Then as she swung around, she saw Gertrude and Pauline watching her, Pauline looking prim and stern, Gertrude smiling sweetly, obviously aware of her grandfather's approval, thinking only of Hildegarde. Hildegarde's heart turned over. This shouldn't be happening to her—to Sister Hildegarde Mutschler who had only been allowed to come along because Father Rapp was kind. This should be Gertrude dancing—this honor belonged to the Rapp family who had received the invitation to the ball.

For a second, her courage was not great enough, and then with a great effort she made her suggestion to the old man who was smiling at her with such friendliness and admiration.

"Herr General," she began. "Please, sir, don't be angry or think I am unappreciative of this honor. But, please, could you ask Sister Gertrude to dance instead? She's Father Rapp's granddaughter, you know. She's the one you ought to dance with."

For a minute she was almost overwhelmed with fright to think that she had actually made such a suggestion. But the general only laughed.

"You're unselfish as well as beautiful, my child. Yes, I'll ask the granddaughter to dance. I hope I haven't offended anyone."

"Oh, no," she hurried to reassure him. "Oh, no. I just. . . ."

"I understand perfectly. I am, to tell you the truth, charmed!"

He danced Hildegarde to the edge of the floor, made the proper and correct request to Father Rapp, took Gertrude, rosy and pleased, from her chair, to dance her sedately across the floor and back. He made no move toward Pauline, nor did anyone expect him to.

They stayed only briefly after this and then, after proper farewells to their host and hostess and guest of honor, they went out into the torch-lit inn yard where a boy was found to fetch their carriages.

The late hour, the strangeness of the city and the events of the evening filled Hildegarde with a mixture of exhaustion and exhilaration. Her head seemed heavy and giddy, but she felt certain that she would never be able to sleep, that all night long the strains of the music, the memory of her dance with General Lafayette and the light and color and splendor of the ball would keep her awake.

The three girls shared one bedroom of the Pittsburgh house, and there were two beds in it—a large bed and a sort of low trundle bed.

"I'll take the little one," Hildegarde offered, not really out of generosity, but out of the knowledge that if she turned fitfully in her wakefulness, no one would know.

"You're sure?" Gertrude asked. Pauline, yawning widely behind her hand, was already in the long white flannel gown, made exactly like the flannel sleeping gown of every other woman in the Society.

"Absolutely sure. I like little beds."

"All right then. If you're sure."

They knelt together for their prayers, dressed alike, their hands folded in an identical way, their dark lustrous dresses hanging neatly and indistinguishable from each other. Their prayers, though said in silence, were almost exactly the same, shaped from repetition, habit, and the pattern of the prayers heard all of their lives.

Their good-nights were said in similar, soft voices, and the silence that followed seemed to enfold them altogether.

But the similarity was not as perfect as it had been before this night. They had been, there at the ball, three separate people—noticed or ignored for their own attributes, no longer safely obscured by the anonymity of the Society. Hildegarde had no way of knowing how this affected Gertrude or Pauline. She only knew that she was intoxicated by it all, that try as she would, she could not suppress the memory of the way people looked at her or the shiver up her arm at the warm touch of the young man's lips. Nor would she ever forget the dresses, the color, the final and unbelievable magic of her dance with the general.

I'm glad he danced with Gertrude, too, she thought contentedly, drowsy in spite of her longing to stay awake. *I'm really glad.* But her last thought before she slept—a thought more rebellious than she could possibly understand—was a wish that her nightgown was not like Gertrude's and Pauline's. Not more beautiful, perhaps, but different—different from everyone else's in the whole, wide world.

Chapter 5

The dust from the Beaver Road settled in a fine powder on the coats of the three men who traveled slowly north through the haze of the June afternoon. Frederick Rapp held the reins of the horses in one strong, sunburned hand, and with the other he pointed out landmarks to the two men who sat beside him in the carriage. General Lafayette's keen blue eyes followed the gestures of Frederick's hand with avid interest, and the young man beside him seemed to watch with equal attention.

The old general's hand dropped with casual warmth born of close association onto the knee of his secretary. "Look well, Auguste," he said in French. "There's much for you to learn here."

Auguste Lavasseur grinned. "As I've been learning everywhere for weeks, mon general?"

"Non! This is different—different from anything we've encountered here—except possibly the meeting with Miss Fanny Wright who was going to join Robert Owen in Indiana."

Frederick looked interested. "My French is poor," he said in German. "But did I understand you to say you visited Robert Owen?"

Lavasseur chuckled. "No. We only met one of his followers in New York. A Miss Wright. I think she was romantically inclined toward the general."

Lafayette laughed easily. "She was only interested in my liberalism," he said. "I am too old and single-hearted to appeal to any woman."

Frederick did not seem interested enough to reply, and in a minute he spoke again as though there had been no interruption in the conversation that had been going on ever since they left Pittsburgh. General Lafayette had been so feted, lauded, and cheered during this tour of the country that it was really an unbelievable stroke of luck which allowed him to spend this day with the Harmonists. Only Lafayette's desire for the experience and George Rapp's calm acceptance of what seemed logical and right had made it possible.

"We're coming to the boundary of our land now," Frederick said. "We have 3,000 acres, all bottom land, arable and well drained. And an excellent slope for water. We have good wells on the higher ground and a fine pump in the village itself."

Lavasseur turned his head to take in the sweep of land indicated by Frederick's hand. "Beautiful country," he murmured. "Is it not, mon general?"

"Like the western part of Germany," Lafayette agreed. "You raise the vine, you say? And do you make wine?"

"Yes to both questions," Frederick said, more than willing to tell of achievement. "The slopes of ground here are very good for the vine. Lots of sun and warmed by the river. Our wine is better than any American wine I've ever tasted. It's more like the wine of Hungary. I wouldn't presume to compare it to French wine, of course."

There was shared laughter, and then Lafayette spoke to Frederick in a serious tone. "Your way of life is not usual here, and although I'm familiar with similar communities in Europe, my secretary is not. Are you willing to answer questions about it?"

Frederick answered readily. "Certainly. You may ask all you please, and I will try to answer competently." There might be reservations in his answers, he reflected, but the Harmonists had a right to shield some things from the unenlightened. One does not share family thoughts with strangers.

"Then," Lavasseur said, "is it truly owned—the land, I mean—by all of you jointly and in common?"

"Yes, truly," Frederick said.

"Not just Herr Rapp—I believe you call him Father Rapp—is the owner then?"

Frederick's voice was easy and placid. "He owns no more than any other man."

"Does he live in the same kind of house as the rest of the people?" Lavasseur pursued.

"No, of course not. He's living just now with

his wife, daughter, granddaughter, and me in an old residence that was here when we came. But by autumn we hope to have completed the *Vosterhaus* which will be his residence. It's larger and more elegant than the other houses, but this is simply for the purpose of providing a fit place to entertain worthy visitors such as you, my general. The world is quick to judge the worth of any community by the condition of the leader, is it not? We want to show that our way of life is a good way."

They were rapidly approaching the village, and the square brick houses could be seen through the trees, while to the right and left of the road stretched the fields of early hay, already losing their green color and beginning to turn golden in the sun.

"Nearly haying time," Frederick observed. "We raise our own crops, you know, and also do much manufacturing."

"Does a man have a choice as to whether he'll be a farmer or a factory worker?" asked Lafayette.

"Yes, but we all work at all tasks," said Frederick patiently. "When it's haying season, everyone goes into the field and makes the hay. When there is less to do in the fields, then more can be spared for the factory work. And of course many of the lighter tasks can be done by the women."

"The women?" Lavasseur's eyebrows rose. "But who then takes care of the children? There are children, aren't there?" he hazarded, remembering rumors he had heard and had always discredited.

Frederick answered swiftly, "Of course, there are some children—those born here or adopted by us. They go to school, learn a trade and work as soon as they're old enough. Very small children are cared for by grandmothers or older aunts if the mother is occupied."

Lavasseur took a swift breath, preparatory to asking another question, but Lafayette's warning elbow against his ribs stopped the words in his throat.

"There," Frederick said, unaware of the action, "down at the end of this street. There's the inn. Father will meet you there for the noon meal since his own house just now is too humble to entertain you. We've reserved a room for you where you can rest until the meal is ready."

Lafayette, accustomed to the cheering throngs, the pressing crowds of people who had surrounded him for nearly a year, looked with great interest at the quiet, serene village through which they rode. There were few people to be seen, no children shouting noisily as they raced in the summer grass, no resemblance at all to the other American towns he had visited. He might almost think it an empty village if it were not for the neatness, order, and prosperity which surrounded him on every side. The gardens were enclosed by neat paling fences and the houses were attractive and sturdy and clean. He didn't really know what he had expected; it certainly wasn't this.

The inn was a large frame building, cleaner than any public inn they had encountered in the smaller towns of America, and the room reserved for them was plain but immaculate and comfortable. Lavasseur, eager to evaluate some of the things Frederick had said, was forced to bide his time. Lafayette, weary from the ride, pulled off his boots and lay down across the woven coverlet. In a minute, he was sleeping heavily, and Lavasseur sat quietly at the window looking out at the strange town which piqued his curiosity.

The meal, tasty but heavy, was eaten leisurely in the small dining room of the inn. Lafayette and George Rapp talked as they ate, but it seemed to Lavasseur, observing Frederick and the other members of the Rapp family, that this was an act of courtesy on the part of the old prophet, for apparently custom kept the Harmonists silent during the meal. A sensitive man, Lavasseur refrained from idle conversation and concentrated on the beef and noodles, the apple schnitzel, and the wine which was really amazingly good.

But when the eating had ceased, chairs were pushed back from the table, and conversation became general. Dr. Mueller, who had joined them for the meal, left after an exchange of glances with Frederick.

"We want you to hear some of our music," Father Rapp said. "Brother Christoph, our doctor and teacher and director of music—a talented man, you can see—has gone to get a few of our girls to sing for you."

Lavasseur's curiosity overcame his prudence. "Is music part of your religion?" he asked.

Father Rapp's eyes were steady and stern. "Our lives are our religion," he said firmly.

"But I mean ritual—"

"Ritual." The old man's voice was clipped. "There is no ritual in real worship. God and our hearts are one. Christ sits beside us."

Frederick cast an uneasy glance at his father. The Harmonists were not a group to proselyte or to even explain their theology to a stranger. It was common knowledge that Lafayette was a liberal, a believer in metaphysics. Surely this young secretary followed the beliefs of his master, so these questions were only idle curiosity. One must not throw crumbs before dogs.

Father Rapp saw Frederick's uneasiness and smiled with reassurance. "If you are curious about our beliefs," he said with the ease born of a surety that the invitation would be rejected, "stay the night. This is our midweek prayer-service night. You could worship with us under the sky."

Lafayette spoke calmly. "Thank you, we will."

Lavasseur looked his surprise. "But, sir," he demurred. "Aren't we expected back in Pittsburgh? You don't even have your valet, Bastien, with you."

"We'll return at dawn tomorrow," Lafayette said. "The inn is comfortable, the company most interesting, and you, my dear Auguste, may act as valet."

The door opened, and Dr. Mueller came into the room followed by eight girls who darted quick, curious glances at the strangers at the table, but there was none of the open acclaim that had been common in other places. Evidently, these girls, like this entire community, Lafayette reflected, were under a special sort of discipline. He was not so falsely modest as to think he was unknown here.

The last girl into the room had hair the color of sunshine, and Lavasseur and Lafayette both recognized her at once even though there were no curls about her face, and her blue woolsey dress had little of the grace or beauty of the silk gown she had worn to the ball.

"My little dancing partner," Lafayette said genially. "How are you, ma petite?"

Hildegarde looked at him swiftly, her face hot with the embarrassment of being singled out, but her eyes dancing with a delight she could not suppress. She did not speak although her smile deepened. Then her glance slid to the man at Lafayette's side, and her breath seemed to stop in her throat. Here was the young man who had asked her to dance, who had kissed her fingers with such delicious and frightening deliberation.

Her hand flew to her mouth, and her eyes widened. Lavasseur smiled warmly, rather enjoying her confusion, although he felt a sudden discomfort when he saw the uneasy way in which she looked toward Frederick. He, too, glanced swiftly at Frederick and was in time to see the stern setting of the lips, the subtle but unmistakable shake of the head.

There was something here that Lavasseur simply could not understand. In France, this girl would be courted and flirted with as naturally as breathing. She would be gay and laughing and sure of herself and her power over men. The gaiety and laughter were in her; he was sure of that. But she was stifled in some way, held down. He looked again at her face— open, shy, yet eager. There was certainly no sign that she *felt* stifled. What was it then? Religion, he supposed. He wished he had the courage to ask blunter questions, unhindered by Lafayette's elbow.

The girls formed a semicircle of innocence at the end of the table, and their eyes fastened on the face of Dr. Mueller. He sang one clear note for them, and their soft voices picked up the note and slid into the harmony. They sang with the ease and the facility of trained singers, although their voices were fresh and natural with nothing operatic about them. They sang portions of Scripture, set to music, and it was oddly incongruous to hear their naive voices harmonizing on the frankly passionate words of the Song of Solomon. Lavasseur had difficulty repressing his smile, although he noticed that Lafayette maintained a careful dignity.

When the music was finished, the girls were introduced to the two visitors, and Gertrude, poised and natural, took her place at the table as a rightful part of the family. The others smiled shyly, acknowledging the honor of the occasion, and then turned to file out of the room.

Hildegarde flung one last look over her shoulder, and there was open wistfulness in her eyes—not envy—but a desire to stay instead of returning to her gardens.

Lafayette saw it. "Can't the little one stay, too? The small Hildegarde? She's such a charming child—as is the Mistress Gertrude," he added with a warm smile for Father Rapp's grandchild.

Frederick spoke quickly before Father Rapp could answer. "Sister Hildegarde has duties to attend to, Herr General. It would not be proper nor right for her to shirk her tasks."

Lavasseur was looking at Hildegarde as the words were spoken. Why didn't she cry out that evidently Gertrude had been excused from her duties? Why did she only drop her eyes and walk quietly away. And then he saw her hands, clenched tightly against the stuff of her skirt, and he felt a sudden and absurd satisfaction. She was not a wooden doll, after all. Somewhere beneath that docile exterior, there were banked fires waiting. With a touch of illogical recklessness, he wished that his might be the hand to stir the sleeping embers, and he knew in a moment of real regret that this could never be.

Lafayette and Lavasseur sat on the last bench that evening when the Harmonists assembled for their midweek service. The river air brought an aching to Lafayette's stiff hip, and he wondered for a minute why he had stayed. But he knew why, of course. He was a liberal, a revolutionist; his sympathy was always with those who dared to break away from the conformity of the established way. There was something of the rebel in these people. He could feel it, and he wanted to know more of what it was. He wanted Lavasseur to be exposed to this strange way of life.

The service began with a hymn, and the singing seemed to drift into the twilight with a sweet purity. Then Father Rapp began to read from the Scripture. The small flame of the lamp on the wooden table which he used for a pulpit moved erratically, in spite of the protecting chimney, and shadows played across the old prophet's face, changing it from sternness to loving kindness, from authority to gentleness.

It had been a long time since Lafayette had been so moved by spiritual words. He had politely listened to several sermons on this tour of America, but this one, delivered under a sky that glowed in the west with the color of summer apples, seemed to touch him deeply. These words were spoken in German, and yet somehow, they seemed to be the words that Adrienne had once spoken. Lovely and beloved Adrienne, his wife for thirty years and now gone from him nearly eighteen years, and yet the terrible loneliness never left him. Even in the midst of the adoring crowd, without Adrienne he stood alone.

But when the sermon began, his thoughts were jerked away from Adrienne. For this man who so obviously believed himself a prophet of God was speaking of the stern sort of ascetic discipline which Adrienne's church had demanded only of its priests and nuns. Not that Father Rapp put it into words; there was no wanton display of a private theology before these strangers. But the old general was sensitive to the nuances of all that was said. He had heard enough about communities of this sort to know the meaning of the words. He felt a sense of disappointment. In view of the obvious material success here, he had hoped for a more practical approach—less mysticism—less perversion of what to his mind was natural and beautiful. His hand crept up to touch the locket he always wore about his neck—the locket on which Adrienne's last words were written, "Je suis tout a vous." Ah, yes, she had been all his and her death had left him maimed and no longer whole.

Lavasseur, less attuned to the meaning of Father Rapp's words, perhaps a bit less proficient in German, tried to listen and tried to understand. But his eyes kept straying to the women, sitting all together, their gaze riveted on the face of their pastor. He could see Hildegarde clearly, her face made tender and shadowed by the deepening dusk. Stubbornly, he tried to catch her attention. He concentrated on her face, willing her to look at him, determined to bring again the heat of blood to her cheeks.

But she did not feel his glance. She was sustained by the words of the man who spoke, it seemed, only to her. This was the way it was with her. After rebellion came compliance, after questioning, submission. She was hypnotized by the familiar voice, the well-known ideas. She was purified, strengthened, lifted up out of herself. It did not matter to her that the world had intruded into this spot of Eden. The young man and the old general no longer caught at her heart.

Lavasseur performed the unfamiliar tasks of a valet with respect and courtesy. He loved the old general, and his hands were gentle performing the nightly rites.

Lafayette pulled up the covers and then spoke abruptly. "They're wrong, you know. I hope you weren't impressed by that tonight."

"I am deeply impressed by their joint effort," Auguste admitted. "It's altogether unbelievable to me that they have accomplished so much in such a short time. Incroyable!"

"They may be incredible," Lafayette agreed impatiently. "I'm not talking about their material success. I'm talking about their theology."

"Theology?" Lavasseur had never heard this word in his master's conversation.

"Yes. Theology. They evidently feel that marriage is wrong. That there is something sinful in the love that exists between man and woman. They're wrong, of course."

Lavasseur only looked at Lafayette. "Oui, mon general," he said fervently. "I agree with all my heart."

"When Adrienne was dying," Lafayette said, his voice soft and full of remembering, an old man's voice. "And she was a saint, Auguste—a veritable saint—pure and lovely and good. But, dying, she said to me, 'I love you in a Christian way, in a worldly way, in a passionate way.' It's all one. She knew. And these people are wrong."

"They don't believe they're wrong," Lavasseur

said slowly, "which may be the important thing, and there's something about them—some dedication and fervor and commitment—which gets things done. More than any other community I've ever seen. I don't agree with them—and yet. . . ."

"But they're wrong," Lafayette said again. "And what's going to happen to the young ones—to that golden-haired child—the pretty one who thinks Rapp is the representative of God? What's going to happen when they find out they're wrong?"

"I don't think they'll ever find out," Lavasseur said and blew out the candle. His voice was confident in the dark. "Look at Frederick Rapp. And that doctor. I never saw stronger men in my life. They. . . ."

But Lafayette was asleep, no longer concerned with the Harmonists, no longer concerned with his young secretary who went to the adjoining room to sit for a long time in the circle of candle flame before he began to write his impressions in his journal.

Chapter 6

The long slow winter of 1825-26 crawled toward spring and then finally thawed and melted into April. Hildegarde, restless from the long days in the classroom and the cloth mill, turned to the outdoor work with relief and a feeling of quick joy. Remembering the errors of the previous spring, she somehow bridled her impatience until the proper planting time, and as a result, the gardens were lovely beyond all expectation. All during the end of May and the early part of June, she stole late-afternoon or early-evening moments to walk across the grass behind the *Vosterhaus*, delighting in the luxuriant growth of climbing roses, the strong, sturdy new growth of the fruit trees and the evident health of the Golden Rain trees. The *Vosterhaus* was nearly finished, and there was a gracious look about it, a stately and settled look that was usually found only in old and established houses.

Not everything in the village was as beautiful as Hildegarde's gardens nor as serene as the Great House, however. There were some minor currents of unrest, the first evidences of impatience over the long wait for the promised Coming. Feeling his people's restlessness, Father Rapp reacted in the only way he knew and understood: he tightened the discipline. There was no cruelty in the old man, but there was no leniency either, for he believed that only the strong, the pure, the dedicated would be fit to live in the city of God when the hoped-for time arrived. With little regard for the opinions of anyone else, even Frederick, he wrote up a new set of agreements and set about getting the people to sign it.

Frederick, more sensitive to the emotions of the brothers and sisters than Father Rapp, suggested caution. "Give them time," he urged the old man. "They are tired from the move, the hard work of the winter, the many changes in their lives. Give them another year."

Father Rapp, cognizant only of the words in Revelation which seemed to speak to him with the sound of trumpets, felt the passing of time with an urgency in him. Three decades had gone by—the decades which to him were so obviously predicted in Revelation, and the time of the Coming was at hand. There was no time to wait!

So in spite of Frederick's cautioning, he insisted on reading the new agreement at a church meeting in early June. He had read it to the leaders—Dr. Mueller, Romelius Baker, Johannes Baker, Gerhard Mutschler—and they had agreed that the conditions were fair and honest, but they were aware of the fact that the new contract gave even more power to the patriarchal head of the community than the original one, and they had also suggested caution. As usual, they had been overruled.

As he read, the people listened with apparent docility. Hildegarde, sitting among the women, listened a little dreamily. It all sounded familiar to her—the statement that each member must give to the Society (she seemed unaware of the fact that it was impossible to distinguish between Father Rapp and the Society) all that he owned and never make full claim to it again, even if he should leave. His goods, his work, his loyalty must be given with gladness and generosity. In return, the Society promised to feed, clothe, shelter, and educate all of the people, even though they might fall ill and no longer be able to contribute. In fact, it seemed a bit odd to Hildegarde that Father Rapp even took the time to read all this. Had they not all agreed to such a situation years before? What was there to gain from a rewriting of these facts, a re-signing of the papers? If Father Rapp read the words and approved of them, that was all that mattered.

But after the meeting, she walked toward home with Maria, and she found that not everyone shared her reaction. Brother Ludwig,

Maria's father, grumbled as he moved along the street, his smallest child sleeping heavily on his shoulder.

"It seems he wants more and more and promises less and less," he said to no one in particular.

Hildegarde was shocked by the fact that Brother Ludwig expressed this heresy without seeming to fear the consequences. Was he so sure that those who listened would be in agreement? If that were so, there was more discord than she had ever dreamed possible.

Peter Kaufmann, a man Hildegarde knew only slightly, spoke in a sharp voice. "This is the last straw. I won't put up with any more. Schreiber has been asking me to leave, and I see now he's right. This is tyranny."

Maria squeezed Hildegarde's cold hand, and the faint light of the stars and the torches carried by a few boys showed that it was not fear that tightened Maria's fingers but excitement. Maria must have heard this kind of rebellious talk before, but the sound of it was new to Hildegarde. Her father and mother had never displayed anything but obedience.

Brother Ludwig laughed softly. "Not enough tyranny to make me want to leave, Brother Peter. Here one eats very well and the work is not burdensome."

"This man controls us like puppets," Kaufmann said. "We are told what to think, what to say, what to feel. No amount of food or shelter can balance such a situation for me."

Peter Kaufmann's voice had risen, and Hildegarde felt a protest crowding to her lips. If it was unseemly for a slip of a girl to speak defiantly to a man, then it was unseemly. But speak she must. No man could talk like that about Father Rapp—no man.

"Brother Peter," she said, and she was as breathless as though she had been running. "You mustn't say those things. You have no right. . . ."

He wheeled on her in the darkness. "No right, missy? And who are you that dares to tell me what I've a right to? Not your girl, is it, Brother Ludwig?"

"Not mine," Ludwig said, shifting the sleeping boy to a more comfortable position. "Maria wouldn't dare. Or Jacobina either. It's the Mutschler girl, I think."

As if I haven't been in his house a hundred times, Hildegarde thought hotly. But now to this Kaufmann man who says such horrible things, he talks as though I were a stranger.

"Yes," she said swiftly, her voice strident with her anger and stiff pride. "Yes, it's Hildegarde Mutschler. I'm not afraid to say so. You've got no right to talk so about the Father. You've. . . ."

Maria was tugging at her hand in misery. "Hildegarde, *shhh,*" she whispered. "You mustn't."

But Hildegarde had reached the point where no cautioning of Maria's could silence her. She snatched her hand from the restraining fingers and took a deep breath, preparatory to further angry words.

A man's voice stopped her. "Never mind, Sister Hildegarde. Brother Johannes and I heard it all. This is something for men to handle—not a girl."

She whirled toward the speaker. Conrad Feucht was directly behind her, straight and stern, and beside him was Johannes Baker, smaller and pinched together, breathing raspingly in the night air. But there was strength in the pair of them—in Conrad's young assurance, in Brother Johannes's calm purpose.

"Yes, Brother Conrad," she said, no less angry but certain that the words of these two men would have a greater effect than any words of hers.

"Save your breath, Brother Conrad," Peter Kaufmann said. "And you, too, Johannes. Nothing either of you can say can stop me or change my mind. I am no longer blind and shackled. Be a slave if you want to. I'm finished."

"You are indeed," Brother Johannes said, and his words wheezed in his throat. "You are finished and doomed. A man putting his hand to the plow and turning back. . . ." He sagged suddenly against Conrad and started to fall.

Hildegarde had suspected for months that he was sick, but the sight of his collapse was like a blow. Since earliest childhood, he had been one of the revered ones, part of the fabric of her faith.

"Help me," Conrad said sharply.

None of the men or boys in the group moved with the sure swiftness that was Hildegarde's in that moment. She leaped to Conrad's side and helped him lower the suddenly limp body to the ground. She snatched her shawl from her shoulders and put it under the head which seemed so heavy on its inert neck. Conrad's hands moved in the dark, and she seemed to know exactly what to do so that her fingers only assisted in the unbuttoning of the jacket and shirt and never got in the way of Conrad's skilled movements. Heedless of the damp grass or the crowding people, she pulled the shirt away from Conrad's face as he laid his ear on the pitifully thin chest.

"He's dead," Conrad said.

She felt his cheek move away from her hands, and it was the first she had been aware that she was touching him. Her fingers were only concerned with the still, frail body on the ground. With a single sob, she began painstakingly to button up the shirt as though she were afraid he might get cold there on the grass.

There was a stir among the people, and Father Rapp's voice was heard.

"What is it? Someone said Brother Johannes. . . ."

Conrad spoke quickly but with compassion in his voice. "He's dead, Father. His heart. . . ."

His words suddenly faltered. Was he going to say "broke," Hildegarde wondered. And was it true? Had Peter Kaufmann's anger and rebellion and arrogance been more than the gentle little man could stand? If that were true, then. . . .

She scrambled to her feet. "Father, Father, listen," she began.

But Conrad stopped her. His hand caught her

wrist with so imperative a gesture that she winced away from him.

"She's upset, Father," he said smoothly. "And no wonder. She helped me in a way no one else seemed able to do. And she's only a girl."

There were enough torches now that Hildegarde could see clearly—the old prophet's stern, sad face—and Conrad's warning look. Weren't they going to tell him? She glanced around swiftly but Peter Kaufmann was gone. Shouldn't they stop him? He ought to be punished.

There was a sudden stir, and the people separated to let Romelius Baker through. He came swiftly and knelt at his brother's side. For a minute there was complete silence, then Romelius stood up.

"Well, Brother George," he said to Father Rapp and was able to say no more.

"We'll see him again soon," Father Rapp said and put his arm across Romelius's shoulders. "Very soon, my brother."

"Several of you help me carry him," Conrad said authoritatively. "We'll take him to his house."

Hildegarde stood in bewilderment. It had all happened too fast. She saw several boys, young Fritz Baumann among them, bend to lift Johannes gently from the ground. Conrad started to move away with them, then suddenly turned back to her.

"Thank you," he said, "for your help. She's a brave girl, Father."

Father Rapp turned from Romelius. He nodded slowly. "I know," he said. "I've been watching her grow."

The unexpected praise, the new grief, and the entire action of the past minutes swept over Hildegarde with such a surge of emotion that she started to cry. A hand touched her shoulder, and she turned to find her mother watching. Here was security, here was comfort; Hildegarde buried her face against her mother's shoulder, feeling the strong arms around her. She was a little girl again, and all her bravery and competence dissolved in her tears.

Johannes Baker was buried the next day. Only the leaders of the community and the close friends of the family attended the simple funeral. Wrapped in pure white cloth, the body lay in a plain hexagonal wooden box awaiting the eulogy of Father Rapp. There was no room for grief in the words spoken above this man who had given his life and love to the brotherhood for nearly thirty years. There was, instead, a sense of exultation that one more member of the family had traveled the road that led to God. The natural human loneliness of family and friends was only a minor part of the emotion that filled the hearers of the eulogy and the speaker of the confident words.

The procession which moved toward the burying ground was solemn, but there was no sound of mourning. At the cemetery, the box was lifted off the bed of the black-curtained carriage which served as a hearse and gently lowered into the ground. One by one, the shovelfuls of dirt were dropped onto the box until at last the hole was filled and the ground was level again. Nowhere was there a marker on a grave. In this final act, all members were rendered completely equal and from now on were known only to God.

Hildegarde watched the people coming back from the cemetery. Each one paused only long enough to take Romelius by the hand, and then each resumed his normal activity. *So life goes on,* she thought. *Men like Peter Kaufmann leave in bitterness and anger, and men like Brother Johannes die and leave us forever. But life goes on. It ought to slow down at least, but it doesn't. It goes on just the same as it was.*

But it wasn't the same, and she knew it. There was a rupture in Eden, and some of the innocence was rubbed off for her. The shocking discovery that not everyone loved Father Rapp as she did had blurred the edges of her serenity with uncertainty. For a few days, her gaiety was submerged, and her eyes were as somber as those of Romelius Baker.

In July an event occurred which washed the somberness out of Hildegarde's eyes and replaced it with the usual sparkle. Father Rapp received a note from Frederick List, the German economist, saying he was planning to visit Economy within the week, and he wanted to include his impressions of the place in the book he intended to publish when he returned to Germany. The entire village reacted with a wave of hospitality, and extra effort was put forth to clean and beautify houses and gardens which already shone with cleanliness and glowed with loveliness.

Hildegarde worked feverishly in the gardens, vanquishing the smallest weed, seeing that the walks were smooth and swept, the grass clipped neatly and the stone Grotto free of its many climbing vines. The day before List's arrival, Gertrude came across the gardens seeking Hildegarde.

"We're going to have a tea," Gertrude announced without preamble. "Here in the garden. Brother Romelius says the weather will be fine, and Grandfather thinks that it might be a nice thing to do for Herr List."

Hildegarde clapped her hands, scattering bits of dirt in all directions. Any break in the normal routine was welcome.

"We're going to be the hostesses," Gertrude said calmly, but her eyes were dancing. "You and I."

Hildegarde looked her shock. "Us? Why not your grandmother? Why not Aunt Rosina? Or—or—anyone else?"

"Grandmother has one of her headaches and will be weak tomorrow—she always is the next day. And Aunt Rosina hates that sort of thing—you know how shy she is. Grandfather asked me and of course I said yes, and then he said to ask you. He said, 'Hildegarde has the feeling now.' I don't know exactly what he meant, but I know he's been talking to Brother Conrad about you."

Hildegarde's cheeks flamed. "It's nothing," she said.

Gertrude turned practical. "We'll have to have

tables carried out and chairs, and the girls in the kitchen will have to start baking ginger cakes so they'll be ready. And there will have to be fresh bouquets—and lots of things. Will you see to the flowers and chairs, Hildegarde?"

"Of course. I'll ask Brother Frederick to assign some boys to help me carry chairs."

"Good," Gertrude said. "If you'll bring that little blue teapot of yours, I'll get Grandmother's pink-sprigged cups, and the ginger cakes will be on the Adams plate. There should be wine, too. I'll run and order that right now."

With a quick wave, Gertrude was gone, and Hildegarde turned to see Maria watching her. There had been a coolness between the two girls since the night of Johannes Baker's death, and Hildegarde had felt that it was due to Maria's embarrassment over her father's actions. Her own emotions had been too chaotic to let her natural generosity take over, and so Hildegarde had allowed the coolness to continue. Now, with the joy and excitement of tomorrow facing her, she pushed away the cold feeling and smiled at Maria as she used to smile.

"Will you help me with the flowers?" she asked. "No one can fix them as you can."

Maria's face was rosy and quick tears filled her eyes. "I've been so unhappy, Hildegarde. I was afraid you were angry. My father—he—well, he is my father, and I. . . ."

Impulsively Hildegarde moved over to Maria and kissed her cheek. She was as quick to forgive as she was to get angry. "It's all right. It's not your fault. We're still friends, and you'll fix my flowers, won't you?"

"The most beautiful bouquets I can possibly fix," Maria assured her. "You won't have to think about it again."

The next morning was crowded with work and last minute preparations. Brother Frederick sent the four young men that Hildegarde requested, and she assigned tasks to them.

"This is a party," Hildegarde chided one of the boys who placed the chairs in rows, "not a church meeting. Put the chairs in friendlier positions—so people can talk."

"Here, Sister Hildegarde," a young man said. "I know what you want."

Hildegarde looked up into the face of Jacob Klein. She had known him always, of course, but had seldom talked to him since she had come to Economy. She had been aware several times recently that he had been looking at her across the church, but she had never paid much attention. Here in the sunshine, in her happy mood, however, his voice made a sharp impression on her. It was a deep, strong voice, making her aware of how much he had changed.

"Thank you, Brother Jacob," she said.

"I'm happy to do what *you* want," he replied, and to her surprise, a clear dark red suddenly ran up his cheeks and onto his forehead.

He must be very shy, she thought, and to set him at ease, she smiled her friendliest smile at him. Rather than putting him at his ease, her smile only seemed to increase his confusion. When he turned to the chairs, she saw that his hands were suddenly clumsy as though they were trembling.

He certainly is nervous, she reflected with compassion. Then seeing that he was fixing the chairs as she wanted, she felt free to run home to dress herself in a fresh cotton dress.

When she came out of her house to cross the street again to the Great House, she stopped to pull several monthly roses from the bush beside the side door. She twisted the short stems into her braids, wishing for a mirror to see how the delicate buds looked against her hair.

She found the mirror in the eyes of the honor guest, Frederick List, a round little man with hair that flew about his head like dandelion down and round blue eyes that looked too innocent and cherubic to be the eyes of an economist. Still, his achievements were known, and Hildegarde was impressed. She greeted him shyly, quite unprepared for his reaction.

"I have rarely seen a rose wearing a rose," he said, beaming at her. "But here in the wilderness—I use the word 'wilderness' with levity, Herr Rapp," he added as an aside to Frederick, "I have found that lovely combination. I am grateful to you, Fräulein Hildegarde, for affording me this pleasure."

My face must be as red as Jacob's was this morning, she thought, as she smiled at their guest. Unable to think of the proper words to say in response, she offered tea or wine to the men standing before her and saw to it that they had ginger cakes to eat.

List's compliments were still ringing in her

head when the little tea ceremony in the garden was finished. The summer sun, the color of the leaves against the sky and the distant satin of the river seemed to whirl with List's words in her brain until she was dizzy—as dizzy as she had been as a child when she had taken the bottle of wine from the cupboard and consumed nearly half of it before her mother caught her. The dizziness spun her on the necessary errands of cleaning up with a light-headedness that bore no resemblance to the practical calmness of her actions of the morning.

Jacob Klein watched her, the way she moved as though she were dancing, the soft color in her cheeks that seemed to match the roses in her hair, and his heart beat chokingly at the back of his throat. He was not a strong man nor an aesthetic one, and he knew it. His bouts with temptation had been bitter and violent, and only rarely did he feel that he had conquered the inherent evil in his nature. And it was always the sight of Hildegarde which tore him to pieces— filling him with human desire and yet making him want to fall to his knees in the purest kind of devotion.

He was balancing two heavy chairs when she danced past, laughter spilling from her like a fragile waterfall. She stopped in obvious admiration.

"Brother Jacob, you're so strong."

"Thank you," he said stiffly, and she saw the color mount again to the edge of his hair.

Something prompted her to pursue the subject. "I've watched you work in the fields," she said. It wasn't really true; she had noticed him no more than any other man. But the width of his shoulders, the strength of his arms told her the sort of work he could do. "If we had more men like you, Brother Jacob, the Society would be even better than it is."

He stared at her in mute joy. She had noticed him. But before he could think of any word to say, she turned and whirled away and he heard her laughing voice as she called to Fritz Baumann.

I'm a sinner, Jacob thought. *I possess such evil thoughts within myself that I even imagine that she possesses them, too. What's the matter with me? I must pray for help. I mustn't stay where I can see her for even another minute.*

He left the chairs where they were and plunged suddenly across the garden and into the street, heading for a place of quiet, a place for prayer.

Hildegarde did not even see him go. If she had, she would not have understood. How could she know that he saw her face in his dreams and woke to a sense of unworthiness and despair and a constant longing that could not be overcome?

Chapter 7

The introduction of the new Articles of Agreement had been so shadowed by Peter Kaufmann's anger and Johannes Baker's death that even Father Rapp finally conceded reluctantly that spring would be soon enough for the signing. He grumbled about the passing of time, and he preached some scorching sermons on obedience, then turned his attention to other matters. By fall, he was so concerned with the harvest, the new printing press that had just been purchased, and the coming of the *Liebesmahl* that nothing else mattered.

The *Liebesmahl*, or Love Feast, was the most solemn and significant occasion of the year. It was a time to accept again the role of being God's special and chosen people, to reaffirm love for God and for each other, to confess the sins of the past year and to ask forgiveness from any member who had intentionally or unintentionally been offended. Religious fervor burned more brightly during the preparations for and the partaking of the *Liebesmahl* than at any other time.

The *Liebesmahl* had been held under the sky in 1825, but by the autumn of 1826, the Feast Hall, one of the first permanent buildings to be erected, was near enough completion that the meal could be served in the *saal*, the large upper room. Built of warm red brick, the Feast Hall stretched more than a hundred feet along Grossestrasse, the street which led to the river. Inside the front and back doors of the building, wide stairs climbed to the second story where a single room, ninety by fifty-five feet, sprawled under the partially completed gambrel roof. Long wooden tables and backless benches stretched along the room, providing enough places for all the Brotherhood to eat. There was an aisle down the center to separate the men's from the women's tables, and at one end of the room a few tables were set slightly apart. These were for children, potential members, or anyone else who had not, for one reason or another, signed the original Articles of Agreement.

The date for the *Liebesmahl* was set for early October, and preparations were begun a week ahead. Apples were brought in for the strudel, the best vegetables were chosen and carried to the many kitchens where they would be prepared and cooked. Future plans included a Feast Kitchen where all the cooking would be done in huge cast iron kettles which would set down into wood-burning brick ovens, but until that project was complete, the side dishes would be prepared in individual homes, and the main dish of beef and pork and noodles would be cooked outdoors over an open fire.

This meant that the great kettles, blackened by previous fires, had to be scoured in readiness, and Hildegarde, who preferred working with her garden or picking apples, was set to the task of scouring them. She managed to escape that sort of thing so frequently that she felt both astonishment and resentment when she found her name on the kettle-cleaning list. Even the fact that Maria was assigned to the same task failed to pacify her at first.

"It's a dirty job," she muttered to Maria as they collected pumice, lye soap, and old cloths. "Why don't they have some of the boys do it, or some of the girls who are too stupid to do anything else?"

Maria looked at her in astonishment. "Am I hearing you right?" she said and giggled. "Is this Hildegarde talking—the girl who said that no one had any right to special treatment except Father Rapp? You must not have been listening that day."

Hildegarde blushed, but her irritation did not dissipate. "This is different," she snapped.

"How?" said Maria. "Because it's happening to you?"

"I'll make you sorry for that," Hildegarde cried with a mixture of mock and real anger. She caught her skirt above her ankles and began to chase Maria who ran, laughing, along the walk.

A stern voice interrupted them. "Sister Hildegarde, Sister Maria, you're supposed to be preparing for the most holy event of our year. This is no time for childish playing."

Hildegarde turned toward Frederick. "We're not playing," she said more sharply than she intended. "We're on our way to scour the kettles." Something made her unable to resist adding, "And get filthy dirty in the process, I expect."

Frederick spoke in a curiously gentle voice. "I don't think it will hurt you any. It might even help you. It seems to me you are too prideful, so I chose you to scrub kettles for your own good."

She knew he was right. She knew his concern for her stemmed from the fact that he felt a responsibility for all of the brothers and sisters. But still, her resentment filled her throat with bitterness. If it had been Father Rapp who had set her to this task, it would have been different. But Brother Frederick—

She disregarded the gentle sound in his voice. "I don't expect to ever be humble enough to *like* scouring pots," she flung out. "I may do it, Brother Frederick, but I *won't* enjoy it."

His face lost a little of its gentleness and seemed to harden.

"Where did you ever get the idea that life is one long time of pleasure? You evidently need some instruction or better still, some discipline."

The words were stern, and her eyes burned with tears of humiliation and chagrin. She had rarely been censored by a superior, and the scorn in Frederick's voice hurt her deeply.

"Yes, sir," she said, and her failure to use the

endearing term of "Brother" was an added pain to both of them.

"I'll speak to the Father," Frederick said. "Since he agreed with me that you ought to do this, then he ought to be told of the way you're acting."

Then she was frightened. Frederick's disapproval might hurt or anger her, but Father Rapp's disapproval would destroy her.

"No, please," she begged. "I'm sorry, Brother Frederick. Truly I am. The devil rules my tongue sometimes, but I didn't *mean* to be saucy."

He stared at the tears on her face. That they were sincere, he could not doubt, but he mistrusted her mercurial nature. She was too pretty, too headstrong, and he knew it. But Father Rapp insisted that it was only her youth, that she would grow into one of the strong, sturdy ones who were the bulwark of the Society. And it was true that her loyalty to Father Rapp was fierce and unwavering. *Maybe I am too much influenced by her looks and her spirit,* Frederick reflected. *Maybe I need to be more forgiving.*

The gentleness came again into his voice. "Don't cry, Sister Hildegarde. Ask God to rule your tongue and your heart. Go and scour the kettles, and I won't have to talk to the Father."

Relief pushed the fear out of her heart and eased the tightness in her throat. "Thank you," she said. "Thank you very much."

She turned with Maria and fairly ran across the grass to where the work was waiting. Frederick, watching her, thought ruefully that she should be cautioned against running, too, but perhaps she had been chastised enough for one day.

Turning, he saw Jacob Klein, whose hungry eyes followed Hildegarde, standing on the path behind him.

"Brother Jacob," Frederick said, more in sorrow than anger. "Are you in need of either confession or prayer?"

Jacob's face, flushed and taut with misery, swung toward Frederick. He seemed unable to control the words which wrenched themselves out of his mouth. "God made her so beautiful," he said.

"She's the devil's tool if she tempts you to worldly lusts and desires. You know that, Brother Jacob. Have you asked God to rid you of this—this evil thought?"

Jacob's jaw set with stubbornness. "Yes, Brother Frederick, I've prayed. More than you can know I've prayed. But my thoughts aren't evil. It's just—just that she's so beautiful."

"Not evil? What do you interpret as evil?"

"I'm not lustful. I. . . ." But Jacob's words wavered and died away before Frederick's searching gaze.

"I'm in need of prayer, Brother," Jacob said humbly. "Not confession. I've never touched her."

"But you've dreamed of touching her."

"How does a man control his dreams?" Jacob cried.

Frederick's hand on Jacob's arm was firm.

"Come, my brother. We'll pray together. God will strengthen you if you let him."

But there was more hopelessness than hope in Jacob's heart as he walked with Frederick toward the church. Sometimes God seemed very far away, and Hildegarde was very near and warm and real.

The *Liebesmahl* fell on a day of brilliant October sunshine. Over the hills, the sky curved in a pure distillation of blue, and the beauty of it ached in Hildegarde as she walked toward the Feast Hall. The emotion of this day had turned all her rebellion and stubbornness into a soft compliancy, and she felt as though she could reach up to touch heaven and hold it in her hands. She had not even thought of Jacob Klein since the day of the tea, and it certainly never occurred to her that his agony should be a burden of guilt on her soul. She knew of only one great sin that would have to be confessed on this day of general confession: her overwhelming sin of pride. And there were only two people with whom she would have to exchange the kiss of peace and reconciliation—Maria and Brother Frederick. They were the only two who had been recipients of her anger and who deserved her request for forgiveness. In reality, the gesture had already been made to Maria weeks ago in the garden, but custom demanded that the words be repeated today. Hildegarde's heart squeezed together in contrition at the memory of her anger toward Maria. Then her thoughts veered to Frederick and the contrition turned to raw fear. She wondered faintly if she would say the necessary words and then touch his cheek with her lips. She would surely die of fright, she thought, and childishly clasped her hands together in the attitude of prayer.

Oh, well, if there were only two. Her mind touched on Peter Kaufmann and she knew an absurd sense of satisfaction that she didn't have to acknowledge *that* anger to anyone. Swiftly and unexpectedly, memory struck her. She had been almost as furious at Brother Ludwig as she had been at Peter Kaufmann. She would have to humiliate herself before him even though he was a man she could not honestly admire. She would have to kiss his bearded cheek which was always redolent of garlic and sausage. Unless she were very careful, her penitence would be a mockery. Well, there was nothing to do but search out the ones who had felt the sting of her anger and her pride. The sooner she found them, the better.

She found Maria first, and the exchanged kiss tasted of tears and love. The ritual words were easy enough to say to Maria, but they were harder to say to Brother Ludwig, especially since he looked his honest amazement at her, having been ignorant of the fury he had aroused in her heart. His hearty pardon, given with condescension, made the prescribed kiss taste bitter on her lips. Slowly and a little forlornly, she wandered through the crowd seeking Frederick.

The people, pardoned and pardoning, were making their way into the Feast Hall, their hearts cleansed and pure enough to allow them to partake of the holy feast, and still she had not found Frederick. Finally, she saw him talking to Jacob Klein, and she stood waiting. She could not hear the words they spoke, but she saw Frederick's hands patting Jacob's shoulders, as though he were offering comfort and assurance. As Jacob turned away from Frederick, he came face to face with Hildegarde, and for a second he seemed to stumble, but Frederick's hands were strong at his back, and he was able to wrench his eyes from her face and make his way into the building.

"Brother Frederick," Hildegarde began timidly, and Frederick swung to meet her. His face hardened, and her heart seemed to fail in her breast. She couldn't know that it was because of her that Frederick had struggled with Jacob, and so she thought the coolness on his face was only because she had been so rude and outspoken a few days before.

"I have sinned against thee." She began the ritual falteringly. "I am not worthy to be your sister. But with God's help I will not be so—" *wicked* was the prescribed word, but she felt her actions needed to be specifically described—"so prideful and haughty again. Will you forgive me?"

With a mental wrench, Frederick tore himself from what he knew of Jacob's feelings for this girl and reminded himself again that he had to be fair, that Hildegarde was probably innocent. She couldn't help it, after all, that Jacob's flesh needed sharp discipline. His eyes lost their sternness, and he answered with the prescribed words of pardon.

Hesitantly, she put her hands on his shoulders and lifted herself onto her toes to touch his cheek. He was objectively aware of the light fragrance of her hair, and pity wrenched his heart for the weakness of Jacob who would be swayed by these physical things.

"Sister Hildegarde," he said suddenly. "God did not see fit to make you plain, and so your responsibility is grave. Unless you are more pure than any girl in this Society, the devil will use you as a tool to tempt weak men. Do you understand?"

Her bewilderment renewed his conviction of her innocence. "I try," she said in a low voice. "It's hard to be always good, Brother Frederick. But I try."

"I'll pray for you," he said kindly, and for this moment there was a real warmth between them, a true blossoming of the harmony that was the foundation on which this Society was based.

The feast of beef and pork and noodles, great varieties of fresh vegetables, apple strudel, bread, and wine was finished at last. The people had eaten together in a feeling of close fellowship, and the food had become a sacrament in the act of eating it. Hildegarde looked at the women near her—her mother, Aunt Rosina, Gertrude, Maria—and they looked back at her with the same love in their faces that she was feeling in her heart.

Suddenly a door, high in one of the end walls,

opened and Father Rapp stood framed in the opening. His voice, compelling and hypnotic, rolled out, casting its spell on every listener.

Hildegarde, mesmerized like the others, seemed to be hovering in a hazy dream. The sound of Father Rapp's words carried her back through the years, back to another time when his voice had been a miracle for her.

Malaria fever had raged through the Indiana community of New Harmony in 1814, and neither prayer nor quinine seemed able to stop the plague which devastated the people. In every house the beds were filled with feverish, delirious people while those who were able to be on their feet nursed the sick with what skill they possessed.

In the Mutschler house, the fever spread like a malignancy from father to mother to children. The youngest boy cried out in delirium and thirst, and the small body stiffened in convulsions. He died before dawn, and Christina Mutschler felt her heart break in her breast, and nothing could comfort her in this hour of sorrow. Her last remnant of hope lay in her two older children, because there would be no more babies to carry in her arms. Wilhelm, the oldest boy, sickened and seemed to hover on the edge of death, but then the fever left him, and she knew that even though he was weak and wasted, he would live. She was able, then, to turn her fierce energy to small Hildegarde who lay moaning pitifully hour after hour, crying for the water which never seemed to cool the blistered lips.

The cries seemed to grow weaker (how often Hildegarde had been told of this), and the hour came when Christina Mutschler gave up hope and yearned in agony over her dying child. But in that moment, the door opened, and like a cool wind blowing, Father Rapp walked into the house—as he walked into every house in the village day after day, using his strength to comfort and to heal. He stood beside Hildegarde's bed, and his voice was vibrant and sure.

"Why are you crying, Sister Christina? Don't you know that God can heal this child if that is his will? Don't you have any faith at all?

"I had faith with the baby, but he died," Christina said, hardly aware of what she was saying. "I'm too tired to have faith anymore."

The old man looked down at the small flushed face on the pillow, and pity and affection softened his eyes. With a rare gesture of tenderness, he put out his hand and laid it on her forehead.

"Kleine Hildegarde," he said, like summer wind blowing across the grass, and the child heard the softness of it in her dreams. "Little Hildegarde, stay awhile."

She had been slipping away, like dark water running over pebbles, so it was not easy to listen to the voice, to hear and come back. But she could not ignore his words either, which in her delirium seemed to be heavenly words.

Hildegarde thought in a hazy astonishment, "It's God I hear calling me. I hear God's voice."

She opened her eyes, lucid and clear of the

fever, and his face was bigger and brighter than anything she had ever seen.

"God looks just like Father Rapp," she said in a small voice, "only more beautiful."

She looked in surprise at the warm tears falling on her hand. She had never seen her mother cry before. She couldn't believe, even seeing it, that some of the tears were Father Rapp's. She didn't even understand that he had called her back from the long journey to death. She only knew that she had heard his voice, and to her it had been the voice of God.

And now sitting on her hard bench at the *Liebesmahl*, she felt the same way. This voice that rolled down over his people from the high door was the voice of God.

After the sermon came the singing, and the loveliness of it soared under the high roof. Hildegarde moved through the hours as though she moved through a dream. It was only when the festivities were finished that she came back to earth to discover that there were hundreds of dirty dishes which had to be carried to the various homes for washing. There were no angel wings to make the task less tiresome, she realized with a sort of wry humor, as she began to gather up the dishes which belonged to their house.

A heavy bowl teetered in her hands suddenly, and she gasped and made a grab for it. Strong masculine hands appeared beside hers and caught the bowl, steadying it, curving her fingers about it safely.

She looked up into Jacob Klein's face, to see nothing but kindness in his eyes, not even a shadow of the agony and desire which had filled him for weeks.

It was only when she saw this new, cleansed, purified look in his eyes that Hildegarde finally realized what Jacob had felt for her before. Now she understood, and in the sweet emotional aftermath of the *Liebesmahl*, she felt pity and compassion touch her heart.

"Thank you," she said quietly.

He left her at once, and Frederick, observing the episode, felt relief explode in his heart. For now, at least, his prayers had been answered. But Frederick was no dreamy mystic; he knew that tomorrow would come for the hot-blooded young man and the arrogant girl—a tomorrow for which neither of them was adequately prepared.

Chapter 8

One midwinter day of 1826, Father Rapp called Frederick, Dr. Mueller, and Conrad to meet with him because a young man had come to Economy that morning with an unusual request which Father Rapp wanted to consider. He knew what custom dictated his action should be, but on the other hand, this might be a rare opportunity which ought not be overlooked.

The men gathered around the plain table in the middle of the room, and Father Rapp introduced them to the thin, yellow-haired boy who had just arrived.

"Brothers, this Martin Schmidt; he was in Wurtemburg not long ago, and he has stopped to bring greetings from old friends. But he also has a suggestion to make."

The three men acknowledged the introduction and their smiles of welcome were so warm that young Schmidt, who had been slightly intimidated by Father Rapp's austerity, began to visibly thaw.

"Tell them what you suggested to me," Father Rapp commanded.

Schmidt hesitated and then spoke bluntly. "I visited with Herr von Bonnhorst in Pittsburgh, and he suggested that perhaps you might employ me for the winter. I'm going on to Indiana to settle, but I'm not really well enough to travel now in midwinter."

Frederick frowned and then made a conscious effort to make his face more pleasant. "Von Bonnhorst is an old and trusted friend. We would accept his references, of course, but he knows that we don't employ outsiders. Our own members do all the work we need."

"Herr von Bonnhorst said you didn't have anyone able to do what I want to do—that is, to teach English to your young people who are going to need it in the future," Schmidt said quickly as though he were afraid his courage might fail if he waited to speak.

For a minute there was no reply and then Conrad spoke carefully. "I think this might be a good idea if your English is really proficient. I'm supposed to be one of the best speakers of English in the village, but I know I'm slow and awkward and sometimes don't understand what is said to me. I, for one, would welcome tutoring."

"Your English is adequate," Frederick said. "We don't need to speak like native Americans, do we?"

"The more business we do with Americans,

the more we need those who speak the language well," Dr. Mueller said. "I tend to agree with Brother Conrad. I certainly wish I spoke better than I do. And I have a few students who would profit from lessons."

"You misunderstand me," Frederick said, casting an uneasy glance at young Schmidt. "I don't mean to insult our young friend here, but it's just not our custom to take in strangers or to have them deal extensively with our young people."

Schmidt spoke up eagerly, his desire for a fair hearing overcoming his natural shyness. "I wouldn't do anything but teach, I assure you. I'm not a follower of your beliefs, I know, but I've heard much of your life, and I would never argue or question your authority. I would only teach English in the classroom and spend my spare time in a quiet room somewhere where I could write and rest."

"How do we even know that your English is really good?" Father Rapp said, paying no heed to the puzzled look Frederick gave him. He knew Frederick was disturbed over the seeming disregard for the fact that Schmidt was not a Harmonist. But English was one subject that had to come from the world—whether or not custom was being violated.

"Here is Herr von Bonnhorst's letter," Schmidt said simply and gave a folded paper to Father Rapp.

The old man quickly ran his eyes down the closely written sheet and then looked up with satisfaction. "I could take von Bonnhorst's word on anything," he said. "If he says you are really skillful in language, then I believe it."

"Thank you, sir," Schmidt said quietly. It was perfectly obvious to him now that any final decision would be made by the old man who sat at the head of the table. He might let the others speak, but he held his own counsel.

"I don't question his ability," Frederick said patiently. "I only question the wisdom of bringing in a stranger to stay and work in such an intimate position as a teacher."

"Brother Frederick," Conrad said, "you, of all people, know the need to speak clearly and plainly with our customers, our competitors, our neighbors. Only a few of us speak English now and none of us very well. Even Brother Romelius has trouble. A winter of studying would go very well, I think."

Frederick shrugged and looked at Father Rapp. There was no point in arguing in front of the young stranger.

"I think I agree with Brother Conrad," Father Rapp said at last after a silence. "I think we'll try it. Could you stay until May or even June, Herr Schmidt? And what would you want as a salary?"

Schmidt knew that these people were not poor, but he felt very certain that they kept a tight drawstring on the purse. Besides, he was not here to make money. He was here because he was tired and almost ill after the long journey. He wanted time to be peaceful, to be quiet, to write a little, to forget the blue-eyed girl in Germany who had refused to come to America.

"A room in your good inn," he said. "Enough food to fill my belly. Some quiet time for myself. That would be salary enough. And I could stay until mid-May, at least."

Father Rapp looked in quiet triumph at his friends. A skilled tutor, some relief for the over-burdened Dr. Mueller, and not even a salary to pay. Good old von Bonnhorst! There was a friend to have at one's side.

"Then it's settled," Father Rapp said, and not even by a quick glance did he indicate that he might feel anxious over contradicting Frederick's opinion. "One of you can take him to the inn to get settled, and we'll begin arrangements for classes. Evening classes, I think, for the advanced students such as you, Brother Conrad. And morning classes for others—such as my granddaughter."

"Let me take him over," Dr. Mueller said. "I have to leave anyhow because I have two music students waiting for me right now in the Feast Hall. Unless you have further need of me, Brother George?"

"No, no need. But perhaps you two will stay a little longer," he added as Frederick and Conrad also began to stand up.

They both settled again into their chairs and when Dr. Mueller and Schmidt had left, Father Rapp turned to them.

"We might as well get this all settled at once. Then I can forget it. We have to decide who will study English."

Frederick spoke evenly, but there was a small line indented at the corner of his mouth as though he were trying to be careful with his words. "I'm sure the Father will agree with me when I say that we should be very cautious in our choice."

Father Rapp nodded benignly. "Of course. I couldn't say anything in front of young Schmidt, but this is why your fears were groundless, my son. Only our faithful members, our dedicated ones will study with this fellow. We don't have to worry that he'll pollute their minds with worldliness."

Conrad smiled and spoke lightly. "You mean, we won't open classes to youngsters like Maria Baumann."

The two older men reacted as Conrad had hoped and allowed their gravity to dissolve in a shared mirth. "No, nor her father," Father Rapp said. "If the Baumanns—or any of our folks like them—want to learn English, they'll have to invent their own method of study."

"I think the evening class should be kept very small," Frederick said, evidently reassured by Father Rapp's words and willing now to join in the plans. "None but Brother Christoph, Brother Conrad, Brother Romelius, and myself, I should think. And you, Father. Do you want to study?"

Father Rapp shook his shaggy head. "I'm not interested in English. My people and my God understand my Swabian; I'll let you deal with the world, Frederick."

"Then, what about the morning class?" Frederick asked. "It'll be a more elementary class, so they can probably have a few more students. I presume you want Sister Gertrude to study, so she'll probably want Sister Pauline. And what about young Jacob Klein? I think he might be very useful to us someday."

"Yes, I agree to all of them," Father Rapp said. "There are a half-dozen boys I have in mind. And I think Sister Hildegarde should be included."

"I don't," Frederick said with such abruptness that the other two men looked at him with astonishment.

"I agree with the Father," Conrad said quickly. "It seems to me she is growing in spirit and in grace. And her loyalty is certainly unwavering."

"I have a very strong feeling about this girl," Father Rapp said slowly, and Frederick felt his heart give a heavy jerk of apprehension. "I think she's going to be very important to our community, to me. I want her to have all advantages."

Frederick knew that he had no real case against Hildegarde. If he told them of Jacob's anguish they would feel only disgust with the desires that tormented the boy, and they probably wouldn't feel it was Hildegarde's fault at all. *But it is*, Frederick thought hopelessly, *she is too gay, too merry, too much in love with worldly things like beautiful dresses and flowers in her hair. She will never be a true Harmonist, and the Father is going to be sorry for this.*

Father Rapp put his hand on Frederick's shoulder with one of his rare gestures of affection. "My son, leave such decisions and things to me. Your genius lies in the business end of our lives. I wouldn't question your advice about certain products. Don't question mine about certain people."

Warmed by the touch of the hand on his shoulder and swayed by the apparent logic in the old man's words, Frederick bent his head in acquiescence. It was not until several hours later that he remembered that he, himself, had suggested Jacob Klein for the class. So now, in spite of his efforts, Hildegarde was to be thrown again in close contact with Jacob and temptation would become a daily torment for the boy. *Perhaps it will prove to be excellent discipline,* Frederick thought, taking on the fashion of Father Rapp's thinking. *Perhaps I was led to say the things I said. Perhaps . . .* but he was not really certain.

Martin Schmidt met with his morning class the following day, and he found twelve students facing him in the classroom on the first floor. They were adults in every sense of the word, except for a childlike naiveté which made their faces look scrubbed and shining, like children's faces.

He consulted the paper on his table and began to read the names printed on it. As each person responded to his name, Martin looked up, trying to associate names with faces. The young men were on one side of the room, and, Martin, shorter and slimmer than most of them, felt a faint sense of relief that they all appeared to be gentle and cordial. There had been a school-room experience in Germany which had left him with a knot on his head and a healthy respect for students larger than he. He turned to the girls' side with more curiosity. Would they all be as plain and stodgy as he had been led by his inquiries to believe? Certainly the two serving girls in the inn last night had not led him to hope for much more.

But here now, here was something different. The golden-haired girl in the back—she was beautiful—but too arrogant and proud for the likes of him. There was a tilt to her chin and a glint in her eye that boded only trouble for a shy, awkward schoolmaster. And that middle girl—did she say her name was Pauline?—there was nothing there beyond her severe, earnest face. He could tell even without talking to her that laughter would be foreign to her, that dullness would be as much a part of her as her thin brown hair. But what of the girl in the front seat? There, now, there was a girl to look at, to ponder over, to try to teach.

Martin looked at Gertrude with a feeling of anticipation. Her sweet, round face, her shining brown hair braided thickly over her ears, her quiet hands in repose on her lap—all these had a calming, quieting effect on his troubled heart. If he were going to forget the girl in Germany, it might very well be Gertrude who could help him do it. Not that he would try to court her, of course; von Bonnhorst had told him there was no courtship here although he hadn't made himself clear about it. But it would be all right to look at her, to rest his tired soul in the placid depths of her eyes. Then, when the winter was over, he could go on his way, cured of his old malady and ready to take his place in a new world.

The lesson went along well enough, and Martin resorted to the tool which he had so often used in Germany to put a point across—the subtle and deft use of humor. He never allowed it to disrupt the discipline of the class, but at the same time there was a definite feeling of a fresh wind blowing through the room. The young Harmonists, used to the stricter discipline of Dr. Mueller, reacted with a quick delight. For most of them, it was their first close experience with someone from the world.

There was one exception. In the back of the room sat a tall slender fellow with blond hair, a blond pointed beard, high forehead, and large dark eyes. He had been born in Europe and had lived in the world until the previous July when he had found his way to Economy, which he considered the lodging for which his soul was destined. His name was Jacob Henrici, and he was not yet a member of the Society, but Father Rapp had sent word to him that he should attend this class. Henrici had received the word with a curious lightening of his heart. Although he had been certain in his own mind for months that his life had to be lived as a Harmonist if there were to be any real meaning in it for him, he had not known for sure that Father Rapp felt the same. Including him in this very special class seemed to elevate his hope more than anything which had ever happened.

Oddly enough, Henrici reacted to Schmidt's humor with less enthusiasm than anyone else. Schmidt, who had noticed that the handsome young man in the back of the room was not dressed as a Harmonist, observed his cool restraint when laughter brushed across the room, and he wondered at it. But he was too accustomed to students to expect identical reaction from all of them. If the tall, blond fellow—what was his name? Henrici? Sounded French instead of German—wanted to act aloof, let him. It was satisfaction enough to see a warmth rise to Gertrude's cheeks, to watch Hildegarde's eyes sparkle with delight, to watch most of the young men lose their somber look. Language was something which was learned best if the students were relaxed. If they were shy or austere, they were usually too embarrassed to attempt correct pronunication. They would have to loosen up a lot if they were going to really try the ridiculous American "r"—the strange "a" that was neither broad nor short. Schmidt turned to his book with no further thought for Henrici.

When the class was finished, the girls left the room at once, and the young men followed more slowly. Schmidt noticed that there was no attempt on the part of any of them to exchange words or looks reminiscent of the coquettish looks he had seen young people exchange at home. He shrugged and reflected that after all it was none of his business. He would teach and rest and maybe write some poetry. He gathered up his books and looked up to see Henrici standing before him.

"May I ask a question?" Henrici was polite but reserved.

"Certainly."

"Do you plan to teach anything except English?"

"No. I've been hired to teach English only. Why?"

A faint flush colored the high forehead under the blond hair. "I only wondered. I had planned—hoped—to teach when I had been here longer. I—I only wondered."

Schmidt spoke casually. "Don't worry that I'll steal your job. I'm only staying the winter and then I'll be moving on. How about you? Do you work here or what?"

Henrici drew himself up and spoke tautly. "No, I don't work here. In my heart I'm as much a member as anyone who was in this room. I'm only waiting until Father Rapp—until we—until the right time comes for joining."

"They do take in new members then?" Schmidt asked.

"Occasionally. They don't proselyte. There's no need."

Schmidt, knowing something of the community from the old men in Wurtemburg, hazarded a quick guess. "Well, if they don't marry and have children and they don't proselyte, then how do they expect to keep the Society alive? When all the present members are dead, what then?" he asked.

Henrici hesitated as though weighing the wisdom of an answer. But the devotion and fervor of a new convert were greater than his normal caution. "There's no need for it to grow or to last beyond the lifetime of the Father. Christ will come again—and soon. Beyond that, what need is there of human plan?"

Schmidt looked into the blazing brown eyes. "I didn't know," he said nervously.

"How could you know?" There was a sort of pity in the handsome face. "Only the chosen ones can know and understand. Only the chosen ones need to know. This isn't any concern of yours. You teach us and then go on your way."

He wheeled abruptly and went out to stride swiftly toward the door of the Feast Hall. He bobbed his head in the briefest of greetings to the two girls who stood in the turn of the hall beneath the steps. Gertrude Rapp and Hildegarde Mutschler seemed as unimportant as the walls of the building in which they stood. Henrici was intent on only one thing: making his heart fit to be a true Harmonist.

Chapter 9

The two girls watched him stride away and then turned to face each other in the dim light of the hall.

"I'm supposed to go over to the factory," Hildegarde said, "but not for awhile yet. Could we take a walk? I love the wind."

"You aren't supposed to," Gertrude objected. "You know you get the lung fever if you get too cold."

"I won't get cold," Hildegarde said. "Come on. We never get a chance to talk."

She hooked her arm through Gertrude's and pulled her out the door into the bitter wind.

"We talk in class and in meetings," Gertrude said.

"I don't mean *that* kind of talk. I mean just you and me."

Gertrude looked surprised. "You mean just talk to make talk? But isn't that a terrible waste of time?"

Hildegarde made an exasperated sound. "Oh, Gertrude," she said. The next words came so impulsively that Hildegarde surprised herself. "I get so tired of being a Harmonist. Sometimes I just want to be me!"

Gertrude's breath drew in sharply. She was shocked and yet she was a little excited, too. This girl beside her was such a mixture of good and bad, and, in a sense, no one knew it better than Gertrude. The thing that frightened the quiet granddaughter of Father Rapp most was that she knew she could be swayed by Hildegarde. Even when the impulsive words of her friend might be wrong, they could not always be resisted.

"How can you be *you*?" Gertrude asked. "Apart from being a Harmonist, I mean? Aren't you all one person inside?"

By now, they had left the Feast Hall and were walking down Grossestrasse toward the river. Their woolen shawls blew back in the wind, but the intensity and intimacy of their talk warmed them.

"I don't know," Hildegarde said soberly. She struggled to give words to thoughts which she never clearly formulated even in her own mind, thoughts which made her restless and unhappy. "Sometimes I feel like I'm two or three people. Sometimes I'm good and being a Harmonist is easy. Sometimes I feel silly and giddy and not like a Harmonist at all. And sometimes I think things—I think things I know I shouldn't think."

Gertrude hugged Hildegarde's arm in a spasm of nervous chill. "I don't understand you at all," she said. "Maybe it's because I live with Grandfather and Frederick, but my mind just goes along the same lines all the time. I think about God—and the silk—and the people. That's all."

Hildegarde didn't answer for a minute, but her thoughts tumbled through her mind, blowing in and out of her consciousness by the winds of memory and guilt and conjecture. Frederick's words at the *Liebesmahl* still tormented her. *Would* she be a temptation to men? Even when she didn't try to be? Was this why Jacob Klein looked at her with an intimacy that jerked her heart? And was she the only girl who had these thoughts? Hadn't Gertrude ever wondered about it at all?

"Don't you ever think about boys?" she blurted out abruptly. "Like Jacob Henrici? Or Herr Schmidt?"

Gertrude looked at her in honest amazement. "No more than I think about you—or Pauline. You know how we've been taught."

"My mind has been taught, but my heart hasn't," Hildegarde said.

Gertrude made a shocked sound but Hildegarde ignored it.

"My heart thinks of many things," she added stubbornly. "I look at people and I wonder. Herr Schmidt, for instance. He's not a member of the Society. What does he think when he looks at you?"

"Please, Hildegarde," Gertrude begged miserably, "you mustn't say things like that."

"Why not?" Hildegarde's recklessness blew as wildly in her as the wind blew. "I can't make my mind be dead. He does think of you, you know."

Tears wet Gertrude's round cheeks. "You make me feel evil," she choked.

Hildegarde looked suddenly contrite. "Don't cry," she said. "I'm sorry. Terribly, terribly sorry. I didn't mean to make you cry. I just saw the way he looked at you, and—I'm sorry, sweet Trudy. Don't cry."

Hildegarde hadn't used the old endearing nickname since they were children, and Gertrude warmed to it and was made even more defenseless by it. She wiped away the tears with the end of her shawl and her voice faltered, dimly and hesitantly. "What do you mean—the way he looked at me?"

Hildegarde knew what her answer should be. She should say that she was only imagining things—that he had looked at Gertrude as he had looked at all the members of the class— with curiosity and friendliness, nothing more. But it wouldn't be true, and besides if Gertrude were mixed up and bewildered over this, then Hildegarde would not be alone in her confusion.

"He looks at you as though you were beautiful," Hildegarde said. "As though you were the most beautiful girl he ever saw."

"I'm not—I don't think—" Gertrude began, and there was misery in her flushed face but there was something else, too. No one had ever told her she was beautiful before. She had always been a pale shadow next to Hildegarde, and now to have these words said to her. . . . Small wonder that her heart pounded in her breast with a strange mixture of apprehension and joy.

"It doesn't matter," Hildegarde said. "I know you're too strong and wise to be swayed by it—but he does think it. I'm sure he does."

They had reached the river and they stood on the snow-covered banks looking at the sullen, gray water that swirled in the heavy center current and piled itself in ice sheets along the banks. Their thoughts were like the water—churning and breaking away from the solid frozen edges of their training.

Gertrude spoke first, and her voice was strong again. "I've got to get back to work. We've wasted enough time, Sister Hildegarde."

The words, the resumption of the term "Sister" ought to reprove her, Hildegarde knew, but there was no withdrawing of the warm young arm from hers. Gertrude wasn't really angry or upset with her. And having said some of the words which she had never said before, Hildegarde felt strangely relieved.

"Yes, I suppose so," Hildegarde said. "I've got to get over to the factory. But we'll talk again someday, won't we? I mean—there's no one else to talk to."

Gertrude knew she ought to say no, that this kind of talking did no one any good, but she didn't say it. Her mind had been stirred by Hildegarde's reckless words and she knew she wanted to talk again sometime, but not until she had time to shore up her own convictions with prayer and study. Then she could hold her heart aloof from temptation.

"We'll see," she compromised and turned away from the river to start back toward the village and the duty that awaited them. Shock ran through her to see Martin Schmidt walking toward them, his head bowed against the wind, his hands deep in his pockets. For the first time, she was aware of his good looks, the pale profusion of his curly hair under his wool cap.

She stood stricken, betrayed by the blood which burned hotly in her cheeks. "I don't want him to see me," she said in a choked whisper.

Hildegarde felt compassion fill her and was moved to pity. "Just pretend you don't see him," she murmured. "Look over toward the factory—he's facing the other way—come on, we'll run like we're in a hurry."

Like frightened rabbits, they scurried across the snow, and in a minute had reached the corner where they could no longer see the water. Gertrude was so flushed and stricken that Hildegarde was filled with regret. *Why do I always say things I'm sorry for,* she thought miserably. But the damage had been done, and none of Hildegarde's tardy pity could erase the seed she had planted in Gertrude's heart.

The winter weeks moved calmly and placidly toward spring, and there was only one event which interrupted the serene sameness of the days. In early March, Father Rapp again presented his new Articles of Agreement for signing, and this time the people signed, women as well as men. Hildegarde signed with gladness, because no matter how confused she might feel about some things she, like most of the others, never questioned the communitarian way of life. She was too devoted to Father Rapp to really associate her periodic rebellion with his sternness. If pressed, she would have named Frederick or Dr. Mueller or even Conrad Feucht as the ones who made life difficult.

But not everyone signed, and even among those who did, there was some reluctance and not a little grumbling. A few refused to sign altogether, saying that the original agreements were adequate for them, and because they continued to give service and devotion to the Society, no further pressures were put on them.

However, in the almost sacred isolation of the schoolroom, none of this business mattered. The students entered the classroom door for the sole purpose of learning, so Martin Schmidt was unaware of any hint of trouble in what seemed to him to be a society of unbelievable serenity. He only knew that as it got closer to the time for him to leave, he felt more and more reluctance in his heart. At first he attributed this to the fact that he didn't have nearly enough time to teach his students all that he wanted them to know. Oh, some of them were learning a great deal, he supposed; Henrici's zeal forced him to scholastic achievement as well as religious fanaticism (or at least that was the word which Martin used in his mind), and a few of the others were making excellent progress. Gertrude, for instance, seemed to possess a natural talent for language, and her sweet, clear voice pronounced the English words with less accent than anyone else in the class.

Listening to her read one day, he faced honestly the real reason why it was going to be more difficult to leave this village in the spring than it had been to leave Germany nearly a year before. This girl who he had once thought might prove to be a solace and a comfort was now a pain twisting in his heart, and her face drifted through his dreams. Martin knew that he could never be another Henrici, joining the Harmonists in true faith and conviction. But what if somehow, someway, he could persuade Gertrude to leave with him? The idea was madness, of course. Or at least so he believed in March. April, with its own pale green madness, made him touch at least the fringes of hope.

Gertrude had moved through the winter months in a strange mixture of anguish and joy. Although she and Hildegarde did not have an opportunity often to speak as intimately as they had that windy winter day, still they had exchanged a few words, a few looks, and this was enough to keep Gertrude's heart disturbed. There were days when she was strong and serene and Martin Schmidt was no more, no less than any other person. But there were other days when a sweet sorrow suffused her heart, and even her prayers could not keep her from seeing the way his eyes softened when they looked at her.

There was more to it than just the fact that the tutor looked at her, more to it than the fact that for the first time it was she who was being singled out and not the lovely Hildegarde. Gertrude was not a scatterbrained, willful girl to be led astray by only the admiration in a man's eyes. There was something about the tutor's mind which spoke to Gertrude in a way she had never experienced before. She had always been intelligent; she had been trained early to be obedient, wise, clever. She possessed musical talent, business sense, leadership ability. But she had never been taught the soft skill of being a woman nor how to laugh nor even how to look deeply into her own thoughts or the thoughts of anyone else.

Now, for the first time, she was in contact with a sense of humor, a sensitivity, an awareness that she had never known before, and she felt an awakening of her own humor and sensitivity in answer to it. Perhaps, had she been younger or older, she might have been able to absorb the mental stimulation without being bewitched by the man. But she was only eighteen, and there was a burgeoning in her which matched the pale, persistent blossoming of April.

It was hard to hide her feelings, especially in the classroom, and she hoped desperately that no one, except Hildegarde, knew of this trespassing breath of romance in a place where romance had been outlawed. But she was not to be granted this wish. Jacob Henrici was aware of something which troubled him deeply.

He could not put his feeling into words, but when he saw Schmidt look at Gertrude or when he saw the sudden color climb into her cheeks, he felt a sort of simmering rage crush his breath. Oh, he knew how the tutor might feel. Had he not felt a touch of it himself when he first looked at the quiet, sweet granddaughter of the holy Father? But it had been only a fleeting thing, dispersed entirely by his growing understanding of what it meant to be a Harmonist. And he knew that Gertrude was completely pure. She had to stay that way. Nothing, particularly a worldly tutor, must touch her mind with thoughts that were unworthy of her. He even toyed with the idea of speaking to the Father about it but he knew he would not dare. Not until he was a member could he presume to approach Father Rapp on so intimate a subject.

There was one other person in the class who, though not at all proficient in the learning of English, knew better than anyone else what was happening. Jacob Klein, familiar with longing and being denied, with dreams that never came true, with wanting what was not for him, felt a great sense of understanding when Martin and Gertrude looked at each other and then looked away again. Jacob longed to help the tutor, to do something to ease Schmidt's longing—perhaps in the hope that such action might do something to assuage his own pain.

But for a long time there was no occasion for Jacob to speak to Martin about anything more personal than the declension of a verb. Then one day something happened which brought them together.

It was a day of soft April sunshine, warm enough that a window could be opened, and bird song threaded itself through all the words said in class until it seemed to Martin that the English words were embroidered with music.

More to hear her voice than anything else, for he felt sure she knew the lesson, he asked Gertrude to conjugate the verb "to love."

"I love," she began obediently, her eyes on the floor. "You love, he loves." Her voice stumbled a little. "We loves, you love, they love."

"Is she correct?" Martin asked the class, his heart knocking heavily in his chest. He knew she would not make an error because she was ignorant of the proper declension. Had she made the mistake because the words meant something to her?

Henrici's hand stabbed the air. "The first person plural should be 'we love' not 'we loves.'" He spoke entirely in English which Martin required of all the students.

"That's correct," Martin said. "Miss Gertrude, will you say it properly please?"

Her eyes flew up to his face, and there was something in them which made his heart stop for an instant. "We love," she said and for just a second their glances clung.

There was a brief hushed period, like the fragment of silence between a flash of lightning and a crash of thunder, and then Schmidt's heart plunged and the thunder was in his ears. There was no denying the way she looked at him. She might be wretched over what was happening to her, but he had surely taught her something besides English. Only—what could be done about it? There had never been any opportunity to speak to her alone, to tell her that he loved her. And there would probably never be.

Somehow he found the strength to continue

the class, to comment intelligently on the lesson, to set them all to writing an exercise. During the writing period, he tore his eyes away from Gertrude's bent head to find Jacob Henrici looking at him. Henrici's eyes were cold and critical, and Schmidt looked hurriedly away. It was then that his eyes met Jacob Klein's and for the first time, Schmidt felt a warmth touch him, the warmth that comes from sharing a thought or an idea. Jacob Klein showed clearly that he understood what Schmidt was feeling, and even more remarkable, that he did not condemn him.

When the class was over, the students filed out, but Jacob lingered behind with the tutor. The two young men stood for several minutes in complete silence, each aware of what had brought them together but hesitant to put it into words. Schmidt was a shy man who did not confide easily in another, and Jacob had been brought up to believe that one did not speak of intimate things to strangers. Being of the world, Schmidt would be a stranger, no matter how long he lived among the Harmonists.

Finally Schmidt wet his lips. "Is it true that there is never any marriage here? Never? Not for anyone?"

Jacob spoke slowly, but his mind was moving more swiftly than was usual for him. If Sister Gertrude were to marry, he was thinking, might there not be a weakening of the rigid rules? Perhaps if Gertrude succumbed to love, Hildegarde could be swayed.

But honesty compelled him to speak carefully. "No, not really true. There are marriages—

sometimes several a year. Sometimes it's because the—the desires of the flesh get too much for a boy or a girl, and a baby is coming. Then the Father marries them, of course. Or sometimes it's only because the boy is afraid this might happen, and he begs the Father to marry him so he won't sin. But it's true there aren't many marriages. It isn't that we think marriage is wicked, but. . . ." Here his voice slowed even more as he tried to find the words to make this thing clear to a man like the tutor. "We believe that the Christ is coming soon, and we want to be pure for him. Or—*they* believe," he added uncomfortably, "this is all very hard for me."

Schmidt was too absorbed in his own misery to wonder about Jacob's confession. "I suppose Miss Gertrude believes this too," he said almost to himself. "Of course, she does. She would never. . . . If only I had a chance to see her alone. Just once. If I could talk to her. If only—but it wouldn't do any good, would it?"

"I know when she goes to the Grotto alone," Jacob said. He wondered if the feeling he had was similar to the feeling Judas must have known. "I could let you know when she'll be there."

Schmidt grabbed Jacob's arm. "Could you? Could you really? I would only talk to her, I swear. But if you would. . . ."

"I'll come to the inn and let you know," Jacob said. "It's a promise."

"Agreed." They shook hands warmly and left the classroom, neither aware of the other's need, each only caring about the pain in his own heart and the fragility of his hope.

Chapter 10

The April twilight turned the distant hill to a pale lavender which seemed to be a reflection of the clump of purple hyacinths blooming beside the graveled walk. Gertrude moved in a dream along the path, drawing the scent of the hyacinths into her nostrils until she felt dizzier than she had ever felt from drinking wine. She leaned down to pick a tiny floweret from the cone of fragrance, and she held it in her fingers marveling at its miniature perfection, at the sweetness it exuded in spite of its size. Her gaze, bemused and soft, swept up to the fruit trees blooming like white lace against the darker hills. April had never been so beautiful. Or had it always been beautiful, but had she been unaware, blind to the loveliness? Then what had changed her?

Oh, she knew what had changed her. She knew too well what voice had called her out of her indifference, her preoccupation with the silk industry and her prayer; whose mind it was that had touched her mind with a new awareness that was as sharp as pain. In a desperate sort of clinging she had tried to hold to the old ways, to say the familiar prayers with deeper intensity, to turn her eyes inward again. But a pale daffodil or a branch of white blossom could stab her heart with sweet and undiminished violence.

This was why she was headed for the Grotto. Maybe when she knelt there to pray she would be safe. The small pastry-shaped shrine in the garden with its thatched roof, rough field-stone exterior, and Grecian-temple interior had blessed her before. Maybe today it would hold and heal her.

Jacob Klein stood behind a tree and watched her move across the garden. As soon as he was sure that she was heading for the Grotto, he turned and ran to the inn with the promised message for the tutor.

A few minutes later, breathless and shaken from his pounding heart—due as much to the nearness of the girl he sought as to his running—Martin Schmidt stood outside the rough bark door of the little shrine. He had never been inside of it, as he had sensed from the beginning that it was expressly for the use of the Harmonists. In fact, he had seen only certain Harmonists come here with any regularity—the obvious leaders of the Society, the women who held some degree of prominence. He had no idea whether this was a regulation or whether it was simply that not all of the members felt the same need for quiet, undisturbed prayer.

Now that he had arrived at his destination, the destination his heart had hungered for, he felt a great reluctance to push open the heavy door. Would she be frightened or angry or cold? But even one of these emotions would be better than this terrible nothingness that seemed to mark their relationship now. His shaking hand pressed against the unlatched door, and he stood staring at Gertrude who knelt on the stone floor, her face lowered with sweet humility over her folded hands. She looked up calmly, evidently used to interruption, but when she saw who stood at the door, her eyes widened and her hand flew to cover her mouth and stifle the involuntary little *Oh!* which had escaped her.

"Don't be frightened," he begged. "I won't disturb you if it distresses you. I only want so much to talk to you."

She got gracefully to her feet and stood waiting, unable to look at him without confusion.

"May I talk to you?" he said.

"Not here," she answered. "This is a place of prayer."

Oh, how brazen! ran the hot thought through her mind, to know, without his saying so, that he does not wish to talk of prayer.

"Where, then?" he asked, glancing quickly over his shoulder, half expecting to see Father Rapp or Frederick or Conrad coming across the gardens.

Gertrude seemed to know what he was thinking. "There's a very important meeting of the men in the Great House," she said. "My grandfather—and the others—they're busy."

"Then could we walk here behind the Grotto? In the garden?"

It was almost dark enough that they would be difficult to identify, she thought. If anyone comes, that is. But there is rarely anyone in the garden. Only the night watchman and he won't be here for an hour or more.

"All right," she said. "For a minute. For only a minute."

He followed her out of the small room and around the little stone building. There, where the flowering trees dropped their branches, he stepped up beside her and caught her hand in his.

"But a minute won't be long enough," he said. "Not nearly long enough to tell you how beautiful you are. Or that I love you."

She pulled her hand away and made a quick little sound of shocked dismay. But you should have known, her heart said, and she felt shame at the way she had withdrawn her hand. You knew he wanted to talk of love. You wanted him to.

"I'm sorry," she said. "I've made you think that I—that I'm something I'm not."

"Something you're not? You mean I'm blind and a fool? You mean you're not lovely and a woman and warm?"

"I'm a Harmonist," she said miserably. "You know what that means."

"Being a Harmonist is for the old," he said passionately, "or the fanatic. Not for you. Not for someone young and sweet like you."

She turned her face away and tried to think clearly. This was madness, and she knew it. Madness and wickedness and contrary to everything she had ever known and believed. Then why did her heart thunder in her breast? And why was she filled with a tenderness that ached in her so that she felt there was no easing for her pain anywhere? If this were sin, then why didn't she feel sinful? Oh, yes, Grandfather had said that sin could wear a winsome face—but surely not like this.

Martin took her arm and turned her so that they were standing very close together, and she felt his breath, warm and sweet, on her face. She closed her eyes, not knowing what to expect, wondering if he would make some gesture which would alter her forever.

But he only stood quietly and then spoke in a whisper. "You are sweet and lovely, like spring flowers. I know you've been taught that a man's love is wrong. But it's not. I swear to you—oh, I swear by all that's good and true—that there is no evil in my heart. How could I love you— you—with anything but purity?"

Still she kept her eyes closed, feeling the heat of tears behind her shut lids, knowing that if she looked at him, the tears would spill down her cheeks.

"Look at me," he begged. "Can't you look at me?"

She opened her eyes and the tears fell, hot and humiliating across her face.

"Oh, don't cry," he said, and there was a pain in his voice. "Don't cry, my sweet, my lieble."

He took her in his arms, unable to resist the need of comforting her. He had thought he would not touch her, not until she came willingly. But he could not bear to see her standing here, her face wet with the tears he had caused. He cradled her against him, like a hurt child. "Don't cry," he said again. "I don't want to make you cry."

She wanted to resist him, to push him away, to stiffen her mind and her body with the memory of words her grandfather had said. But his nearness in the spring night, the smell and feel of him, the strength of his arms was more than she could endure. Her resolve melted away and in its place came a great warmth—made up of gratitude for his nearness and his comfort, a sense of home-place in his arms, and a sweet, strange sensation—different from anything she had ever known. Without meaning to or really wanting to, she let the stiffness flow out of her body and leaned against him.

"Gertrude," he whispered, his voice husky and almost timid. "Could you care for me? Could you ever care?"

She had not been trained in coquetry or flirtation. She knew only honesty. And so she lifted her wet eyes to his. "I do care," she said. "I care very, very much. But I mustn't. It would break my grandfather's heart."

"And if you stop caring," he said slowly, "it will break my heart. So, you see, the only real choice is—whose heart?"

"Oh, no," she cried in soft anguish. "Don't say it so. Couldn't you—wouldn't you become a Harmonist? We could see each other every day. We might talk sometimes. Wouldn't it be enough?"

For answer, he tilted her head with his hand and bent to her lips. His kiss reflected his shyness, his sensitivity, and the gentle, boy's kiss fell lightly on her mouth.

"I've never been kissed on the mouth before," she said. "Only on the cheek. I don't think we ought to—oh, Martin, I'm so very unhappy."

"Unhappy, my darling?" He was carried away by her submission, and the April air ran like a fire in his blood. "Because of this?" And once more he kissed her.

She knew she should push him away. She knew that this was the act against which she had been warned and cautioned, that from this grew the desires which did away with purity. But no one had told her that the touch of a mouth could shatter the pattern of the years and leave her standing in the April night dazzled and shaken.

Finally, Martin spoke gently, "You'll have to go now. They'll be looking for you and wondering. But will you come again? Will you come and make me the happiest man in the entire world?"

Of course not, said her heart sternly. *How ridiculous to even ask it.* But his fingers were touching her face and before she could move, his mouth was on her mouth, and her stern resolve was drowned in a purple wash of happiness and a new longing.

"Tomorrow night," she whispered against his lips. "I'll try—I can't promise. If I come to the Grotto, I'll leave a hyacinth blossom on the path by the door. You'll know I'm the one inside."

"Oh, my darling, my little one." He had never dared dream of this, of her acquiescense, of the feel of her in his arms. He was heady with the wonder of it.

"Good night," she said and slipped from his arms and was gone. He made no attempt to follow her. A man did not win a girl like Gertrude Rapp in an hour or an evening. But before May was over, God willing, he would have her as his wife, even if he had to carry her bodily away from her grandfather and his insane notions of what constituted a godly life. Martin clenched his fists in the darkness, and then loosened his fingers, remembering the size, the power, the magnetism of Father Rapp. *No, I would not be able to prevail against such a man,* Martin thought. *She will have to come to me on her own, or I will never have her.*

He went onto his knees in the darkness, straining over his knotted fists. "Grosse Gott," he prayed, "give her to me. I need her, I need her more than that old man could possibly ever need her."

Gertrude got safely to her room with no one to see her. A quick glance into the mirror showed her that it was a good thing she had escaped observation. The glow on her cheeks, the softness of her mouth, the trembling of her hands would have made anyone see that something had happened to her, something unusual and in need of investigation. There was cool water in the basin on the wash stand, and she splashed it on her face, hoping to cool her cheeks. But nothing could wash off the kisses, she realized in a sort of panic. They were like a stain on her mouth. Surely anyone would be able to see.

With fumbling fingers, she undressed, putting on her muslin gown quickly as though to cover her suddenly vulnerable nakedness. She blew out her candle and knelt by the bed, prepared for long prayer, ready to say the necessary words of penitence and shame. When she felt that God had forgiven her, then maybe she would have the courage to make confession to her grandfather. There was no doubt in her mind as to which of the two she feared more. God would be more benevolent than her grandfather.

She bent her face into her hands and waited for the words to form in her heart, for the shame and remorse to fill her with darkness and the need to confess. But nothing happened. Her nostrils still held the scent of hyacinths, her arms still felt the warmth of a man, and her mouth still trembled in memory of his touch.

"Ach, Gott," she cried in a soft anguish and bit her knuckles. "I should be ashamed, but I'm not. What shall I do? What shall I do?"

But God did not answer her, and she could not stay her mind on him. Feeling more and more the intrusion of Martin into her thoughts, she gave up, at last, any attempt at prayer and crawled into bed. It was the first time in her memory that she had got into bed without praying. She lay, tormented and happy by turn, until the sky began to turn pale in the east. At last she slept, but even in sleep, there was no real peace for her.

Father Rapp's prayers that night held none of the pleading of Martin's prayer, nor any of the penitence of Gertrude's. Instead they were filled with gratitude. He and Frederick and Brother Christoph and Brother Conrad had had a most satisfying meeting. Many of the crops were planted, the mills were producing more and more and the vines would bear well this year. Or at least it appeared so. The unrest that had simmered under the ice of winter seemed dispersed in the loveliness of April. The spirit of the Lord was with him night and day, and he felt confident and vital and strong enough to handle anything that could face him. He thanked God for the peace in Economy, for the faithfulness of the beloved brethren, for the fact that he, George Rapp, vinedresser and stonemason, had been called to lead the people to the Promised Land. A man, so blessed, could only kneel before his God in adoration and praise, with no suspicion of unrest to trouble his serenity.

Chapter 11

Half a dozen times before the middle of May, the hyacinth blossom had been dropped on the path, and the hyacinth-scented words and kisses had been exchanged behind the Grotto. Because their actions had apparently gone completely unobserved, Gertrude was almost ready to really believe Martin when he said that obviously God did not disapprove of their growing love. If he did, wouldn't he make it clear to them? Wouldn't someone see and tell? But the spring dusk seemed a friendly conspirator, hiding them with a sort of tenderness, stretching Gertrude's heart with such joy that she thought it incredible—or a miracle—that her grandfather did not hear its pounding and demand the reason.

Then toward the middle of May, there came an evening of scarlet sunset which held the crisp threat of frost. Hildegarde, fearful for the tender seedlings already set out, spent the evening setting buckets, boxes and burlap sacks over the most vulnerable of her plants. It was nearly dark when she finally felt that enough security measures had been taken, and she headed toward home, cutting across the back of the Vosterhaus garden skirting close to the Grotto. Her mind was entirely on her work, and her feet were noiseless on the grass. A sudden whisper of sound, a sensation of movement jerked her to a stop. Unseen by the couple under the tree, she stood in complete stillness, deep in shadow, unable to believe that the words which she had just heard were true. Surely she had imagined them. Even though she suspected that the tutor loved Gertrude, she was unprepared for the husky pleading in Martin's voice.

"My darling Trudy, say you'll go. I can't leave without you. I can't. I'll die."

Gertrude's answer was so long in coming that Hildegarde was in an agony of suspense and shock. Of course Gertrude would say no, but how would she do it? How could she do it when there had been such yearning in the young man's voice?

The words, when they came, were almost too faint for Hildegarde to hear, and if it had not been for Martin's exclamation of joy, she would not have been able to believe that she had heard correctly.

"Yes—oh, Martin, may God forgive me, I'll come."

There was a silence and Hildegarde wondered what Martin was doing. She had read no love stories, she had never seen any physical acts of affection between the sexes and she was incredibly unaware of the force that made men and women fall in love and cling together. And yet, she had that memory of Lavasseur's kiss on her fingers at the ball, on the night which had lifted her out of pure innocence and shown her that life had other sides and other colors. And there was the way Jacob's eyes moved across her face sometimes with the intimacy of a touch. This much, at least, she knew, and so she stood with thudding heart, shaken as though she were witness to the sudden rending of the universe.

"My sweet," the man's whisper came. The next words were too faint to be understood, but then Hildegarde heard him say, "I have friends in Pittsburgh who will keep us until we can be married. Listen, here's how we'll do it."

But Hildegarde could endure no more. As stealthily as a brush of wind, she turned and moved away from the Grotto, skirting the back area of the garden, working her way along the fence until she came to the side gate. She slipped through and ran swiftly along the road toward her own house.

For most of the night she struggled with the problem that threatened to overwhelm her. What should she do about this thing she had discovered? She ached to help Gertrude, but at the same time she felt a deep compassion for the tutor. It was different with him, she realized. He had not been taught, as the Harmonists had, that physical love was wrong. He could not know that he was doomed by his sin.

Sin? Hildegarde thought of Martin's gentleness, his humor, his kindness. What had these things to do with sin and damnation? Her mind could not find a clear way through the tangled questions, and so she could only close her thoughts with the narrow gate of what she had been taught.

I'll talk to Gertrude in the morning, she decided finally. She might listen to me and understand that she can't go away and break Father Rapp's heart. She just can't.

But in the morning, word came to Hildegarde that she was to spend the day with Dr. Mueller and Conrad Feucht. They were going to concoct medicines and her knowledge of herbs was necessary to them. With reluctance she hurried to obey the summons, comforting herself with a promise to talk to Gertrude the following day.

But that evening as twilight deepened into early night, Gertrude stood motionless in her small bedroom which opened off the parlor. Tonight, Martin had said. They would leave tonight. In the sweet shelter of his arms, she had been strong and certain, but here, in this room, surrounded by the memories of her childhood, she was again irresolute.

It had been an agonizing day, and several times she had felt a great yearning to turn to Hildegarde for help. If there were only one person to whom she could talk without being certain that wrath would follow. Hildegarde would at least be sympathetic, and maybe she would be able to say the words, boned with strength, which would stay Gertrude's feet. But Hildegarde was not in her usual places, and Gertrude dared not be obvious about seeking her.

She tried not to let herself think of her grandfather. She adored and respected the old man almost to the point of idolatry, but she knew that if she let her mind dwell on him at length, she would be reduced to a jellied mass of fear and guilt.

He will never forgive me, Gertrude thought, but she also knew that her grandfather would probably not feel the sense of loss that she would know. He would be shocked and disappointed, but there was such a conviction in him that he was chosen and set apart, he could never feel any sense of human mourning. How often Gertrude had seen him preach the eulogy of his dearest friends with never a tear, never a sign of unsteadiness in his voice.

People have said I am like him, Gertrude thought, *and maybe I was once. But not any more. My heart has learned how to ache and my tears are ready to fall at any hour.*

Her mind moved slowly, figuring it out. *And it's Martin who has taught me. He taught me how to suffer and to feel. This is why I want to go with him.*

She stood very still. Her mouth steadied and seemed to strengthen. *This is why I will go,* she thought. And her irresolution faded away as she began, with steady hands, to pack the small cloth valise with a few items of clothing.

When the packing was finished, she stood and looked around her room with a sense of tenderness. The four-poster bed with its woven

white coverlet, the partially finished needlework on the chest, the small diary on her desk
were all an intimate part of her life but they
would be left here. She would not even take the
needlework, and the diary contained nothing
personal—only statistics on the silk, and exer-
cises in English. Her grandfather would need
the material on the silk, and she would have
Martin to teach her English.

She put a piece of paper on her pillow. There
were only two sentences on it but it would be
enough, and when her grandfather found it, he
would know. "I am going away with Martin,
Grandfather," she had written, "and I hope you
will forgive me and let me come back someday.
I love you all."

She opened a window carefully, pushed the
valise through, and heard it drop quietly to the
ground. There was a soft scuffle on the grass,
and she knew that Martin had been waiting as
he had promised and would put the valise in his
carriage. There were no torches or lanterns on
that side of the house, so he would be safe as he
made his way down the road and across the
field to where he had tied his horse under a
great oak tree.

With pounding heart and weak legs, Gertrude
stepped out into the parlor and moved over toward the dining room and through the kitchen.
Even if anyone saw her, there would be no questions asked. Everyone went outside just before
bedtime to the little building which housed the
primitive plumbing. She made her way along
the path, and just before she reached the

outhouse, she slipped off the path and began to run swiftly and noiselessly toward Kirkstrasse. She knew the way well, and there was no sign of the night watchman. For this moment, she was not even afraid, and she knew that it was most unlikely that anyone would come to her room. She had closed the door and left the room darkened, and if anyone sought her, they would go away thinking she was asleep or praying.

The cautious sound of the tutor's voice told her that she had reached the meeting place and when she answered, she suddenly felt his arms go around her and his eager lips crush down on hers.

Martin had been so uncertain about her coming, even after he picked up the valise, that his emotions were not at all under control as he caught her in his arms. He knew, of course, that she would have to be wooed and won with a patience that no other girl would need. He knew that it would be a long time before she would be able to give him her body with the open willingness with which she had given him her heart. But he had been thoroughly frightened, and when he saw her really coming, he lost the control which had, until now, made him act cooler than he really was. Gratefully, thankfully, he pressed his mouth against her lips, holding her fiercely against him, allowing himself for once the full freedom of his passion.

Gertrude was completely shocked. Somehow she had not let her mind dwell on the physical aspects of marriage, and she had thought only of the depths of Martin's mind, the sweetness of the gentle kisses they had exchanged in the garden. But this ardent embrace was like a blow from which she tried to recoil.

Martin, immediately aware of this, let her go at once, but she had already started to cry. And once the tears began to flow, all the torments and anxieties and guilt which she had been suppressing, came sweeping over her like a flood. Her strength dissolved abruptly, and although she allowed Martin's hands to lift her into the buggy, although she did not struggle or resist, she felt as though her heart was breaking. This was sin and she knew it. Martin tried to comfort her, but all of his gentleness and anguish could not stop the torrent of grief and shame which huddled her, sobbing and defenseless, in her corner of the seat.

Pauline Speidel, who was living for several months in the Great House, taking her turn at working in the kitchen, had spent a long, fruitless hour in prayer. Her small, rigid mind was convinced she was a sinner because she had spent vain hours repairing a particularly pretty shawl, rather than discarding it and wearing the plainer one which lay in her box. Now, although she had earnestly and ploddingly asked forgiveness of God, she could find no peace of mind. She felt unworthy and depressed and nothing seemed to comfort her.

She knew that Gertrude was wiser than she could ever hope to be, and Gertrude had a calm, sane way of looking at things which seemed to make plain the crooked ways of Pauline's small, petty theology. She decided, finally, that foolish as it may appear, she would go to Gertrude and ask for prayer and counsel in order to smooth out her thorny heart and let her sleep.

She moved quietly along the hall which separated the center part of the house from the room where she and several of the other girls slept. It did not occur to her to act secretive because of course she had nothing to hide, and besides there was no sort of police system here which guarded the members against transgression.

Outside Gertrude's room, Pauline paused, intimidated by the closed door and the fact that no candle light shone from under it. Gertrude must be asleep or deep in prayer and in either case, she should not be disturbed. But Pauline's need was greater than her normal caution and with a soft apology, she pushed open the door.

"Gertrude," she whispered. "Are you sleeping?"

Silence was her only answer and she hesitated on the threshold, straining to see in the dark. Something made her uneasy, and she turned back to the sitting room where several candles still burned, for evidently Father Rapp or Frederick was still up and about.

She flashed the light of the candle and saw the neat, empty room. At first she felt only disappointment that Gertrude was not there, ready to listen, to advise. She started to back out of the room, supposing that Gertrude was with Father Rapp, when the candle flame shone on the piece of paper which lay on the pillow. Not knowing why she dared do such a presumptuous thing, though later she was to believe fervently that it was divine intervention, she picked up the note and read the incredible words.

For a minute she thought she would surely faint. Blood hummed in her ears and sharp daggers of pain ran up the sides of her head. That such a thing could happen was almost on an equal in her simple mind to the idea of God tumbling from heaven, and she was staggered and bewildered. Her first instinct was to run crying to the only real authority she knew— Father Rapp.

But a sudden and unexpected cunning filled her. Her sense of sin had undoubtedly brought her to this room, so it must be God's will that she, Pauline, find the errant one and bring her back. And *without* the knowledge of Father Rapp. If she could bring about this miracle, the old man would be spared anger and sorrow. His mind must be allowed to dwell on higher things, Pauline thought reverently. This quest was hers to perform, and, God willing, she would find Gertrude and bring her home.

But where to begin? She was completely incapable of formulating any plans, of trying to guess what Gertrude might have done, where she might have gone. Helpless and frightened, Pauline stood with the guttering candle in one hand and the scrap of paper clutched in the other.

Hildegarde will know. The thought came as vividly and clearly as though someone had said the words to her. There was a brief thrust of jealousy that perhaps Gertrude had confided in the willful Hildegarde whom Pauline considered to be a bad influence. But the jealousy was put aside in the great need of this hour. In spite of her own feeling of distaste and reluctance, she had to go to Hildegarde now, this minute, in the darkness. Because even if Gertrude had not confided in Hildegarde, Hildegarde's mind would be able to guess what plan was taken. And why not? Hildegarde will go herself someday, Pauline thought spitefully, with some hot-blooded lout like Jacob Klein. She is no better than he is even if the Father *does* approve of her.

It was not until a few minutes later, hurrying through the dark street with her dress pulled hastily over her nightgown, that she realized she still held the note. When she finally felt it in her hand, she knew a great sense of thankfulness that no one else would come into that room and know that the granddaughter of a prophet had been tempted by the world.

Her concern was so great that she was unaware that anyone else was on the street until she plunged around the corner to meet Conrad Feucht face to face. The young doctor, like all the other men in the Society, took his turn as night watchman several times a year, walking the streets, calling the hours, warning the brethren of the impermanence of life. He gazed in dismay at the disheveled girl who stood in front of him. Had he been asked to name the one

Harmonist girl who would never run through the streets at night, he would probably have named Pauline.

"Sister Pauline. Are you in trouble?"

She was too frightened and shocked to be reticent. Besides, he was one of the leaders, young as he was, and there was a certain solidarity and the hope of comfort in finding him beside her. Again, she felt a great assurance of God's presence. This could so easily have been a lesser man who could have spoiled everything.

In a whisper that threatened to get hysterical, she poured out her story and Conrad's reaction was all she hoped it would be. He was shocked and concerned but at once anxious to help.

"You think Sister Hildegarde will know?" he asked.

"She'll know," said Pauline stubbornly. "That one. . . ."

But Conrad interrupted. "Then I'll go to the Mutschler door and ask young Brother Wilhelm to take over my watchman duties, and you can speak to Hildegarde through her bedroom window. It would be better if no one knew, particularly Brother Gerhard, what we are up to. He is too close to the Father, and if we hope to bring Sister Gertrude to her senses. . . ." His voice trailed off, but Pauline did not hear the lack of resolution in it. How could she know that the young doctor, well aware from his studies and ministrations to men of the needs of the body, felt a deep and aching compassion for the brothers and sisters who stumbled and fell.

They carried out his plan and while Frau

Mutschler scurried about to wake her son and get his warm jacket, Pauline tapped on the window of the room which Hildegarde shared with her mother.

Hildegarde, aroused by the noise at the door, heard the tapping and felt a sudden and unexpected fear until Pauline's shrill whisper quieted the fear and hurried her into some clothes.

Frau Mutschler came into the room before Hildegarde could slip on her shoes, but the girl had no need to try to deceive her wise and compassionate mother. Without even thinking about it, Hildegarde knew her mother would understand, so she only said, "There is trouble and they think I can help."

The mother nodded. For nineteen years she had lived with the knowledge that this child was in danger from life, but tonight was not the time to be afraid. Whatever had happened had not happened to Hildegarde. "Keep warm," she said, "and let me know if you go beyond the yard. Be careful not to wake your father."

As Pauline poured out her troubled and frantic story, Hildegarde felt a strange mixture of guilt and excitement. The guilt came from the certain recognition of the part she had played in this, but the excitement was something she didn't really understand. It had to do with the forbidden thought that Gertrude had escaped, and that they had no right to bring her back.

And so at first, she did not speak. She knew what they wanted to know, of course. She could hear, plain in her memory, the whispered voice of the tutor, "I have friends in Pittsburgh. . . ." But what should she do? Where was her duty? To Gertrude as a Harmonist? To Gertrude as a woman? She stood, torn and hesitant, unable to make a decision.

"Sister Hildegarde." The voice was stern, and she looked up startled. She had not known, until now, that Brother Conrad was here. "If you know where Sister Gertrude is, you dare not hide that knowledge. It is your duty to. . . ." He felt, rather than saw, her stiffen away from him and he knew, immediately, that "duty" was the wrong word for this girl. He had made his voice so stern because he had been shaken by the sight of her golden hair, mussed and lovely in the moonlight, and he had been angry at his own weakness.

With effort, he softened his voice. "Please tell us. If Sister Gertrude does something on impulse and is not allowed the opportunity to change her mind, she will live in grief until the end of her days. You can see that, can't you?"

The sweet reasonable tone moved her as anger never could. The thought of Gertrude's grief was unendurable. And Conrad said that all they wanted was to give Gertrude a chance to change her mind. The habit of years, of succumbing to a voice of authority, formed her answer.

"Yes," she said softly, so softly that Conrad had to bend toward her in the night and the scent of her hair brushed his face. "Yes, I know. I'll tell you. I'll help you find her, if you want."

Chapter 12

Hildegarde could not, with her scanty knowledge of romance, have any strong feelings that she might be assisting in a plan to strip Gertrude of her happiness. She had only a vague, nebulous feeling that Gertrude had started on a road to freedom and they would be stopping her. Still, Conrad might be right in thinking that Gertrude should be allowed to reconsider if she chose. And having committed herself by telling Conrad that she would help, she gave herself entirely over to the idea of going after Gertrude. It was simply part of Hildegarde's nature to do anything she did with complete abandon.

So it was really her feet which ran most swiftly toward the small barn where Conrad and Dr. Mueller kept their horses. It was her hands which helped harness the fast little mare, and her voice which whispered encouraging words to Pauline who was reduced to a terrified sort of snuffling.

Conrad, moving swiftly and efficiently in the darkness, was more aware of the girl beside him than he had ever been before. He had known for many years that she was no ordinary girl, that she possessed the quality of vibrancy which could make her a strong and faithful member of the Society or which might bring her to grief. He could not be unaware of her beauty, but when her pale hair was braided tightly in its customary braids and her slender body clothed in the dark blue which blurred all the women into a sort of monotony, she was less disturbing than she had been when she ran out of the house, disheveled and warm from sleep, her hair, newly washed, a shining fragrance in the night. Now, even though she moved with the same strong purpose that had marked her actions the night of Johannes Baker's death, there was something about her which troubled the young doctor. He sternly tried to remind himself that it was only the light perfume of her hair, tied loosely at the back of her neck with a piece of string she had pulled from her pocket. He reminded himself, with cool clinical detachment, that the darkness of the night, the sense of adventure and secrecy which surrounded them would heighten any man's awareness. This should mean nothing to a Harmonist.

But his mind was still moving in curious and forbidden ways when they got into the buggy and started cautiously down the dirt road that led toward Pittsburgh. As soon as they were safely past the last house of the village, Conrad spoke urgently to the little mare, and she moved swiftly through the night, the lantern on the dash lending only a fitful, erratic light to the road. Conrad was grateful for the fact that the wide buggy seat allowed the three of them to sit without touching. By the time they had found Gertrude and four of them would be crowded in (somehow he never doubted that she would be returning with them) his mind would be in order and he would be indifferent to Hildegarde's nearness.

They had traveled less than an hour when Hildegarde's voice came sharply to his ears. "Look, up there, in the moonlight, see that moving patch, like a shadow. Could that be them?"

Pauline's voice was muffled and despondent. "I've cried so much I can't see well enough to tell what it is."

Conrad, peering in the direction of Hildegarde's pointing hand, was inclined to agree with her. "It might be," he said. "It's hard to tell from here, and it doesn't seem to be moving very fast. You'd think they'd be racing as though Satan were on their tail."

"Speak for yourself," Hildegarde said, and a soft giggle escaped her.

Conrad felt a quick delight touch him. This kind of humor was so rare among the Harmonists, though so dear to his own heart, that the discovery of it was a heady sort of thing. A more sober reflection might have warned him that this reaction on his part was more dangerous than any momentary distraction brought about by the sweet smell of loosened hair in the night.

But there was no time for sober reflection. A

touch of the whip made the mare increase her speed, and in a minute, Hildegarde's shadow took on the sharper lines of form, and the tutor's buggy was ahead of them in the night.

Martin, certain that their plan was flawless, that Gertrude's absence would not be noticed until morning, had felt no need to race toward their destination. It seemed of far greater importance to him that the girl beside him be persuaded from her tears and regret. It would never do to bring her, tearstained and sobbing, to his friends who had been led to believe that they were to be host to a happy bride and groom. So he looped the reins loosely over the whip socket, letting the horse jog slowly along the road, and he turned his attention to Gertrude. With gentleness and restraint, he pled his case. So concerned was he, so threatened by the fear of her rejection, that he had no fear of any other intrusion. He did not even hear Conrad's horse until his buggy was overtaken by the mare.

But Gertrude heard the sound of hooves, and her heart squeezed together with sudden chill. It would be her grandfather, of course, angry and righteous, and all her penitent tears, all her renunciation of the love which had tempted her away from her duty, could never heal the breach that would be between them. She would do anything, she thought in quick terror, anything in the world to undo what she had done. If only, somehow, somehow, she could erase this action from her grandfather's memory so that he could look at her as he had always looked, without anger or sorrow.

She stiffened away from Martin's touch, and in that minute, the tutor heard the approaching horse. His instinct was to reach for the reins, to speak sharply to his own horse. But Gertrude, aware of this, held him back.

"No," she begged. Even in her fear and distress, she knew that it would do no good to run away. The time for running was gone.

And Martin knew it too. He felt engulfed in total defeat, drowned in the bitter taste of it. *I should have known*, he thought in a great surge of sorrow, *I should have known it would be like this.*

Conrad's voice came out of the darkness. "Sister Gertrude, are you there? May we talk to you?"

Not Grandfather's voice, Gertrude thought, weakly, hardly daring to hope. But if he were in the buggy, no one else would have presumed to speak. Who, then, had come after her?

"Who is it?" she quavered, sitting away from Martin, pulling herself into herself, no longer the girl who had felt the stab and ache of life.

"It's Brother Conrad," Conrad said, "with Sister Hildegarde and Sister Pauline."

"Just you three?"

"Just we three. Will you talk to us?"

"No," Martin whispered in her ear. "Oh, Trudy, no. They can't make you go back. They can't take you like a sack of meal. Don't leave me now. Oh, my darling, my lieble. . . ."

Pauline's voice came insistently, interrupting the pleading whisper. "Sister Gertrude, this isn't for you. Your home is with the Father, with all of us."

And Conrad's voice moved smoothly into the short silence that followed. "We're waiting for another Bridegroom, Sister. You haven't forgotten, have you?"

For a minute Gertrude didn't answer. She knew with a great certainty that if she went back now, she would never leave again. There would never be, for her, the promise, the sweetness, the torment of love she had known so briefly with Martin.

But at home I will be safe, she thought, *safe from sin and safe from temptation. What I must renounce is small compared to what I will gain.*

But only if Grandfather doesn't know, she thought. "Does he know?" she asked. "My grandfather, does he know?"

Pauline spoke eagerly, puzzled that Hildegarde, for once, was letting her do all the talking. "No one knows but us. I still have your note here. No one will ever know, sister. Come back with us—we'll take you home."

Gertrude could feel the trembling of Martin's hand against her arm, but she would not let herself look at him. She had made her decision and it would only be weakness to look back. In a very real sense, she had made her decision in the moment when Martin had kissed her with such desire, but she had been cowardly enough to let him take her away. Now, she knew she must never be cowardly again.

"Yes, I'll come," she said. "Brother Conrad, will you help me down?"

Conrad handed the reins to Hildegarde and with a strange mixture of compassion and relief churning in him, he stepped down to help Gertrude. Of course, it had to be like this. It was possible for any girl in the village to run away—but not Gertrude Rapp. He knew it as they all knew it. But pity for the tutor, rejected and silent, touched his heart.

Hildegarde sat shaken and still. In her usual eager, impetuous way, she had planned a speech of persuasion that she thought would sway any runaway. But she had not bargained for the sight of Martin's face in the dim, flickering light of the lantern. She had not expected the anguished line of his mouth, the glaze of pain in his eyes. She had not expected the glimpse of his trembling hand stretched toward the empty place where Gertrude had been. In the face of this, her little speech seemed silly and so she sat in unexpected silence.

Martin made no move to protest. He had recognized long ago that unless Gertrude came of her own free will, she would not come at all. What had he to offer against the strength of her training and the fanaticism of these people? Only a heart full of love—a puny weapon in the face of such an offensive.

Gertrude squeezed in between Hildegarde and Pauline, and Conrad waited a minute before he clucked at his horse. Was there no word of farewell to be said?

Then Martin spoke. "Good-bye," he said. "Good-bye, Trudy."

Pauline's breath drew in sharply at the use of the intimate name, but Gertrude answered in a clear, little voice, drained of all emotion.

"Good-bye, Martin," she said. "I'm sorry—but good-bye."

Conrad heard the brittle tone and knew that further delay would only intensify the pain of this moment. His hands hauled hard on the reins, and his urgent command started the little mare in a quick wheeling turn which headed them toward the village.

For several minutes, there was no sound at all. Then Pauline began to pray breathlessly, with tears clogging the words. "Gross Gott, we thank thee for our sister. We thank thee for letting her see the truth. Bless her, God, and. . . ."

Gertrude's tears were like an explosion, more terrible because they had been preceded by such calm. The intensity of her sobs shook her so hard that Conrad could feel the tremors even though Hildegarde sat between them. Pauline's voice murmured on and on, but it was Hildegarde's arms which held Gertrude, trying to keep her from breaking apart with grief.

Gradually, Gertrude's tears lessened and then stopped. Hildegarde felt the trembling go out of Gertrude, and she seemed to sense the strength that flowed in to take its place. Is it Pauline's prayers, Hildegarde wondered with a queer sense of detachment, or is it just because she is Gertrude Rapp and nothing can break her, after all? But Pauline's prayers don't touch me, she went on in her mind. I only want to tell her to stop crying and blow her nose. And I'm not a Rapp. What would strengthen me if this happened to me?

They stopped the buggy several hundred feet

from the Great House, and Conrad and Hildegarde sat in complete silence, waiting to see if there would be any sound when Gertrude and Pauline slipped in the kitchen door. There was no sound from the sleeping house and in only a minute a candle flickered in the front room where Gertrude slept.

"She's safe," Hildegarde said.

"Yes. He'll never know she ran away. No one will know," Conrad said, feeling that maybe Hildegarde needed reminding to hold her tongue. Then he felt a touch of shame. Was he trying to make himself believe she was a scatterbrained girl so that she would seem less attractive to him?

He clucked softly to his horse and they moved around the corner to stop in front of the Mutschler house. The fact that they were alone in the night did not seem to even enter Hildegarde's mind. She was completely obsessed by all that she had seen this night, and she knew herself to be profoundly moved and shaken and altered by the events of the past hour.

She made no move to get down from the buggy. "When I said 'safe'," she mused softly, "I meant safe from Father Rapp's finding out. But I didn't say it. Only you said the same thing. But it isn't the kind of safety we should have been thinking of, is it?"

He felt uncomfortable, knowing he should hurry her into the house, knowing that she was too affected by this night. But she deserved an answer, too.

"We were wrong," he said, trying to keep his voice stern. "We should have been far more concerned about the safety of her soul. We were wrong."

She turned to look at him then, and he was shocked to see that her face was streaked with tears. Her eyes looked heavy and sad in the dim light.

"What about him?" she asked. "What about Herr Schmidt? He isn't safe from anything."

Shall I say his own sin blinds him? Conrad thought. But he could not bring himself to say the words.

"I don't know," he said helplessly. "He's of the world, so I can't judge him or know his heart."

"He loved her," Hildegarde said. "He looked at her—like. . . ."

Conrad heard the questioning and the pain in her voice, and he knew he had to be strong for her.

"Don't use the word 'love' loosely," he said sharply. "You have been taught the right way, Sister Hildegarde. So has Sister Gertrude. This—this intruder will go away and everything will be all right. You are positively not to even think of it again."

Out of long habit, she had bent to his authority once this night, but she was different now.

"My mind is my own, Brother Conrad," she said coldly. "If I think of tonight, it is my own affair."

Before he could answer, she had jumped out of the buggy and was gone, swiftly and silently into the second side door that led into the bedroom where her mother lay waiting. Once inside, the tears came with a nervous chill which made her teeth chatter even after her mother had wrapped a cover around her. Wisely, Frau Mutschler asked no questions but only held her child—her beautiful, willful, frightened child—until she was asleep.

Conrad watched her go and then turned the head of the horse toward home. He had failed her, of course. He had not been as wise nor as stern nor as positive as he ought to have been. Father Rapp or Frederick would have handled it better. Even Dr. Mueller might have known better what to say. But a reluctant grin tugged at the corners of his mouth. Even *they* might have been taken back by her fire, he thought with something almost like admiration. She will bear watching, that little one. Lots of watching from now on.

During the days that followed, Hildegarde tried again and again to establish some sort of contact with Gertrude, to get Gertrude to admit by word or glance that something had happened. It almost seemed to Hildegarde as though that dark chase had never taken place, as though Gertrude had never wept despairingly in her arms, as though Martin Schmidt had never sat hunched with loss in the lantern light. There was an unbelievable quality of solidarity about Gertrude which Hildegarde could not even chip away with questioning looks or attempts to speak of the subject.

Knowing of her own moments of regret and penitence and fervent promises to be better, Hildegarde had some idea of the night Gertrude must have spent in anguished prayer. But what Hildegarde could not understand, what she would never really understand, was the total calm and resignation which had come to Gertrude before dawn had lightened the sky. Gertrude came to believe during that night of prayer that her grandfather's unawareness of her defection was a miracle, vouchsafed to her, however unworthy she might be. There was, of course, no answer to this but to give herself wholly, unquestioningly, to the will of God—to pledge her life totally and unswervingly to his service. All of the weakness had been washed out of Gertrude in that searing hour of recognition of her sin. From this hour on, until her death, she would walk serenely, safely, joyfully on the path her grandfather had chosen for her.

She ignored Hildegarde, then, not out of cruelty or fear, but out of an unawareness. She had sinned but she had been forgiven. She had too much of her grandfather in her to torture herself with needless and repetitious recrimination. So when she looked at Hildegarde, she did not see the questions trembling on her lips or the anxiety that filled her eyes. Her smile in Hildegarde's direction was sweet and amiable and gave not the slightest opportunity for an exchange of words or thoughts.

Hildegarde, robbed of her one confidante, allowed the defiance which had shaped her cold retort to Conrad to build and build. She wasn't like Gertrude, she could never be like that, so why try? With deliberation she sought out Maria Baumann. Part of her reason for spending time with Maria was because she knew that Gertrude frowned on the association, but part of it was because Maria could make her laugh. And laughter was the thing Hildegarde hungered for all during that long, hot summer. If there were to be no clear answers for her mind, then at least her heart could be merry.

Chapter 13

By late September, the purple grapes hung in heavy, fragrant bunches on the vine. Espaliered vines, trained to climb along the brick houses above the first story, held the choice grapes, juicy and sweet from the heat of the bricks that retained the sun's warmth after the sky was dark. In one corner of the park that stretched between the *Vosterhaus* and the river, trellises rayed out from a central arbor in such a way as to catch every bit of the sun, and outside the village, acres of ordinary vineyards ran in meticulous rows parallel to the road. The harvest was a good one in the autumn of 1827, and everyone who was able to walk or carry a basket was called out on the day of grape harvest to help pick the heavy fruit and take it to the grinder for the grinding. The actual pressing was not done for ten days after the picking, but there was still an air of festival in the gathering of the brethren to perform this task which bore less resemblance to drudgery than most things which had to be done.

Hildegarde and Maria were assigned to the *Vosterhaus* garden, and for the first few hours they picked with a will, enjoying the hot September sun on their heads and the unusual freedom which allowed them to talk freely. This corner was small enough that only the two had been assigned to do the picking. Frederick, who assigned the pickers, had suggested that they start in opposite corners and work toward the center, and they had complied with the suggestion for a short while until they were sure that everyone else was busy and then Maria had come to Hildegarde's corner and they had continued their work, facing each other across the vine.

They talked with animation of little things and in only a short time their mouths were stained with the purple fruit and their conversation had taken on the sweet, tart taste of the grapes.

"What would you say," Maria asked with a sidewise look, "if I told you that I might not stay here forever? That I might go away?"

Hildegarde stopped with her hand poised over a bunch of grapes. "Here? You mean here in the garden?"

"No, dummkopf. I mean here in Economy."

Hildegarde's hands began to move again, automatically doing the task of picking, but her mind darted in quick circles. Was this to be another leaving like Gertrude's had been—unfinished and incomplete?

"You couldn't leave," Hildegarde said at last. "You haven't anywhere to go."

"I do, too. My brother is in Pittsburgh. I could go to his house. He'd take me in."

"But why?" Hildegarde said. "You know we have to stay here. We have to be ready."

Maria shrugged. "I don't even try to understand the Father. I never have. What he talks about isn't for the likes of me anyhow."

"Of course it is. It's for all of us."

"Oh, come on, Hildegarde. Do you think things can be the same for Brother Frederick and someone like me? I'm not made like he is—he and Brother Christoph and Brother Conrad. I'm only a girl. And my mother—my mother. . . ."

She stopped and dark blood colored her face and neck. Hildegarde looked at her with sudden excitement.

"What about your mother?"

"Nothing. Only she says—well, she says that women are supposed to have babies, not just wait for the Coming."

This was blasphemy! Hildegarde felt a matching stain run up her neck and face. It was true enough that Frau Baumann had borne child after child and seemed to feel only joy and pride in them, but somehow Hildegarde had been able to accept this without thinking about it. It had seemed like a sort of accidental thing that happened in spite of what surely had been an earnest desire to comply with the Society's stand on celibacy. It had simply never occured to Hildegarde that the Baumanns had deliberately had children because they thought it was right and moral. This shocked her far more than the thought of an occasional guilty sin might shock her.

"You mean," she gasped. "You mean that your mother—that she *wants* to have babies?"

Maria looked ashamed and defiant at the same time. "Yes. She and my father both do."

The last sentence was only a furtive whisper, but it sounded in Hildegarde's ears like an explosion. She stared at Maria, her mouth open, her hands suspended in the air.

Maria, as motionless, stared back. Her confession had come almost as unexpectedly to her as it had to Hildegarde. Now that the words had been said, the restriction of natural reticence seemed broken. The words poured forth.

"And my brother. You know he and Mathilde left the Society to get married. My parents weren't sad or angry or anything. They only sort of smiled and said it was God's will that some people live happy—and some people live saintly."

"But we're to be both happy and saintly. Look at Father Rapp—how he's happy," Hildegarde argued.

But Maria's young voice was scornful. "Happy? He's contented, I guess, and besides it's different with him. He's not like us. He's not like me anyhow. And I don't think he's much like you."

"Well, Sister Gertrude, then," Hildegarde said. "She's happy."

"I don't know about her," Maria said stubbornly. "I don't know whether she's happy or not. I only know about me."

"Aren't you happy, Maria?"

Maria shrugged and slipped a grape into her mouth. "We laugh at our house, Hildegarde. Do you laugh at yours?"

"Yes. Sometimes."

They were silent for a long time, but Hildegarde was thinking furiously of all that had been said. She had, of course, been aware of the difference in the atmosphere at the Baumann home, and as a child she had loved to go there, finding the relaxed freedom refreshing and pleasant. But she had attributed it only to the fact that there were young children there and that Frau Baumann had stayed home more than most women to care for her family. After the night when Johannes Baker died, Hildegarde had avoided the Baumann home, because she felt that Brother Ludwig was faithless and weak. Now, with the memory of Maria's words, she was revising her opinions—wondering if the faithlessness were due to something more dangerous and more serious than weakness.

"Anyhow," Maria said at last. "Don't be surprised if you hear it. That I'm gone, I mean. I wouldn't want you to think I hadn't told you."

Hildegarde stared at the round, determined face across the vine. "But what would you do? I mean, you aren't really ready to live in the world, are you? What would you do for food—for money? You can't stay with your brother forever, can you?"

Maria looked down at her hands, suddenly

confused and shy. "I don't intend to stay with him forever. I have—I have other plans."

Hildegarde's heart knocked sharply against her chest. "You mean you—you. . . ."

"I don't know," Maria said quickly, suspecting the word which evidently could not be forced out of Hildegarde's mouth. "But maybe. If I want to."

"Who?" Hildegarde asked bluntly.

Maria's voice was lost in shy confusion. "I can't tell. If the Father asks you, I don't want you to know. I want you to say you haven't any idea."

Hildegarde felt as though she were drowning in a sort of desolation. What was happening all around her without her being aware of it? She had suspected nothing about Gertrude and Martin until she had heard them whispering in the garden. She had never dreamed that Maria wanted to leave the Society. And Maria and Gertrude were her closest friends. Was she blind? Too occupied with herself? Or was she just too stupid to know what could stir the heart of a girl?

Hildegarde was not a humble girl. She had grown up, knowing that her looks and ability and charm had gained many special privileges for herself. She had grown to expect it as her due. But whatever had come to Gertrude and Maria had certainly not come to her.

The noon bell rang suddenly and Maria jumped. "You won't tell, will you?" she said nervously. "Will you, Hildegarde?"

"Don't be silly," Hildegarde snapped. "I'm not a gossip."

"Oh, I know," Maria tried a more placating tone of voice. "It's just that—I shouldn't have told you, I guess. But you're my friend."

With an effort Hildegarde pulled her mind from its customary obsession with her own concerns and tried to focus on Maria. "I know. It's all right. I hope you'll be happy—whatever you decide to do. But be sure, Maria," she added abruptly. "Some have gone, you know, and had to come back."

Maria's chin went up. "I know how I feel," she said. "I won't come crawling back."

Hildegarde saw the strength of the determined little round chin, and she was reminded of the strength that had implacably shaped Gertrude since that night in May. They were opposite strengths, stiffened by opposite beliefs. And Hildegarde did not know—could not know— which was right.

By midafternoon, Hildegarde was weary from the hours of picking, and her head was aching from the constant sun. Maria had been moved to another place to pick, and Hildegarde was finishing up the last of the arbor to which she had been assigned. Part of her headache was due, she thought, to the emotional confusion which she had been feeling for the past several hours. She held her hand to her forehead and wished suddenly that she could lie down in some cool, dim room and not have to think about anything at all.

"Are you tired?" a voice said.

She looked up to see Jacob Klein looking at her and there was something on his face which made her knees feel weak and caused her hands to fumble on the grapes.

"Yes, tired," she said, trying not to look at him, but feeling her eyes drawn to his face against her will.

There was tenderness in his eyes, but there was something else, some intensity she could not define nor understand. For a minute, she considered turning cooly on her heel and moving away, but something stayed her. Here was her chance to find out the answers to the questions which had been plaguing her. She could find out what this thing was which had shaken Gertrude and Maria from the pattern set for them. The fact that Jacob Klein had no appeal to her as a person—the fact that she would never have sought him out meant nothing to her, of course, because she did not know at all the nature of love.

"Yes," she repeated letting her eyes rest steadily on his, "I'm tired. I'm not used to this kind of work, you know."

He moved a step nearer. "Oh, I know. You're too small for this heavy work, too. . . ." The word that hammered at the back of his tongue was "lovely," and he knew he did not dare say it.

She had the grace to laugh in a depreciating way. "Oh, it isn't so terrible, really. I guess I've been spoiled."

She wanted him to deny it, and he did. "Not spoiled," he said hotly. "Why should you be treated like the rest? You're not like them at all."

This was the kind of attention she hungered for and received so seldom. She never questioned communitarian ownership of material goods, but she longed for recognition of her own self.

Again he came closer to her. "I could go to Brother Frederick and ask him to let you go," he said. "I can finish up here."

She basked in the ardent admiration in his eyes. "But you must have something else to do?" she said.

"I was sent to draw off the old wine," he admitted. "In the wine cellar. But that can wait."

She thought with longing of the cool, dim, quiet wine cellar, and an idea leaped into her mind. "I know," she cried. "Let me go and draw off the wine, and you pick. That way we'll get the work done, and I can get out of the sun."

"Fine," he agreed heartily. "If anyone comes, I'll say you had too much sun."

She started to move away then suddenly realized that their arrangement had done nothing more than take her out of the sun. They were still to be separated and she was no closer to finding out what she wanted to know than she was before. The sense of disappointment she felt had nothing to do with Jacob personally, but it was sharp and insistent.

She smiled her sweetest smile at him, wondering if her hair were mussed or if her face and hands were dirty from the work of picking.

Jacob was only conscious of the purple grape stains on her lips and the kind way she was looking at him. A great pulse throbbed through his body, and the sky seemed to spin over his head. All the prayers and counsel of Frederick dispersed as though they had never been, and Jacob stood there in the vineyard with his longing and his desire.

"You're beautiful," he said chokingly.

She felt the hot blood rush to her face, and her training told her to drop her eyes from his, to turn and run. But her perverse curiosity held her in her place, hot and breathless, enduring his hungry look.

In spite of the churning of her blood, her mind was cool and calculating. *What would he do,* she thought, *if I were to touch him, if I were to let my hand touch his hand?*

The air was still and heavy, and there was no sound of voices or movement. They were alone in the garden. With a show of great timidity but with careful deliberation, she moved forward and laid her hand on his. She remembered the tingling that had gone up her arm when Lavasseur had kissed her fingers. Is this what was happening to Jacob?

His face flamed, and she saw the heavy pulse beating in his temple, but she was too excited at her own daring to be afraid.

"Thank you," she whispered. "Thank you for being so kind."

Some instinct, buried under the dust of her training, roused itself and told her that this was enough, that she should go now. With a quick squeeze of her fingers and a deepening of her smile, she turned and began to run lightly across the grass toward the wine cellar under the tailor shop which was situated just across Grossestrasse from the vineyard.

She was both excited and puzzled as she ran. There was no doubt but what she possessed some strange power over Jacob, and this knowledge was heady. But was this what had made Gertrude run away? Maria, maybe—that little scatterbrained one—but Gertrude? Gertrude would never be so foolish as to leave just because a man looked at her with his blood warming his cheeks. There must be more to it than this.

She ran down the steep stone steps into the dim cavern which kept out the summer heat and winter cold with its walls, which were three feet thick. There was the sharp yet musty smell of wind and cordial. Hildegarde waited a minute until her eyes had accustomed themselves to the gloom.

She was reminded of the day she and Maria had drawn off the wine together and had tasted too much. What a scolding they had received when Frau Mutschler discovered their flushed cheeks and bright eyes. Remembering, Hildegarde giggled a little and then a wave of desolation suddenly engulfed her. What was it going to be like with Maria gone? There would be no one to laugh with anymore. Gertrude, with her new serenity and solidarity, would never again walk by the river and listen to the revolutionary words that churned in Hildegarde's mind. There would be no one to listen, no one to share the feeling that laughter was good.

She moved finally to the barrel which needed to be drawn off and began to work the bung loose. A sound on the step jerked her toward the door. At first she could not tell who it was there on the steps. From the size she thought it might be Brother Frederick, and she began hastily to fashion an excuse that would make sense to him.

Then the intruder spoke, and she recognized Jacob's voice.

"Hildegarde," he said. "Are you there?"

Not Sister Hildegarde—just Hildegarde. Oddly enough, this shook her more than the touch of hands had done.

"Yes," she answered tremulously. "Is something wrong? Did someone come looking for me?"

"Yes," he said, coming toward her. "I came looking for you."

"I don't understand," she faltered. "You knew I was here. Have you changed your mind about wanting to finish the grapes?"

"I've changed my mind about a lot of things," he said, and she could hear his breath, loud in the dim cellar. "I've been a fool not to know it before. Listen, Hildegarde, I love you. I need you."

"Oh, no," she breathed. She had not really believed that her actions in the garden would result in this. She had withdrawn her fingers from Lavasseur's warm hold, and that had been the end of it. Now, with Jacob looming large between her and the daylight at the head of the steps, she knew that the simple act of withdrawing would be denied her.

If she wanted to withdraw, that is. The questioning, the wondering, the curiosity still twisted in her. So, while there was still space between them, while he was still dazzled by the sudden loss of bright sun, while she still might have twisted from him and escaped with a laugh and a light touch that might have meant nothing, she waited to find out what would happen.

With a sudden groan, he reached out to her and gathered her tightly against him. At first, she was too surprised to resist. She certainly had never expected anything like this. A touch, an impudent word, a look—these, perhaps, but no more.

He bent his head, and his mouth on hers was savage, ruthless, starving. For a few seconds, she was stripped of all will and struggle, she was drowning in astonishment and fear.

Then she began to fight. She was shocked and horrified by this passion which had in it nothing of gentleness or sweetness. She remembered the time when the tame moose in Father Rapp's garden had suddenly gone berserk and had killed the female in the frenzy of mating. Hildegarde, wide-eyed and terrified, had seen the attack and her dreams had been filled with violence for weeks. Smothered in Jacob's embrace, she could see only the blazing eyes of the mad moose, the wicked flailing of his hooves.

Her fear strengthened her, and she tore herself out of his arms. Stumbling on the uneven floor, but feeling pursued and hunted, she struggled toward the steps.

"Hildegarde, wait. Listen," he called pleadingly, but she only plunged upward to daylight and safety.

"What's going on here? Sister Hildegarde, are you all right?"

The voice rolled upon her with the crash and suddenness of thunder on a summer day. For a second, she felt sure she would lose her balance and crash down the steep steps to land, broken, on the cellar floor. There was even time to think fleetingly that death might be easier for her than this instant of time which seemed to grow large all around her.

Then she balanced herself and groped desperately for the words to say to Father Rapp who stood between her and the September sky.

Chapter 14

Father Rapp stared at the girl, seeing her flushed face and the distress in her eyes. As always when he saw the Mutschler girl, his heart warmed and softened. She was nearly as dear to him as Gertrude was, and he had a strong feeling that she was meant for some great thing in the Society. So frequently had he experienced this feeling that he had come to look on it as God's will that he give this girl special consideration. It might be, it just might be that he could use her talents in other ways than just in the greenhouse and garden. He would pray about it, he decided.

While these thoughts raced through his head, Hildegarde came up at last with words to say— words that were not really untrue but might allow her to escape detection. He must be kept out of the wine cellar somehow; he must never know that Jacob was down there with that hot look in his eyes.

"Oh, Father," she said faintly. "I was drawing off the wine, and I felt suddenly very ill. I think I've had too much sun."

She did not have to pretend to be weak and unsteady on her feet. Between the sun and Jacob's fierce embrace and the terror of seeing Father Rapp, her knees were trembling so much that she could barely stand.

He took her arm to steady her, and he felt her trembling. To his fond eyes, her flushed face looked only feverish, and he drew her into the shade.

"I'll walk with you over to the apothecary shop," he said. "I saw Brother Conrad heading that way only a minute ago."

Her heart sank. She had a sudden wish that it might have been Dr. Mueller who would see her. Conrad was too astute. But she dared not protest.

"All right, Father," she said meekly and discovered that she really did need his strong hand to hold her steady as they walked toward the building which housed the doctor's office and the apothecary shop.

The shock of seeing Father Rapp had blotted Jacob out of her mind for a minute, but safely away from the wine cellar, the memory of that violence came sweeping over her, and she suddenly began to cry. There was no use trying to deny the fact that part of the sin, the devastating sin, was hers. She had deliberately touched his hand, she had tempted and teased. Her ignorance of what this would do to him was no excuse. And her motives had been reprehensible. She had used Jacob as a tool to solve a problem. She had not thought of him as a person, and so her sin was compounded by heedlessness and cruelty.

Oh, God, please, she thought in despair, wanting to move away from Father Rapp's sustaining hand, feeling that he would be contaminated even to touch her. But she knew that if she shook off the hand, she would fall, weakened by fear and self-loathing.

She stumbled weeping into the cool hallway of the store building and walked back to the small room where Dr. Mueller kept his instruments. The room was empty, and for a minute, she thought she might escape an examination. But Father Rapp gently forced her to lie on the black leather-covered table.

"You lie here," he ordered her, never suspecting that her tears came from anything but illness. "I'll fetch Brother Conrad at once. He's likely in the apothecary room."

She lay shaking with sobs as the old man left, wanting desperately to get down from the table, to run and hide but aware of the fact that she was physically unable to move.

Was this what had tempted Gertrude and Maria—this dark shame, this feeling of humiliation and fear that had filled her as she struggled in Jacob's crushing hold? Oh, surely not. Not Gertrude. She would never want to leave for such as this. Not even Maria—Maria might be heedless but she was gentle and sweet. She would not want to be—to be—"mauled" was the only word that came to Hildegarde's mind.

Father Rapp, followed by Conrad, came back into the office. Conrad's eyes took in Hildegarde's condition—the uncontrolled trembling, the hot, flushed face, the inflamed eyes. He took her wrist in his cool hand, and her pulse raced erratically under his fingers. But she didn't seem to be the type of girl who would suffer from a little sun. Not in September. And not when she worked in the garden all summer.

"Did you have malaria in New Harmony?" he asked abruptly.

Father Rapp answered for her. "Yes and badly. Complicated with lung fever. She nearly died."

Conrad made an assenting noise with his lips and tried to get Hildegarde to look at him. But she kept her face turned away and when he pulled it around to face him, she squeezed her eyes tightly.

There's something more than sun here, he thought. *This girl is in some kind of shock. Maybe I can provide a countershock.*

"It may be a sort of relapse," he mused, seemingly to himself. "I think several large doses of cochane root might bring her around."

Her eyes flew open. "Oh, no," she gasped, "not that horrible stuff. I'd rather be sick."

So, he thought. *She is not really sick at all.* His feeling was a mixture of curiosity, sympathy and a sort of amusement. He felt sorry for her, and yet he felt that like a naughty child, she should not be allowed off scott-free. He didn't suspect the happening in the wine cellar, but he suspected something.

"Well, a dose of salts at least," he conceded. He watched her wry face with amusement. "And then go home and lie down. Bathe your forehead with witch hazel. If you're not better by evening, have your father fetch me."

With a feeling akin to enjoyment, he watched her gag down the dose of salts, and when she tried to walk with cold dignity out of the room, he was close to laughter. He swung his eyes toward Father Rapp who was moving to assist the girl, expecting the same gentle amusement to be on the old man's face. To Conrad's amazement, there was nothing but concern and affection there. Conrad frowned a little, reflecting that he had known for years that Father Rapp was not always objective in his treatment of the brothers, nor was he impartial. But this Mutschler child—she was transparent as a pane of glass—pretty and headstrong and capricious. Surely, the Father could see it. But watching the large hand gently steadying the faltering girl, Conrad had to accept the fact that the wise old prophet did not see the girl as others might see her. Was he wiser than the rest, Conrad wondered, and able to see virtues not obvious to others—or was it just barely possible that he was capable of a fond fatuousness that had no basis in fact at all? Shaking his head over the difficulties of the question, Conrad turned back to his work.

Father Rapp walked all the way to the door of the Mutschler house with Hildegarde, leaving her there alone with some reluctance.

"You'll be all right?" he said. "You won't fall? You'll lie down at once?"

"Yes," she promised. "At once, Father. I'll be all right. I feel stronger already."

She was almost desperate in her desire to get away from the old man. His honest concern for her was like a whip across flesh already cut and bleeding. She simply had to be alone to sort out her thoughts and try to pray. She knew that if she were as good as she had been taught to be, she would be on her knees before him, now, this instant, confessing everything she had done. But she simply did not possess that kind of courage. She could endure anything, she thought, but seeing the disillusionment in his face.

"Then I'll go," he said. "If I see your mother, I'll send her home."

"No, please," she begged. Her mother's eyes were as discerning and disconcerting as Conrad's had been. "Please, Father. I only want to sleep. We need the workers for the grapes. Tomorrow it might rain."

He looked at her fondly. *Even in her sickness, she cares about the Society,* he thought. He, who was usually able to ferret out insincerity like a dog can scent a rabbit, saw only what he wanted to see in the flushed little face.

"All right then," he said. "To bed. I'll inquire tonight to see if you're better. God bless you, child." He smiled his warmest smile, turned on his heel and left.

Hildegarde went into the cool, quiet house. She had only enough strength to cross the living room and enter the narrow bedroom she shared with her mother. There, without removing her

dress or washing her fruit-stained hands, she
flung herself across her bed. The ropes under
the thin mattress protested softly at the sudden
jarring fall, and then all was quiet. For a little
while, the girl was too sickened and ashamed to
even cry, but at last the healing tears came and
finally she slept. Even in her sleep, her breath
came in ragged little sobs and the tears dried
streakily across her cheeks.

When Father Rapp and Hildegarde left the wine
cellar door, Jacob stood staring up against the
sky, so filled with emotion that he could not
move. There was relief, of course, relief that
Father Rapp had not come down the steps and
discovered the cause of Hildegarde's tears and
trembling. But there was more than relief. There
was a hot anger at the girl, anger which blended
with the emotion that Jacob, from his training,
could only know as lust. She had been deliberately provocative in the vineyard; even an inex-
perienced man like himself could not be wrong
about that. The smile, the touch of her hand, the
look in her eyes—they all added up to invitation. He was sure of it. She had been a fire in his
blood for two years, and only prayer and Frederick's counsel had kept him safe this long.

Or had it been the prayer and counsel? Had it
not been, after all, Hildegarde's indifference
which had kept him safe? And when the indifference disappeared, when she smiled at him
and touched him, all the discipline dispersed in
a blaze of longing that had made him follow the

girl into the wine cellar, heedless of any danger of their being caught.

He had been sure she wanted him to follow her. She might struggle a little; he expected that. But it would be only a token struggle, a tantalizing prelude to her capitulation. He had never expected at all the fierceness of her fight, the way her hands had scratched and pushed, the frantic fear which had made her struggle like a wild cat in his arms. He had not thought she would run from him in disgust and terror.

Now, angry, frightened and terribly aware of the desire which pounded in him, he stood shaking in the cellar, trying to quiet his pounding heart. He could not stand here like this forever; someone would surely come and he must at least give the appearance of working. And yet his hands were trembling so much that he knew he could not handle the utensils which held the wine. Nor did he think his legs could haul him up the steep stone steps into the sunlight.

He sat on an overturned keg and put his head in his hands. He had learned something this afternoon, something he should have known always. He was not a Harmonist by nature. He did not have the kind of mental discipline which the Father and Frederick had; he could not make his blood run cool and thin and quiet. Passion was only dormant in him when he tried to be like the others; it was never vanquished. His blood ran hot and fast and lusty; to dam it up was to invite future disaster.

He would have to leave. It was as simple as

that. He would have to leave his parents and his brothers and go out into the world where he could find a girl to wife, a girl to give him children and make him into the kind of man he wanted to be. Surely God would not forsake him altogether; there would be some reward for the years of faithful service.

A girl to wife, he thought with terrible aching. But what girl other than Hildegarde? Even with the anger still in him, he knew he loved her, loved and wanted her and no other girl would do.

His mind moved ploddingly. Frederick would have to give him some money if he left, a little anyhow; that was part of the agreement. And he was a skilled worker; he'd find work in Pittsburgh or Wheeling. He felt a cold wave of fear at the thought. He never in his life had to be concerned about money or food or clothes or shelter. These things had been taken care of for him. How would he manage?

Well, others had done it. Some, anyhow. Some had come back, it was true, whining and crawling and confessing their "sin" because they could not cope with the world. But he was different.

The anger and the desire were ebbing away, and his tired mind shied away from the memory of what had taken place in the cellar. Memory went back, instead, to the vineyard, to the touch of her hand, the sweetness of her smile and her friendly words. Perhaps it wasn't really as final as he had first believed. Perhaps—in another time and another place—he might make her kiss him, too. Maybe, given the proper circumstances, he could bend that proud spirit and gentle that fierceness until she would melt obediently to his will.

He had to have her. There was no use deceiving himself any longer. He simply had to have her.

A month went by. Hildegarde tried to avoid anything that would make her remember that shattering experience which had actually made her ill, so that her words to Father Rapp had not been a lie after all. For several days, she had stayed in bed, listless and wan, crying intermittently, unable to eat any of the food her mother brought solicitously to her. Frau Mutschler nursed the girl gently and lovingly, and so there were no accusations made, no explanations required. Everyone seemed willing to believe it was the work of grape harvesting coupled with some unknown ailment.

By the time Hildegarde was able to be up and out again, another shock was dealt her. Maria had really gone. There was no hue and cry; it was rather obvious that the elders in the Society only breathed a sigh of relief when one of the Baumanns left, but Hildegarde was deeply shaken by the event. It was not only that Maria was gone—Maria with her sparkle and her laughter—but the fact that Maria had left for something which had become dark and loathsome in Hildegarde's mind. Unable to reconcile what she had experienced in the wine cellar with what she had formerly felt for Maria, Hildegarde simply put it all out of her mind. She could not think about it without crying, so she resolved not to think of it at all.

She stayed away from the Great House, away from Father Rapp, and the slightest glimpse of Jacob was enough to send her running in the opposite direction with a thudding heart and an overwhelming feeling of guilt.

Fortunately, this was a busy time in the gardens. The little box hedges had to be carefully covered with straw, the annual plants had to be taken from their beds, the perennials pruned or covered or banked. There seemed not to be enough hours in the day to get everything done, and when night came, Hildegarde was too tired to do more than say her prayers, half asleep on her knees, and then tumble into bed, too tired to even be aware of her dreams.

Although she had avoided meeting Jacob face to face, she had not escaped his vigilance, and he learned that she often worked until dark in the greenhouse and then, feeling perfectly safe on the dark streets—for was this not a village of perfect peace and harmony?—walked to her home alone. It was not far—just across the garden and then a block down Kirkstrasse. But the garden had many wide trees with deep, black shade under their spreading branches and they offered the kind of hiding place Jacob sought.

The *Liebesmahl* was postponed until the very end of October this year, and Jacob wanted a confrontation with Hildegarde before the feast day came. He had to know how it was going to be with him. Would he still be here, confessing to a sin he did not really feel? Would he be gone alone and cast out from the girl he wanted? Or was it just dimly possible that they might be gone together? He had to find out and there was only one way possible to him.

The nights of the last week in October were crisp and cold, and the moon was not yet in its first quarter, so the darkness lay thick on the land. Lantern light showed the movements of Hildegarde's busy little figure through the walls of the greenhouse, and Jacob, standing beneath the wide oak tree, watched her movements with a feeling of breathlessness. Soon, he thought, and his heart thudded in his throat.

The lantern flame was suddenly blown out, and the door clicked shut. Hildegarde's feet moved surely down the graveled path, and Jacob moved to meet her.

His impulse was to grab her, sweep her into his arms without a warning, but some shred of wisdom held him back.

"Hildegarde," he whispered. "Hildegarde, wait."

She stopped but she was poised to run, and he felt it in the sudden taut stillness. "Who is it?" she said.

"It's me—Jacob. No, wait," he cried softly, seeing her start, "Wait, my sweet, my little one. Wait."

She knew she should run, that even a second of hesitation might make it too late to get away, but the anguish of his voice snared her feet.

"Jacob, you know this is wrong," she said. "Let me go past."

But he was close to her now, there was no longer any chance to run away. His hands, fumbling for her in the darkness, brushed across her breast and caught at her shoulders. She drew in her breath to call out, but his mouth had found hers and she could not make a sound.

At first, he was as fierce as he had been in the wine cellar, and she began to fight, to struggle for her life. But suddenly, the heat, the savagery was gone, and his arms cradled her against him, and his mouth was soft and sensuous against her lips.

Something tore through her body, some emotion remotely like the tingling she had felt when Lavasseur had kissed her fingers but multiplied a hundredfold. She was melting, aching, straining against him, letting her lips soften and mold themselves to his.

Then she was truly afraid. All the other fear she had known at times in her life, lumped together, could not compare to this fear.

Because now she knew what was meant when they spoke of temptation and the lure of sin. She almost hated Jacob; everything in her mind cried out against him, and yet her wicked, weak body was curving itself closer to the man who held her.

Oh, God, she thought in total despair as she felt the warmth of his hand move caressingly down the curve of her back.

Chapter 15

Father Rapp spent a long time in prayer that evening. He had grown too old for kneeling for such long periods, but on this night, he disregarded the stiffness in his knees and gave himself entirely over to God. There was always much to fill his prayers—praise and glorification as well as humble petitions and sometimes fierce, importunate demands. His prayers on this night had dealt with the usual things and now were concentrated on the girl, Hildegarde. She had filled his mind so much during recent months that he was beginning to believe that God really had a mission for her to perform, a role for her to play in the coming of the kingdom. Why else would her face appear to him in his hours of solitude or her voice sound suddenly in the middle of his meditations?

He was too rigidly disciplined, too dedicated to his beliefs for this occurrence to have any meaning other than a holy one. Hildegarde's beauty or sparkle made no impression on his conscious mind except that he would not, if he could, change the way she looked or the silver of her laughter. He thought of her as a child—a willful, spirited child—and it was his duty to guide, train, and use her to the glory of God.

He knotted his old hands together, straining to open his mind and heart to God's will. Hildegarde must have been brought into his mind for a purpose, he reflected; if only he could determine what the purpose was. His memory flooded over the years—gathering pictures of her—but he saw only the things he wanted to see: the times of humility and devotion, the fierceness of her loyalty the night Johannes Baker died (Conrad had reported later how she had leaped to Father Rapp's defense), her concern for the Society (like that day of the grape picking when she would not let him take any workers from the field even though she was obviously ill). Some inexplicable blindness in him closed his mind to the fact that she had a temper, that she was heedless and merry when she ought to have been sober and respectful. He even refused to heed the gossip that said that she was not above smiling in a way guaranteed to sway young, weak men from the goal of purity which was preached and taught. If he honestly could not see fault in her, he reasoned, then it was God's way of showing him that there really was no fault.

But for a long time, it had not been made clear to him how she could be used for the kingdom.

Surely it was not enough that she plan and plant gardens, that she assist Gertrude in the silk experiments, that she work, as other women worked, in the ordinary tasks of the Society. There must be something else, something for which she was destined!

And finally, as the evening wore on, and the intensity of his prayer increased, a great silence came to him, and into the silence God spoke. As plainly as though he actually heard the words, Father Rapp felt God tell him that the time to work on the Holy Experiment had come at last—and Hildegarde was to be his assistant! No longer should he spend his time on the study of alchemy and the mysterious process that would produce the Philosopher's Stone that could turn base metal into gold so that they might have enough wealth to build the New Jerusalem. The time had finally come for *action*, and Hildegarde's talent would be used at last.

That was what God had been trying to point out for months, and only the old man's frailty had kept him from seeing this revelation before. How else explain the girl's cleverness with books, her obsession with science, her apparent ability to comprehend the essence of what he said when he preached, so that he often found himself speaking almost entirely to that small face, lifted like a pure flower, drinking in his words as though they were dew from heaven?

The vision slowly faded, and Father Rapp came back into himself, back to the awareness that he was stiff and cramped and chilled. He pulled himself awkwardly to his feet and stood for a few minutes, gazing dazedly around the familiar room, as though he were in a strange place. It seemed to him, sometimes, after such prayer experiences, that he had touched upon the borders of heaven, and it was actually painful to come back to his mundane, earthly life.

But the conviction did not leave him. He had never been more sure of anything than of the fact that the Holy Experiment must begin at once, and that Hildegarde would be his assistant. Gertrude would help, too, but not Frederick, as he had once thought. God had not brought Frederick into his mind for one second during the hour of prayer. And certainly one does not question God's ways. Frederick would probably be hurt—he had always been excited about the search for the Philosopher's Stone—but he would have to be told that God had other plans for him.

Now, where to begin? The old man looked around the room. Why, he must tell Hildegarde, of course. Should he go to her house? She would no doubt be there, or would she? Hadn't he seen her lately, working long after dark in the greenhouse, readying the plants for the coming winter? He'd try the greenhouse first since it was only a stone's throw from the Great House.

His stiffness nearly gone, he walked across the grass, taking a shorter, diagonal way and avoiding the gravel walks which would have announced his coming with a grating under his shoes. So he came in silence to the dark shadow under the trees where he dimly discerned two bodies, straining together in the darkness, smirching, with this act of physical desire, the purity of the Divine Economy.

"What goes here?" he barked, his voice rough and commanding.

The cry that came from the girl was pure anguish, and her struggle to release herself from the grasping arms of the man who held her was instant, wild, and tormented. Perhaps he had been wrong, Father Rapp thought. Perhaps it had not been mutual passion which he had come upon—but an attempt at rape. The girl was obviously frightened to the point of hysteria.

Then the young man spoke, and the words hit Father Rapp like a blow to the heart. "Hildegarde," Jacob said in a hoarse whisper, "Hildegarde, meine. . . ."

"Hildegarde!" Father Rapp repeated, and the horror and incredulity in his voice gave Hildegarde the strength she needed to tear herself out of Jacob's arms, and then, suddenly weak and broken, she fell in a sobbing heap at the feet of the old prophet. It would have been easier, she thought in a fuzzy sort of terror, to feel the eyes of God upon her than to know that Father Rapp had been witness to Jacob's passion and her spineless sin.

"Father, Father," she gasped, her voice strangling in her throat, "save me, save me."

Hildegarde was not wholly rational in this moment of terror and self-loathing, but she did know that her cry was a plea for spiritual salvation, for absolution from evil.

But Father Rapp, in his fondness, heard only a

practical cry to be saved from the brutality of a man. Instinctively, he lunged toward Jacob, swinging his arm in a hard, tight arc. Jacob, although shaken and reeling from the past few minutes, dodged the blow which would probably have knocked him to the ground if it had made contact.

"Father, wait," Jacob gasped. "You don't understand. We love each other. You have no reason to strike me."

"How dare you?" Father Rapp said, barely above a whisper but with such blazing anger tamped down in the words that they seemed to sear the night air like hot gasses. "How dare you speak to me with such impertinence? How dare you accuse this child, this innocent girl of the unspeakable things which crawl in your own heart?"

Jacob winced back from the soft fury of the words, but his arms, his whole body retained the hot memory of Hildegarde's body curving to his, her lips softening and responding to the bruising force of his mouth. It didn't matter what this old man said, nothing could change the fact that Hildegarde had clung to him with a passion that equaled his own. If no one had come, if the empty darkness had sheltered them sufficiently, he might very well have had her, there on the grass, and his agony and hunger would have ended.

And so he spoke with a courage that would never have been his before this moment. "I dare to say it because it's true. I love her, and she loves me. We want to marry."

Father Rapp stood in frozen stillness. He finally spoke to the girl who groveled at his feet. "Is this true? Is he speaking the truth?"

She was nearly fainting from fear and yet she knew she had to speak. Of course, she didn't love Jacob; he was coarse and violent, insensitive and evil, and so he couldn't possibly understand the drive that had made her body respond to his passion.

But she had to say something or her silence would be interpreted as assent.

"I don't love him," she said at last, choking on the words. "I don't love him."

The old man's voice dropped even lower. "You swine! You not only soil her body with your touch, but you defile her name with your foul and lying tongue."

"That's not so," Jacob cried wildly. "She kissed me. She did! I'd swear before God that she did not struggle against me until you spoke and startled her."

Hildegarde knew Jacob was telling the truth, just as she knew that if she admitted it, she would lose everything in the world that she valued—her place in the Society, the love of Father Rapp, the regard of everyone who mattered. Yet if she denied Jacob's words, she would be condemning him to the unrelenting wrath of Father Rapp. She would in a very real sense be casting Jacob into outer darkness.

She was not a saint. She had neither the courage nor the strength to take on herself the condemnation she deserved, just to protect Jacob. Besides, her mind hastened to reassure her, part of what Jacob said *was* a lie! She did not love him. She could never, never love him. The thought of leaving the Society and living in the world with this crude man was enough to make her want to die.

"He lies," Hildegarde said, her voice muffled against Father Rapp's shoes, her mind already starting to blot out the memory of what she had done. "He grabbed me, Father, when I came from the greenhouse. I couldn't get away. I tried to fight him, but if you hadn't come. . . ." Her voice trailed away, leaving its dreadful indictment hanging in the night air.

"Hildegarde," Jacob cried. "Tell him the truth. Tell him how you kissed me. Tell him. . . ."

"Enough!" rasped Father Rapp. "Get out of my sight. Don't touch either of us again with your unclean breath, your foul desires. Get out. You'll be dealt with later. Just get out."

Jacob stood hesitating for a minute, but he knew defeat when it faced him squarely. Hildegarde was truly lost to him now. She didn't love him as he loved her. If she felt even a fraction of that love, she could not lie there like a craven coward, telling half-truths, letting him bear the entire blame, knowing full well that he would be sent away, deprived of all he had worked for during his adult years. His passion burned out, and in its place was a mixture of scorn and regret and loss that tasted bitter in his mouth like gall.

"You haven't heard the last of this," Jacob said, "neither of you."

He turned and left them abruptly, crashing

through the trees like a young bull, bruising himself against the trunks, trying to ease the pain inside him by battering his body—as medieval monks had applied the whip of self-abasement.

When the sound of Jacob's leaving was gone, Father Rapp and Hildegarde remained without moving. They were both in a state of shock, both feeling whipped and torn by the emotions that had been unleashed. Then, slowly, a strange sort of peace began to fill the night. Hildegarde's spasms of weeping slowed and diminished, and she felt hollow and light—like a skull, she thought with amazement, a skull that has been scoured down to the pure hardness of bone and was open to light and air.

Father Rapp was exultant. This girl had to be bruised by that lout's clumsy touch, so that she would know once and for all that she was not destined for that. She had to suffer, all chosen souls must suffer, so that she could be cleansed.

Very gently, be bent and helped her to her feet. "Did he hurt you?" he asked.

"No," she said. "Or not that it matters. I'm all right."

"Come to the Great House," he said. "I'll give you a small glass of wine to settle you after your fright. It wouldn't do for your parents to see you so—so shaken."

She nodded, and he felt, rather than saw, the movement in the darkness. They walked side by side, not touching, for he sensed her new steadiness. He had been privileged, he thought, to see a soul saved from evil this night. Not only saved from evil but filled with a great strength. She was now fit for anything. She was committed and cleansed. What a partner she would make for the Holy Experiment!

They went into the back kitchen, where candles burned dimly against the night. He glanced at her quickly and was even more reassured by what he saw. Her eyes had the fixed look of one who has been in the presence of God. There was no hysteria in her face, no wild flush on her cheeks. Her hair was not even disheveled. She was, he thought objectively, very, very beautiful. But this did not cause him to feel the slightest compassion for Jacob, who had fallen victim to this beauty. She was beautiful as the statue of Harmonie in the Grotto was beautiful—as all things are beautiful which come from God.

He poured out two small glasses of dark, sweet wine and handed one to her.

They drank in silence, standing in the kitchen.

At that minute, a step was heard in the formal dining room, and they turned to see Frederick coming toward them. The look of utter astonishment on his face was totally ignored by the old man.

"We have both had a shock," Father Rapp said to his son. "Sister Hildegarde has been accosted by that brute, Jacob Klein. I was led by God to find them, I believe, and to save her."

Frederick glanced sharply at Hildegarde and then back at his father. "Jacob has been battling his passion for a long time," Frederick said. "I don't think Sister Hildegarde has helped him any."

Hildegarde felt a momentary crack in the shell of peace that had enclosed her since Jacob crashed away, and fear flowed in to touch her with cold. Frederick was too discerning, and his feeling for her was not warm. She knew that.

But she forced her voice to remain calm. "I didn't know of any so-called 'passion,' Brother Frederick. You might have warned me."

Deliberately, she pushed away the sudden memory of the scene in the wine cellar, the many times she had caught Jacob's eyes, hungry and hot, on her face.

"Or me," Father Rapp said. "I'm the spiritual leader of my people. Why didn't you tell me?"

"The boy was in enough agony," Frederick said. "I thought my prayers might suffice. I thought your influence on Sister Hildegarde might be enough to keep her—safe."

The slight irony on the last word escaped no one. Hildegarde felt a faint flush on her cheeks and she turned again to her glass of wine, to sip its dark sweetness. When she and Father Rapp had been alone in the kitchen, it had been almost like a sacrament, and she resented the intrusion of Frederick, almost as much as she feared his probing gaze.

"Nevertheless, he has gone too far," Father Rapp said. "He has to leave here. At once."

Frederick opened his mouth and then shut it again when he looked at Hildegarde. He would not degrade himself to the point of arguing in front of this girl.

"If you've finished with your wine, Sister Hildegarde," Frederick said, "I'll see you safely home. You may be frightened."

Her chin went up. "I'm not afraid," she said, and her eyes, steady and calm again, met Frederick's squarely. "It's only across the street. Thank you! Father, pray for me."

Father Rapp smiled at her. "I *have* been praying, child. You have a special mission. I'll talk to you about it tomorrow. The *Liebesmahl* will mean more to you if you know what's facing us."

Hildegarde felt a queer little jerk in her heart. What could he mean? But she only bobbed her head briefly to both men and walked with a strange, new dignity out of the kitchen door.

Back in the Great House, Frederick struggled with the words that he wanted to say. He wanted to warn the old man, to tell him that he, Frederick, knew Hildegarde's nature and that she couldn't be trusted. Oh, he had seen the glory that sat so sweetly on her this night—but what had brought it on or what would scatter it to the four winds one day, he did not know. He only knew that she had too much of the world in her to be what Father Rapp believed her to be.

Before he could shape any words of warning, however, Father Rapp spoke abruptly: "God has spoken to me regarding this child. She will be my assistant in the Holy Experiment. We'll talk of it later, after Jacob is gone. Good night, my son."

And he was gone, out of the kitchen, heading for his own room where no man dared to go, not even the beloved son.

Frederick stood in utter silence, stunned by Father Rapp's last statement. Surely he had misunderstood. The coveted position would not be taken from him so lightly. It *could* not. But Father Rapp had been explicit enough, Frederick thought bitterly as he blew out the candles. He felt, in that moment, that his birthright had been stolen from him—traded involuntarily for a mess of pottage which would feed no one.

Chapter 16

The watchman, crying the hours, had gone by several times since Frederick had walked, sagging and defeated, into his own room. For a long time, he had simply sat quietly, letting the waves of hurt and disappointment break over him like a rising tide, but his own strength of character, acting as a leveling agent, had reduced the waves until he was able at last to bear them and to think.

It was not, Frederick kept assuring himself, jealousy that made the thought of Hildegarde becoming Father Rapp's assistant such a bitter thing. True, he had assumed that the Father would ask him to be the chosen assistant; true, he had spent hours studying everything that had been written about the alchemy which might produce a Philosopher's Stone, and true, he had even dared to dream of the way they would share in its miraculous discovery if their experiments were successful. But that wasn't the entire reason for his present grief. Most of his pain stemmed from the fact that Father Rapp was so blind to the faults of that little— little. . . . Frederick's mind failed to come up with a word scalding enough to label the girl but still decent enough to shape itself in his thoughts. But he, Frederick, knew her for what she was. She was irreverent, seductive, heedless, worldly. Her honest affection for the old prophet, her unwavering loyalty to him were only, Frederick believed, because she liked the importance of being accepted by the Father and Gertrude, almost as though she lived in the Great House like Henrici or Frederick, himself.

Frederick's sober mind could not comprehend any virtue in merriment or laughter. His dedication to the Holy Cause was so unswerving that he felt it almost sacrilege to be too happy. Oh, he was warm to those he loved, his smile was ready when actions pleased him, but his fervor was never far enough below the surface of his mind to let him feel any approval for girls like Hildegarde Mutschler and Maria Baumann. The Society was well rid of the one; if only Hildegarde had been lured away by Jacob's passion. Then peace would surely reign.

There was no doubt in Frederick's mind but what Father Rapp would send Jacob away, penniless and unblessed. All the prayers, all the counseling, all the struggle to hold the young man steady had failed, and Frederick's efforts had been wasted. And all because of Hildegarde, Frederick thought almost savagely. All because she smiled and tilted her eyes up and looked beguiling.

Moreover, people would talk. Frederick knew they would. Jacob had friends, and already there were some who said that Father Rapp was partial and prejudiced. The mutterings that had been heard when the last articles had been signed, the mutterings that said Economy was becoming more of a patriarchy than a brotherhood, would be revived.

Frederick's mind plodded on. He had to do something. He had to stop this insane business before it went too far. There was no one to whom he could go for advice. His mind touched briefly on Dr. Mueller, on young Conrad Feucht, on Jacob Henrici. The doctor, in spite of his loyalty, had already expressed the opinion that the old man was getting too dictatorial. He would probably welcome a display of weakness, of fallibility in the old prophet, hoping that the people would be more inclined to think for themselves. As for Conrad Feucht, Frederick had an uncomfortable feeling about him. He suspected that if he went to Conrad, the young man might only laugh—his laughter was too ready, anyhow—and say that Frederick was putting too much emphasis on an unimportant action. Surely, what Hildegarde did or didn't do could hardly matter to the Society. She was only a child. Conrad was probably as blind to Hildegarde's potential danger, Frederick thought glumly, as the Father was.

As for Jacob Henrici, well, Frederick had his pride, after all. Henrici was too new to the Society, too much in the Father's favor, too much the fervent, dedicated convert to be realistic about anything. Besides, Frederick had the uncomfortable feeling that Henrici had also been dreaming of being the chosen assistant. He might accuse Frederick of being jealous.

There was nothing for it then but to go to the Father himself. Directly. Oh, not face to face— the old man's temper would only blaze and there would be hot words between them which could never be unsaid. Frederick had had his fill of that long ago when there had been quarrels over how the Society should be managed. If they, the two leaders, could not live in harmony and love, how could they ever demand that the others follow the preachings?

No, he would write to him, now, tonight, in spite of the fact that it was well after midnight. And the Father would read the letter in the cool of the morning and then, knowing how Frederick felt, they could discuss the whole thing with restraint.

Frederick dipped his quill into ink and began to write.

Father!
This is the first time since I have known you that I am declaring myself against you, and I would not do so now if I were not so concerned about the Friendship. I have always been your loving and loyal friend and son, but now I cannot keep silent.

I am writing concerning Hildegarde

Mutschler who, I fear, has bewitched you so that you think of her as pure and holy when, in truth, she is the exact opposite. When I heard you say tonight that she was to be your assistant in the Holy Experiment, my heart broke in my breast. She is impure, Father, and her touch—even the brushing of her breath—will condemn your work so that you will fail. She is too worldly to ever be anything but a hindrance to you.

For a long while, Frederick paused, biting the end of the quill and thinking seriously. Did he dare go on and say what he wanted to say? Would the Father be given the grace to know that Frederick wrote only out of love, not out of condemnation? At last his pen moved again.

There are those who have criticized you already, Father, who say you are not fair in your treament of the brethren. They say you cast out some as sinners and let others stay in spite of the fact that they do not abide by the teachings. Your harshness toward Jacob Klein will not go favorably, my Father, any more than your quick acceptance of Henrici, putting the latter over the heads of men who have given years of service to the Society. Please, Father, don't make this situation worse by doing what is bound to bring criticism on your head.

Another long pause, and then slowly, deliberately, Frederick wrote the most difficult words of all.

> If you choose this girl as your assistant, I know that some (not only from the world but from our own) will say that she has an unhealthy and false influence over you. They may very well accuse you of having her as your damsel. And she will only laugh and lie her way out of it, while the condemnation will fall on you. And you have been chosen by God, Father, to lead us—not to let a little strumpet lead you into faithlessness. Oh, Father, I plead with you. . . ."

Frederick sat looking at the words he had written. They were true, every one, and yet—yet, he knew that he did not dare deliver them to Father Rapp. The old man would only get angry as he always did when his pronouncements were questioned. And this night had not been an ordinary one. Frederick realized that. There had been a radiance on the old man's face—the kind that came only when he had seen a vision. And Hildegarde was different, too. Her eyes had not slid away from Frederick's as was her custom when she thought he was seeing too much. Instead, they had met his with level steadiness and her chin had been high.

Maybe a miracle *had* happened. Perhaps she had really been changed "in the twinkling of an eye" and God had cleansed her. Even as he thought these things, Frederick knew that he didn't really believe them. What he believed was what was written in his letter. But he was helpless, bound by the chains of loyalty that had held him for so long. There was a sudden crushing breathlessness across his chest, and he bent, breathing harshly, over his desk, waiting for the feeling to pass. It had come to him before, and he knew that someday it would not pass.

"Oh, God," he prayed suddenly, "let me live until I have done my work. Keep me well until she is gone. Oh, God. . . ."

The heaviness lifted slowly, and Frederick's breath came in a sort of ragged sobbing. His hands wiped the pen carefully, and then, trembling slightly, they lifted the paper and tore it into a hundred pieces which he dropped into the stove where a few dull embers glowed. A blaze leaped up, and the letter, the warning, the criticism were only ashes.

Someday, Frederick thought with regretful premonition, *I will write a stronger letter than this, and it will be delivered—but it will be too late, forever and ever too late.*

The next day, the judge and jury, the accused and the accuser sat in the small trustees' room behind the main parlor of the Great House. Father Rapp, as judge, had stated his case against Jacob, and the jury, consisting of a dozen men of the Society, had listened in silence. Hildegarde, sitting behind Father Rapp, could not see their faces clearly because the windows were behind them, but she felt sure that their attitude was not one of total sympathy toward her. Jacob's industry had been a valuable asset to the Society, and her own mercurial disposition had never been of equal value.

At first, Jacob sat in a sort of humble silence and let the old man's wrath roll over him like a flood. Then his mind began to function more clearly. He watched the new look on Hildegarde's face, a face that had been rinsed pure of the sparkle, mischief, and gaiety that had always drawn him like a magnet, and he realized that he had been duped. She was a tool for Father Rapp's maneuvering. She was no different than Gertrude or Pauline or any of the other mealymouthed women who moved at the old prophet's whim.

His anger began to grow, to blaze, to build and at last he could no longer be silent.

"She led me on," he said hotly. "I don't care what claims she makes to you or will ever make. She led me on by her smiles and her looks."

Hildegarde looked at him evenly. In this new, pure state of hers, nothing seemed to really touch her. "If I misled you by my friendship," she murmured, "I'm sorry. I beg forgiveness."

Jacob looked at her and even in his anger, he could not hold his heart from jerking in his chest. "That day in the vineyard," he said. "That was innocent friendship?"

Stung, Hildegarde cried out without thinking

of what she was saying. "I did nothing," she cried. "You followed me to the wine cellar—you're the one who. . . ."

There was a strange sound from Conrad Feucht, and Hildegarde's eyes swung to his. She felt the guilt stain her cheeks as she looked into eyes that were too knowing. She could almost see his mind tying loose ends together and coming up with knowledge that she had thought would always be secret. So *that*, she could almost hear him thinking, was what brought on the faintness and the weeping and the chills. Fear. And guilt. Her eyes slid away and she clamped her lips tightly together.

The silence stretched out tautly after Hildegarde's impulsive words. No one else, of course, not even Frederick, knew what had been admitted, and Father Rapp's mind was on other things. Conrad had the generosity to say nothing, to finally move his eyes away from Hildegarde's face, and Jacob Klein sat quietly. There was, he thought, no use fighting any more. They were conspired against him. No one would defend him.

But Jacob was wrong. Two of the men began to support his cause, to argue his value to the Society, to point out that other young men had succumbed momentarily to the flesh but had been allowed to stay.

Their arguments fell on empty air. Father Rapp listened with an expression that told the speakers that their words did not get past the surface of his ears. In his eyes, Jacob was guilty. If there had been, in the minds of these trustees, the idea that such matters could be decided in a democratic fashion, they were learning rapidly that they had been mistaken.

Then Jacob turned, with an odd dignity, to Frederick. "Brother Frederick," he said, "you know how I have struggled, how I've prayed and worked. If I've failed, it's not for lack of trying. Tell them. Tell them I deserve at least a remuneration for my time. I deserve something better than to be kicked out like a stray mongrel without any payment for my years of service."

Frederick spoke softly but firmly. He looked at Jacob, but it was plain that his words were intended for Father Rapp. "Yes, I know, Brother Jacob. I have prayed with and for you. I know your struggle. I know that the girl—was, well, perhaps innocent but not so unaware as she would seem. I feel you should get some consideration."

"Some?" Dr. Mueller spoke sharply. "The boy has been clearly sinned against—in addition to his admitted sin. He deserves fair payment."

Father Rapp's voice was harsh. "Let's have no more talk. I have made up my mind. He goes. Out into the world where he belongs. And nothing—I say, nothing will be given to him to soften his going. Let him learn, as Adam did when he left the Garden, how it is to earn his living by the sweat of his brow."

Jacob stood up, and although his legs trembled, he found voice to say softly. "You have not heard the last of this. I'll sue. I'll make you sorry you didn't listen."

He would have said more, but Frederick's

eyes, sad and filled with warning, seemed to stop him. He whirled on his heel, but this brought him face to face with Hildegarde.

For long seconds he looked at her, and then he laughed—a bitter burst of sound. "At least when Adam left the garden," he flung over his shoulder, his eyes never leaving Hildegarde's face, "he didn't go alone. And God probably paid him in good coin."

Father Rapp turned white. "Blasphemy!" he shouted, leaping to his feet. "You dare!"

But Dr. Mueller's hand was on Jacob's arm, pushing him toward the door, and several other men formed a sort of innocent barrier between the furious old man and the young heretic. Frederick's hand, on his father's arm, was soothing and strong. And Hildegarde, in her total stillness, seemed to act as a brake on the old man's passion.

Abruptly, he shrugged his shoulders, as though ridding himself of even the memory of Jacob Klein. It was like a horse flickering an annoying gnat from his side.

"Well, he's gone," he said with satisfaction, watching the group of men leave the Great House. "In a day or two, it'll be as though he never was."

"With his family here?" Frederick said slowly. "And his friends? Does it mean nothing to you?" And then he stopped, his eyes swinging to Hildegarde and the others in the room. Does it mean nothing, he was going to say, that the men who took Jacob's part are important in the Society, that they, too, influence minds and control actions? But he couldn't bring himself to say these things in front of this girl and Feucht and Henrici.

"You worry too much," Father Rapp said lightly. His anger was gone, and he was confident and serene again. "You've always worried too much. And haven't I always been right? Always?"

Frederick looked steadily at his father and the heaviness crushed across his chest again. *No*, he ached to say, *no, you haven't always been right. You're wrong about this girl. You're wrong!*

Instead, he bowed his head in acquiescence. "Yes, Father," he said. "I only hope we won't have legal and expensive demands from Jacob. He may make financial trouble for us."

"Then you must solve the troubles, Frederick," Father Rapp said. "That's your genius, my son, solving our troubles. As for me, I'm going to devote myself to things spiritual—to the search for the Philosopher's Stone as I told you. No more talking about it—now we will be *doing* the experiments. You, my child." He turned to Hildegarde who had sat in frozen stillness after Jacob's departure, afraid to leave, afraid to stay. "I've decided you'll be my assistant. A vision came to me last night. Are you ready?"

The almost casual words seemed to explode in the small room. Henrici's head jerked up like a frightened horse, and Frederick had the sour satisfaction of seeing the pain and disappointment in the boy's dark eyes. Conrad's look of amazement was tempered by the strange amusement that seemed to touch his mouth always when Hildegarde was the subject of discussion. It was as though he knew something about her no one else even guessed—something funny and clever and even precious. It worried Frederick but it wasn't anything he could isolate and defeat as he had struggled to defeat Jacob's passion.

Hildegarde looked steadily at the old man who faced her. She had moved in a trance-like calmness since that devastating scene by the greenhouse last night. She had, unbelievably, slept sweetly and peacefully after she had returned to her own home. She had wakened this morning feeling strong and clean. All the things that had tormented and delighted her for years seemed to have disappeared like early morning mist. She was changed, she was different, and she knew it.

But to be Father Rapp's assistant. That was a miracle beyond her wildest hopes and dreams. Was she ready for that? Her eyes moved slowly across the faces of the men in the room. She saw the bleakness in Frederick's and Henrici's eyes and guessed at once that they had coveted the position. She saw the faint laughter glimmering behind Conrad's eyes, and she turned away from it. That was in the past. She must not be shaken by jealousy or affection or even the anger she had seen so clearly on the faces of the men who had gone out with Jacob. She must look to Father Rapp and to him alone.

"Yes," she said coolly. "I'm ready." Then, feeling like a character from some biblical story, she couldn't resist adding the words of drama. "Here I am, Father. Use me."

Father Rapp smiled and nodded briefly. "Go, my child. Go with God. I'll call you when I need you."

She went without a look at anyone. She skirted the knot of men who stood, still talking, outside the kitchen door and her eyes hardly registered their last glimpse of Jacob. He looked up, but his face was the face of a stranger.

Hildegarde walked, almost unseeing, through the gardens that blazed with the late colors of autumn. The trees still wore their colored leaves like a glory, and the last zinnias and marigolds burned against the hedges and fences. But Hildegarde's eyes were turned inward, inward on the color that leaped and blazed and glowed in her heart. She had forgotten the weakness, the cowardice, the fear. She was touched by the hand of God, and she walked in a burning beauty.

Father Rapp and Frederick were alone at last. Frederick knew it was futile, but even so, he tried to say something of what filled his heart. "You've made a mistake, my Father," he said humbly. "You've given your critics a weapon to use against you. You should have been more impartial in your judging of the affair. You. . . ."

But Father Rapp interrupted. His voice sounded more surprised than irritated. "Are you God, my son," he asked, "that you would tell *me* what to do?"

Frederick looked at the old man. No, he was

not God. He was only a man—weak, frail, beginning to be ill, and frightened. And perhaps he was wrong. Perhaps God would move in mysterious ways to prove that the old prophet's ways were infallible, after all.

Frederick shook his head, and Father Rapp's voice was very gentle as he reached over to pat the arm of the younger man. "I'll pray for you," Father Rapp said, "so that you'll know what to do if Jacob makes trouble. And you pray for me—that we may find the Philosopher's Stone quickly and hurry the coming of the kingdom."

And so they parted in peace, but each knew that nothing was exactly as it had been before— nor would it ever be again.

Chapter 17

OCTOBER 1828

The autumn sun slanted through the deep-silled windows of the laboratory to lay like gold dust on the plain square table. Hildegarde stood in tense concentration, ignoring the patina of nature's gold, her eyes fixed on the odd container in the middle of the table. It was her turn to check the contents, to see if the miraculous alchemy was starting to work, to determine if the lump of common lead was starting to metamorphose into gold.

She really dreaded lifting the lid. During the first months of the work, she had come to this moment of the experiment with a feeling of wild anticipation and a fervent conviction that this time they would be successful. But the months had slid by—winter had warmed into spring, and spring had burned into summer, and summer had cooled into autumn, and always the hoped-for miracle had failed to occur. Small wonder that the fervor, the devotion, the conviction had slowly waned until now she approached this particular point of the test with reluctance.

She felt cramped and weary, stale and dusty from the months of study and application of study. It was no longer enough to remind herself that she was Father Rapp's confidante and almost constant companion.

She was, she realized with startled dismay, becoming bored with the whole confining, repetitive process. She was tired of working hard and thinking sober thoughts and being with people who were either old or so serious that they didn't even know they were young.

As the rebellious thoughts tumbled through her mind, she looked surreptitiously over her shoulder. She sometimes felt as transparent as a pane of glass—so that if Frederick or Jacob Henrici or Gertrude were to suddenly come in, they might be able to see into her mind. Not that they came to the experiment room often. Gertrude came when she could spare time from her other work, and Frederick appeared occasionally, but that's all. The only person who came in with any frequency was Conrad Feucht who brought chemicals or books or his knowledge. But he came only when Father Rapp was there, and his words were purely technical.

Well, she was alone now, and the moment could not be postponed. Hildegarde felt a fleeting sense of regret that she was not filled with anticipation and excitement. It was just not right to feel so negative, and she knew it.

Her hands were steady and careful in the prescribed motion that exposed the lead. For one fleeting second—briefer than a heartbeat—she was deluded by the glinting of the sun into thinking there was a glow in the lead itself. But practiced caution made her move the container into a place untouched by sun, and the glow was gone. The lead was dull, unresponsive, unchanged from its original state.

The experiment had failed again!

When this had happened a year ago, Hildegarde had wept and prayed in soft anguish. Six months ago, she had felt only the crushing weight of defeat. But during the long hot summer and the wine-sweet days of autumn, a new emotion had been building up in her. She hadn't tried to analyze or even understand her changing emotions, so she was totally unprepared for the thrust of blazing anger that suddenly stabbed her.

"O, verdamm no a mahl!" she said softly and hotly, not even knowing where she had heard the expletive, hardly aware she had the words in her vocabulary.

"Sister!" The voice at the door jerked her around so quickly that she nearly lost her balance. Had it been Father Rapp, she would have undoubtedly felt the old shame, the old desire to recapture her purity and piety. Had it been Frederick, she would have felt the touch of fear that served so often as a disciplinary measure. But it was neither of these; it was Conrad Feucht who stood in the doorway, looking at her with a comical mixture of pure shock and reluctant amusement on his face.

"How do you even know such words?" he said, trying to make his voice stern but he was still struggling to suppress the desire to laugh that had filled him when he had first heard the ridiculous sound of swearing in the soft, pretty voice.

"The experiment failed again," she said, her voice still hot. "I just get so—so. . . ."

His voice broke in smoothly. "This isn't a place for anger, Sister. Not here where the Holy Experiment is. . . ."

"Is a failure," she finished for him, but the heat had left her voice, and the dull red of shame was belatedly coloring her cheeks.

"Temporarily," Conrad said, but it was an effort to make his voice confident. His studies had not led him to the same conclusions that Father Rapp had reached, and he was certain that his own faith was not strong enough to bridge the blank space between science and miracle. "Isn't the Father here?" he said, looking around the room. "I was sure I saw him coming in this direction."

Hildegarde smiled, and Conrad was much too sharply aware of the dimple in her cheek, the sudden glint in her eyes. "Do you really think I would have let my—my disappointment—come out in words if he had been here?"

He knew he should be stern. He ought to accuse her of levity in a room dedicated to holiness. He ought to tell her that perhaps she was the deterrent in the experiment. He ought to send her, shamed and humiliated, to her room. But he could not. She brought out a perversity in him, and so he avoided ever being alone with her. But today had simply happened.

"I guess I should have known," he admitted and returned her smile. "Do you know where he is?"

"He said he'd be working on correspondence, so he's probably in his room. Or the office. You can find him there probably."

"And you?" he said. "I thought you usually helped him with his letters."

"Not always. I had to work in here."

"Well—I'll look for him." He turned to leave and then looked back. "Don't be discouraged, Sister. Or if you must feel cast down at times, take my advice and don't be so—so vocal about it."

This time she looked properly sober. "I know. I'm always doing the wrong thing. Everyone knows it."

"Perhaps not *always*," he said, and with another smile he was gone.

She stood feeling a little dazed. It had been so long since there had been any teasing or laughter in her life that for a minute she hardly recognized it. When it finally registered on her that he had been teasing her, she felt a strange warmth. He was really very kind, she thought gratefully. She had been wicked, unforgivably wicked, to say such words in this room, and he had not condemned but had seemed to understand that she was only tired and let down.

She carefully covered the lump of lead, made

the proper notations in the notebooks, set up the preparations for the next step, and then got ready to leave the laboratory. She opened the door, which was always left locked when no one was there, stepped out into the trustees' room, and then turned to lock the door.

"Wait, Sister."

She looked up to see Frederick coming toward her. He came so rarely to this room that she must have shown her surprise.

"Do you want something?" she asked.

"Only to check on the progress of the experiment," he said stiffly. "Must I ask permission?"

She felt the queer little lurch in her heart that was part fear and part resentment. She wished desperately that Frederick did not do this to her, but she felt his disapproval as strongly as though it were something tangible she could touch.

"Of course not, Brother Frederick. I only wondered if I could help you. The experiment was a failure." The last words were said baldly, unemotionally, but they brought Frederick to an abrupt stop.

"Again?" he said, his eyes bleak. "Are you sure?"

"I checked carefully as always," she said stiffly.

Frederick spoke cooly. "I've never questioned your technical ability," he said with only the slightest emphasis on the word "technical."

"But my spiritual ability?" she said, quickly, amazed at her own daring. "You question that?"

He only looked at her, and it seemed to her that he was judging her again as he seemed to judge her every time they met.

For a year, she had endured it in silence, but today her emotions were rubbed raw, and the words tumbled out of her without her being able to stop them.

"Ever since Jacob Klein left," she choked out, "you've treated me like an evil sinner. You saw the letter he sent by Herr von Bonnhurst as well as I did. You know he cleared me of any guilt. He said I was innocent—that I didn't return his feelings. Yet you treat me with contempt. Why, Brother, why?"

She stood, shaking and panting a little, alarmed at her insolence but feeling a sense of relief at saying the words that she had kept bottled up for months.

"You saw the letter?" Frederick said slowly, seeming to fasten on only those few words.

"Of course, I saw it," she returned impatiently.

"Then it's true. You *do* see the Father's correspondence. He shares even that with you?"

Her courage began to dissipate before the dark look of pain in the eyes of the man who faced her.

"Only the letters he thinks I should see," she said, stumbling a little on the words.

Frederick glanced away from her, and she watched the way his shoulders sagged. For a minute he was quiet and then he spoke softly, "Sister, whether or not you are as innocent as you say—or even as Jacob—I don't know. I only know that if this experiment is ever to succeed, it must be touched only by hands of holy people. Are you pure enough, Sister? Are you?"

For several seconds she endured his scrutiny, and then her eyes dropped before his. No matter what mood ruled her—piety, impatience, anger, scorn—there was always some thin thread of self-honesty that forced her to see herself as she really was. It was her own peculiar agony that she could not totally justify her sins. She had persuaded Father Rapp and her parents and many others that she was truly good; she had never wholly persuaded Hildegarde Mutschler.

Frederick seemed satisfied. He merely nodded briefly and turned to leave.

"You don't want to go into the room before I lock it?" Hildegarde said in a muffled voice.

"No, Sister. Lock the door and guard the key." There was an obvious irony in Frederick's voice.

For a brief second, in spite of the feeling of self-abasement that his question had brought out in her, she felt a quick, bright shock of anger, and her hand itched to fling the key at his head, to stamp away from the discomfort of shame that he always made her feel.

But the discipline of the past year held her steady and she said nothing at all. Her hands trembled as she turned the key in the lock and then thrust the key into the deep pocket of her blue-checked apron that covered her dark blue skirt. She turned away from Frederick and walked swiftly through the trustees' room, down the central hall, through the dining room and into the kitchen. Several of the girls were working at the tables, preparing dinner, and their soft talking buzzed like bees. With only a nod to acknowledge their presence, she hurried through the back door onto the long veranda and down onto the cinder paths that led across the back of the Great House and on out into the garden.

It was not until she was walking toward the pavilion that the words she had heard in the kitchen really registered on her mind. The girls had been talking about Maria Baumann! Hildegarde stopped abruptly, deliberately pushing her angry feelings about Frederick to one side, and trying to concentrate on the words that had fallen so unheeded on her ears as she fled through the kitchen.

Maria Baumann. She had definitely heard that. And something about—about a baby. Well, that was to be expected, of course, even though she had not known of a baby coming. But then except for the church or community gatherings she had not been with any of the Baumann family during the past year. Her steps slowed even more. There had been something else—maybe not even said in actual words—but the implication was that Maria was here in the village. Now.

Hildegarde knew, as everyone knew, that sometimes the outcasts came back—sometimes to publicly confess their failing and plead for reinstatement into the Society—sometimes only to visit their families. But when it was for a visit, it was done in secret, hidden from the eyes of the men who were in authority. Not that there was any real danger, but it took a courageous person to stand up to the scorn and wrath in Father Rapp's face, and those who ran away seldom possessed such courage.

Had Maria come back at any other time, it might have meant little to Hildegarde. In spite of their old friendship, Hildegarde's new piety might have kept her away from the house of the transgressor. But today's events had stirred up a sharp rebellion, and she was suddenly wildly tempted. What would Maria be like now? And a baby—a baby. What would a baby be like? There had been so few babies in the Society that Hildegarde had never been involved with any of them. She had never held an infant in her arms. What would it be like?

Her year of discipleship had done many things to her, but it had not quelled the impulsive side of her nature. She spun around on the path and started running down Grossestrasse toward the Baumann home. In a minute, she slowed down to a walk because she was prudent enough to know that there would be little achieved if she called attention to herself.

At the Baumann house, she slowed even more and was aware of the fact that her heart was beating fast and light up behind her throat. Was it just the idea of seeing Maria again (how long ago it seemed that they had stood opposite each other in the garden vineyard, their mouths stained with purple, and their eyes wide with the shock of Maria's words ["My mother says women are supposed to have babies"]) or was it because she was doing something of which she knew Father Rapp would disapprove? Well, whatever it was, she was here. She slipped through the gate that fronted on the street and walked to the entry door that faced the back yard. It was closed—an unusual thing on a day of such brilliant sunshine (unless they had something to hide, Hildegarde thought), and before her courage could desert her, she knocked on the closed door.

There was a sudden silence. She had not really been aware of the normal stirrings of people within the house until she knocked, but now in the startled stillness, she was aware of the abrupt cessation of the stirrings. She knocked again, and the silence continued for a second until it was broken by an unfamiliar sound—a thin, high wail. The baby.

Hildegarde knocked again. "Maria," she called in an urgent, low tone. "I know you're there. Let me in. I want to see you."

There was the sound of feet moving across the floor, soft voices making hushing sounds, and then the door was pulled cautiously open. Hildegarde looked into Frau Baumann's face.

"Sister," she said breathlessly. "I know Maria is here. I want to see her. Can't I please?"

"Is anyone with you?" There was real fear in the face of the older woman.

"No. No one even knows I've come. Let me in quick before anyone sees me."

Hildegarde saw the hesitation, the reluctance in the woman's face, and she understood. After all, she must seem like Father Rapp's spy.

"I'm only Hildegarde," the girl said, stripping

herself of all authority, all prestige. Not Sister Hildegarde, not Father Rapp's assistant—but only the child who had once played with Maria.

Frau Baumann stepped back and Hildegarde slipped into the entrance hall. Instinctively, she turned toward the steps that angled steeply up out of the hall toward the upper bedrooms. Her eyes questioned the older woman and a nod confirmed her instincts. Lightly, she ran up the steps and across the first room. At the door of the furthest room she stopped.

Maria was standing facing her, almost like a young animal at bay, her skirts spread wide to shield whatever it was that lay on the narrow bed behind her. At the sight of her, all of Hildegarde's old love came plunging up out of her heart, all the delight she had known with Maria, all the joy of the young years. She felt the foolish smart of tears in her eyes as she flung her arms wide.

"Oh, Maria," she cried and ran toward her.

Maria's response was as automatic and as warm. It was as though the past year had never been, as though their friendship had never been disrupted by the long separation. They hugged each other breathlessly, heedless of the tears that wet their faces.

"You look beautiful," Hildegarde said at last, pulling away to look at Maria. "Absolutely beautiful."

"You always look beautiful," Maria said, laughing a little. "But you're thin. Are you working too hard?"

Hildegarde just shook her head, gazing without embarrassment at the girl facing her. There was something about her—some warmth, some sweet roundness in her face, a new softness.

"You haven't found the world as harsh as they say," Hildegarde said, and it was a statement, not a question.

"I'm well cared for," Maria said, smiling. "And—well, I've got a new reason to be happy."

She stepped aside, and Hildegarde looked down at the bed. The baby was very small—she had no idea of its age—but it was completely beautiful. The little round head was covered with black ringlets of hair, and the wide eyes which stared so solemnly at her were dark blue. The tiny fists, flailing the air, were curled like flower petals. The dress was long but the little legs had kicked at it until it was bunched up about the knees, and the small feet made sturdy kicking motions.

Hildegarde stood in total silence. She had never seen a child as young as this, and she felt suddenly more reverent than she had ever felt in the laboratory. She made no effort to understand why she felt as she did; she only knew that she was seeing the miracle that had been denied her a few minutes ago when she had lifted the lid off the container of lead.

"His name is Johannes," Maria said, her voice proud and yet anxious. "He's three months old. What do you think of him?"

Hildegarde found her voice with difficulty. "Oh, Maria, he's the dearest thing I've ever seen in my whole life." She moved closer to the bed and almost timidly put her hand down near one of the waving fists. She touched the tiny hand, and it was as though an electric shock went through her. The incredibly small fingers were satin soft but they fastened around her finger with an amazing strength.

"Do you want to hold him?" Maria said.

"I don't know how," Hildegarde admitted humbly.

"Here, I'll show you," Maria said warmly. "Sit on the edge of the bed—so." Her hands, capable and deft, scooped up the baby and she placed him in Hildegarde's arms. "Bend your elbow to hold his head," she went on, laughing at Hildegarde's awkwardness. "His neck wobbles, but he won't break. Don't be so nervous."

Hildegarde laughed, too, but her arms felt stiff and awkward.

"Hold him closer," Maria said. "There—tight against you. That's the way. Now—relax. He won't fall."

Hildegarde was silent, adjusting her arms until the baby felt cradled and secure. She bent over him, and was sharply aware of the sweet, milky smell of him, the unbelievable softness of him against her body. She, who always had words for every occasion, was mute before this event. Slowly she became aware of a dull aching in her breasts—a feeling so foreign, so inexplicable that she simply tried to ignore it. But it was too strong to be put aside. Something in her body yearned and ached over this child. Was this part of the worldliness against which she had been warned? But the baby was so pure—so innocent—so beautiful!

She looked up at Maria, tears flowing from her eyes.

"I'm sorry," Hildegarde choked out. "I don't know why I'm crying."

Maria only nodded wisely. "You're not used to babies," she said. "You were too young to hold my brothers when they were tiny—and—well, you worked with gardens, not ever with any of the children. And there never were very many, this young."

"But why?" Hildegarde said as though Maria were an oracle and she only a child.

Maria perched on the edge of the bed beside Hildegarde. Neither of them seemed aware of the fact that Frau Baumann had slipped out of the room.

"A woman's body was meant to have babies," Maria said. "I'm not talking against the Society, Hildegarde. Maybe it's possible for some to be pure and holy. Like Sister Gertrude—or Sister Pauline. But for me, no. I—I'm happy being married. I can't feel it's sinful to—to love someone and to have his baby. When—when little Johannes was born, I felt more holy than I've ever felt before."

These were the most serious words Hildegarde had ever heard from Maria. The old levity and silliness had changed to a new maturity, a new conviction. And yet, the red mouth still curved with laughter, the dark eyes glowed with joy. The entire thing was simply beyond Hildegarde's comprehension.

And so she made no effort to answer, to argue, to question. She only held the baby, rocking her body a little, looking up occasionally to smile at Maria—but mostly just gazing at the child who had fallen asleep against her breast.

Frau Baumann came back with small glasses of sweet wine and dark, spicy ginger cookies. Hildegarde would not put the baby down, so she only sipped at the wine as the three of them began to talk.

For nearly an hour she sat, holding the baby, and learning something of Maria's life in Pittsburgh. The man she had married had also been a Harmonist but he had found work in one of the glass factories—and while they did not always live as well as they had lived in Economy, they were comfortable and happy.

Finally, the baby woke and began to cry, turning his head with a blind, seeking gesture toward the warmth of Hildegarde's body. She looked helplessly at Maria and then watched with a mixture of embarrassment and wonder as Maria took the baby, unbuttoned the front of her dress and pressed the small, seeking mouth against her nipple. Maria was modest, of course, and her shawl quickly covered the small face and her bared breast, but Hildegarde could hear the loud sucking sounds and the small contented grunts that the baby made between swallows. Hildegarde felt a sense of awe that Maria's body—the unworthy part of man as she had been taught—had formed this beautiful child and was now nourishing him and keeping him alive.

Hildegarde didn't stay any longer. She lightly touched the sleeping child's soft cheek, hugged

Maria tightly, smiled at the older woman and then hurried down the steps and out into the October afternoon. She started slowly down Grossestrasse and her thoughts whirled through her mind like the crisp, bronze leaves that swirled about her ankles.

Maria *had* deserted her calling, she *had* lost her claim to the chosen few, she *had* sinned. Everything that Hildegarde had ever been taught made her accept those facts. And yet—and yet. . . .

She suddenly pushed aside her serious thoughts. Nothing really mattered except the lovely realization that she had been vouchsafed one miracle on this golden day—the miracle of seeing Maria's child—even if the lump of lead had remained unchanged.

Chapter **18**

During the weeks that followed Maria's visit to
the village, Hildegarde went about her work
with her usual concentration, but there was
always the secret of the baby in the back of her
mind. She found that in the midst of an experiment, there would come to her, unbidden, the
sharp memory of the feel of the child in her
arms, the unfamiliar, sweet scent of him in her
nostrils, the way his wide gaze had shaken her
heart. She tried to put it out of her mind, but she
was not always successful.

Her confusion was complicated by the fact
that the experiment continued to go badly. She
and Father Rapp conferred over the books on alchemy, Conrad Feucht made suggestions that
brought no positive results, and the smell of
failure seemed to lie dankly in the laboratory.

Early in November, when in spite of all of
their effort and prayer, the lump of lead was

again found to be unchanged, Hildegarde turned to Father Rapp in despair.

"It just isn't going to work," she said. "No matter what we do, nothing works out."

He didn't even look up from the book he was studying. His patience with this inanimate thing seemed unlimited, quite unlike his impatience with members who failed to live up to his standards. "Never mind, child. It'll work in time. God has willed it so."

"Sometimes I wonder if it's me," she said in a small voice.

"Nonsense! I had a vision. Don't talk foolishly."

"Father," she said humbly, "I have to talk to you. I really do."

"Then talk."

"Not in here. Could we go into the trustees' room?"

He looked up at her and frowned. He hated to be interrupted in his work, and yet he knew his greatest work was with the souls of his children, and if Hildegarde had a problem, he must listen to her. "Very well, " he said reluctantly. "Come on."

They left the laboratory, closing the door on their failure, and sat facing each other in the room she had chosen. He sat on one of the wooden chairs at the table, perched on the edge of it, but she settled herself determinedly in the settee at the end of the room.

"Well?" he said.

"Father, I'm worried. I'm worried about the experiment, about the fact that Brother Frederick makes it clear that he doesn't approve of me, about the fact that we fail. I'm worried."

He stared at her for a minute. "Worrying should be left to me," he said almost gently. "I'm the one who knows what is right and what is not. Except for this experiment—and I knew it would be very, very difficult—we're prosperous, aren't we? The brothers and sisters work together and share the goods and their labor. For the most part, there is love and brotherhood. Why do you worry?"

"Brother Frederick . . ." she began, but he interrupted brusquely.

"Frederick is a good man, but he's not the one God called to lead the people. He also worries too much about certain things. He should concern himself with the businesses, the vine growing, the trading. I've told him so."

"He doesn't like me." She said the words softly, but she should have known what the reaction would be.

"Nonsense! We're a group who are all one. We love each other without exception. Frederick may think you too young to be working with the the Holy Experiment, but he likes you. There's no question. You're being foolish and sentimental."

The quick tears filled her eyes. She couldn't bear for him to even be impatient with her.

At the sight of her tears, his voice gentled. "Always there are some who question, my child. There are people in this valley, people in Pittsburg who think we are foolish or impractical because we share everything in common, because none of us owns personal goods. But are we foolish? Are we impractical? Do we starve or go cold?"

"No," she said.

"Of course not!" His voice was hearty again. "We are warm and well dressed, our houses are built better than any other houses in this area; we eat well. And so I prophesied. If I'm right about this, how can you question my feelings about the Philosopher's Stone?"

"Oh, not your feelings, Father. I'd never question you. It's just me. I sometimes think. . . ."

He stood up abruptly. "That's your trouble," he said. "You think too much. Let me do the thinking. You do what you're told. Now—go and take a walk or something to blow the cobwebs out of your brain. You're tired. Tomorrow we'll come back to the laboratory with freshness. Go, now. No, never mind about the locking up. I'll take care of it."

She was by no means satisfied with the conversation. She had so many more things she wanted to ask, but he was impatient already, and if she persisted, he would only get angry. She hadn't been questioning their way of life, but he had interpreted it that way. She wanted to know about herself. Even though she resented Frederick's attitude, his question, "Are you pure enough, Sister? Are you?" kept repeating itself in her mind.

She managed a small smile and an inclination of her head to the old man and then she got up and walked from the room, feeling her confusion like a churning ache in her.

If only there was someone else she could talk to! She remembered the day she and Gertrude had stood on the cold, windy riverbank and had shared, not just words, but ideas. Hildegarde had dared to say her thoughts then, but now she dared talk to no one. Her mother would understand many things, but her pride in Hildegarde's position would surely prevent her from being able to be really objective. "Of course, you're good enough," she would say.

And "Of course, you aren't," Brother Frederick would say. And Gertrude—what would Gertrude say? She would probably gaze at her with wide, clear eyes and say, "But surely you know yourself, Sister. Only you can know that."

But that was the whole trouble, Hildegarde reflected mournfully, pulling her shawl closer to cut out the chill November wind. I don't know myself. I'm not even sure that I really remember exactly what happened about Jacob Klein. Sometimes I feel that he was like that moose, mad with his evil longings and I was only afraid and repulsed. But sometimes—sometimes I know that I was too kind to him that day in the garden. I was only young and foolishly curious, but I wanted him to—to do something.

But if Father Rapp had a vision. . . . Her steps slowed and her mind worked furiously. Was it at all possible that Father Rapp could be wrong? He had been so positive that only Jacob had been sinful, and Hildegarde wholly innocent. If he were infallible, wouldn't he somehow have known about what happened in the vineyard and in the wine cellar? Or if not that, wouldn't he suspect the weakness that sometimes made her think wrong things—like how tedious it was to always dress and act exactly like everyone else—and to wonder and wonder how Maria could be so serene, even happy, if all men were coarse and almost cruel as Jacob had been?

She had to have someone to talk to. She felt sometimes she would die if she didn't find someone who would listen, who would say not yes or no but, "Well, I think perhaps. . . ."

She glanced up at the gray, lowering sky. It looked almost as if snow was imminent. Maybe she ought to run over to the gardens to see that all the winter precautions had been taken, that the tender boxwood hedges were covered with straw, that the herbs were moved into the greenhouse. Since she had been working on the experiment, she had been relieved of much of her gardening responsibilities, but she could not forget her beloved plants.

She hurried over to the garden and spent an hour or two talking to the boys who did the work now, checking to see that they were doing all that needed to be done. Always in spring or summer she had found healing for her mind and soul when she worked with the garden, and even on raw autumn days, like this one, she had found a curious solace that she never seemed to find in the laboratory. It occurred to her that perhaps she was a person who had to make things grow if she were to feel content. Or keep things safe for growing, she thought, pressing earth against the bulbs which were stored in the dark corner.

A small sound jerked her hands back, but it was only a cat, her sides swollen with young, who had found a bed in the corner and was indicating her resentment at being disturbed.

"This is no time for kittens," Hildegarde said softly, her voice faintly shaky from the small fright. "Why didn't you have your babies in the spring, like normal cats, and not have to find a place out of the cold?"

The cat slitted her eyes at Hildegarde but made no effort to move. She was lying in a peculiar fashion, and her sides seemed to be moving. Dimly, in the shadowy light, Hildegarde saw a ripple move along the cat's body, and the small pink mouth opened as though she were going to cry, but no sound came. Hildegarde knelt on the damp earth, staring at the animal. She was going to have her kittens now, and if Hildegarde stayed where she was, pretending to be busy with the bulbs, she might see them born. She had never seen a cow drop its calf or a dog produce a litter of pups. Rural though she was, the process of birth was something that had always happened when she was not there. Perhaps she had never even cared before, never even thought about it. But now, she knew that she wanted to see this thing. She wanted to know what happened.

She glanced over her shoulder, and the boys were all gone. The day was sliding toward chill twilight, and she knew she ought to start home, but the cat held her. She found a small lamp, lit it, and placed it on the ground beside her. She folded up several burlap sacks and knelt, watching, talking foolishly and crooningly to the cat, aware that her heart was pounding. The feeling that filled her was not one of morbid curiosity. Birth among animals was not to be confused with human action at all. Yet, in her mind, there was a feeling that if the kittens were born, it would be a sort of miracle, a beautiful thing to see.

The minutes slid by, and the cat's sides moved with her labor, and then, with one sharp yowl, the cat strained, and a small, damp bundle lay between her hind legs. For a few seconds, while the kneeling girl held her breath, the cat lay supine, limp, and then she twisted to get the small sac-enclosed kitten in her mouth. She pulled it up close to her face and then, almost quicker than Hildegarde could see, she slit the sac. Hildegarde watched it shred the sac into wisps of membrane which the cat ate quickly, biting the umbilical cord deftly. The kitten looked dead, wet and dark, curled into a bundle. The cat began to lick it, over and over, turning it and twisting until it began to emerge from her ministrations as a tiny, fluffy creature with miniature paws and snub-nosed face. The cat butted it—roughly, it seemed to Hildegarde— until its head was close to the cat's belly. Suddenly, the tiny thing seemed to come to life. Its small head moved of its own accord with the same blind, instinctive gesture that Maria's baby had used, seeking the source of nourishment. With the cat's help, the small mouth found the waiting teat, and there was a soft sucking sound. Hildegarde hardly saw the emergence of the afterbirth, the unpleasant business of the cat devouring it so that the birthing nest remained clean with only small spots of blood. The girl was too intent on the kitten. Here was life where ten minutes ago there had only been pain.

Two more kittens were born while Hildegarde knelt on the cold ground. She was speechless and almost mindless before this spectacle of birth. The cat's instinctive behavior, the emergence of individual life, the fact that the three kittens were all different, each one beautiful in its own way, kept her a captive audience to the small drama.

How long she would have knelt there, she was never to know. The door of the greenhouse opened suddenly, and a man's voice called softly, "Is there someone here? Why is the light burning?"

It was Conrad Feucht, and his voice brought her guiltily to her feet. She realized that it was black dark outside and that perhaps her mother was worried about her. Well, maybe not. She might only think Hildegarde had been delayed at the Great House.

"It's me—Hildegarde," she said breathlessly. "I'm coming in a minute."

"Oh, Sister. I didn't know who might be here so late. Why are you working here in the dark and the cold?"

"I hadn't realized," she admitted with a little

laugh. In the dim greenhouse, with the birth of the kittens fresh in her mind, she found herself talking as casually as though he were her own brother. "I've been watching kittens being born."

He moved over to where she was and stood in silence looking down at the mother cat and her young. At last he spoke. "You saw the whole thing? It didn't sicken—or distress you?"

She didn't even look at him, although there was no embarrassment in her at all. She couldn't seem to tear her eyes away from the kittens. "Oh, no! I thought it was—like a miracle."

As soon as the words were out, she realized that she had spoken her heart. Not only spoken her heart but to a man and one of the men who went out into the world. Her breath caught with apprehension. What would he think? What would he say?

Fearfully, she slid her eyes up to look at him, but he was staring down at the kittens. He bent over and touched one of them with a very gentle finger.

"Yes," he said. "A miracle. Birth is always that at least."

She stood beside him, her throat tight with emotion and excitement. Here was someone who understood. Here was someone who felt something of what she felt. Maybe he would talk to her. Maybe he would listen to the questions which tore her to pieces.

"Brother Conrad," she said, her voice shy and hesitating. "I'm wrong, perhaps, to speak to you. Here in this place. Alone. But I'm so troubled. I need to talk. I have no one—no one to talk to."

"The Father?" he asked, his voice calm, but there was no calmness in him. He should never have opened the door. He should have—but that was foolish. He had to check on the lantern because of the danger of fire. His being here with this girl was not something he could have foreseen nor avoided. *Even if I had wanted to,* he added honestly in the depths of himself.

"The Father doesn't *listen.* He knows everything and he never asks questions and he has no patience with me when I do."

Conrad made a soft sympathetic sound. He knew. He had tried to talk to Father Rapp himself in times of self-doubt and had met the same impatient lack of compassion that Hildegarde had met.

"Could I talk to *you,* Brother?" Hildegarde said swiftly before her courage failed. "Would you listen? Would you help me?"

Conrad knew what his answer ought to be. He was fully aware of the fact that this child—no, this woman—should be sent to Frederick or Romelius Baker or even Dr. Mueller (in spite of the doctor's growing disillusionment with Father Rapp's increasing authority). She needed someone who was old and whose heart did not twist suddenly when she smiled or when she said the words that no one else in the village would say. Who else would think the birth of kittens a miracle? Who else would take the time to watch? Conrad knew, without doubt, what his answer *should* be. But he was caught up in the spell cast by the mother cat nursing her kittens, the eager beauty of the face tilted up toward his, by the aching hunger to communicate with someone who saw life—differently. They needed each other, Conrad knew, but the need should be ignored.

"Here?" he said.

To his amazement, she laughed. "Here? And have Brother Frederick find us and send you packing—as though you were another Jacob Klein. And, as important as you are, you could demand even more money than Jacob did—and get it, as he did."

"You know too much," he said and laughed with her. "Where then?"

Her laughter dissolved into a sweet sincerity. "My heart is honestly troubled, Brother. I won't bother you with silliness. Could we meet along the Beaver Road, do you think—quite by accident, of course—and could we walk along and talk? Some day when you're free. I won't bother you for long."

"Tomorrow," Conrad said before he could discipline his tongue. "Tomorrow after the noon meal. I have to go into Beaver in the early morning. I'll be coming back about then. We could meet out beyond the vineyards."

"You won't mind?" she asked anxiously. "I don't want to trouble you."

"It won't be any trouble," Conrad said, his voice stiff and formal in his attempt to keep the joy from showing. "I'll be happy."

She smiled at him, a dazzling smile that tilted

his heart. "Thank you, Brother, thank you for not scolding me tonight for staying here so foolishly."

"Is it foolish to see a miracle?" he said, his voice soft and teasing.

The look she threw him was pure gratitude. "Oh, no," she said. "And I have seen—oh, such loveliness!"

She touched the cat's head. They both knew that she was not referring to the kittens' birth in her last remark, but neither of them said anything.

"I'll hurry now," she said primly, "and, if you'll be so kind, you may put out the lamp. I would not want—we shouldn't—the dark—" she floundered, not brave enough to say that they must not be there together in the dark.

"Of course, Sister," he said. "Hurry or your parents will be wondering." She was nearly to the door when he added, "I'll see you tomorrow."

"Thank you," she flung breathlessly over her shoulder. The door closed behind her and she fled across the paths toward Kirkstrasse. She looked back only once to see his tall, dark silhouette bend over the kittens again. She could imagine his long, clever hands reaching out to touch the soft bits of fur, and warmth filled her. She would have to come very early to the greenhouse and give instructions to the boys that the cats were not to be disturbed.

When she glanced back again, the lamp had been blown out, and there was nothing to be seen. But, oh, the things to be remembered, she thought! The kittens' birth, the coming of the man and his kindness, the wonder of finding someone who felt as she did. And tomorrow they would talk. Tomorrow she could put her doubts, her worries, her fear into words and someone would listen and understand.

Chapter 19

The hour after the noon meal was usually devoted to minor duties, brief rest, study or meditation, so it was not difficult for Hildegarde to leave the Great House, skirting the far side of the garden near the granary so that there was no chance of her mother seeing her, and then to make her swift but cautious way down the streets that led to the Beaver Road. The day was chilly, but the sky blazed with a pure brilliance. When buildings or trees sheltered her from the November wind, the sun poured a delicious warmth on her shoulders. She had never, she thought, felt so alive in her entire life. It was all she could do to keep from pulling her skirts to her knees, as she had done when she was a girl, and running like a colt. But she managed to maintain a decent dignity as long as she was within the reach of any prying eyes.

Finally, when she was alone on the Beaver Road, the excitement of the glorious day, her unusual freedom, the anticipation she was feeling all combined to strip away her inhibitions, and she began to run, laughing like a child, feeling the wind in her face but loving it, even though it made her eyes sting until they blurred with tears.

Conrad saw her running toward him, and a strange feeling of fear and foreboding filled him. She was a creature shaped for joy, he thought, but she had been held down, suppressed, molded into a form that was not her own. He knew that she was intelligent, too. That was not enough to shake his soul. Nor was Hildegarde's beauty sufficient to make him turn from the plow to which he had set his hand. But if today showed him, as he was beginning to suspect it would, that she was sensitive and curious and questioning, then what would keep him safe for Father Rapp's fold? Conrad had been lonely all his life, and he had been able to bear it only because he thought no one else knew the same loneliness. What if this girl shared his peculiar kind of aching solitude?

He slowed his horse, and at that moment Hildegarde saw him coming. She stopped running, smoothed her skirts that had been blown by the wind, brushed her hands over the curls that had been loosened under the pleating of her bonnet, and by the time he reached her, she was a model of decorum.

He swung himself from his horse, loosening the bridle, so that the animal could lower its head to crop at the frostbitten grass as they walked along.

"Good afternoon, Brother Conrad." Her voice was breathless from running but solemn enough to reassure him.

"Good afternoon, Sister. Shall we walk away from the village for a short distance? This will give us more time to talk."

She nodded her head, fighting for composure so that she would not sound like a silly child, breathing hard from running. For a few minutes they walked in silence, and the only sound was the chewing sounds of the horse and the sudden, shrill call of a cardinal.

When Hildegarde spoke, she was calm enough to satisfy anyone who might have heard her. "It was good of you to meet me, Brother. I'm sorry it has to be hidden this way. If things were different, I'd like to just sit in the schoolroom and talk. . . ."

If things were different. . . . Ah, that was the whole problem and they both knew it.

"I'll be glad to help," Conrad said. "If I can, I mean." He kept his voice deliberately cool and formal.

The sound of his words intimidated Hildegarde momentarily. She looked at him with apprehension, and he knew at once that he had been too cool. He had destroyed the warmth that had seemed so natural the night before.

He decided suddenly to stop fighting and forget his own difficulties. The girl needed something, and perhaps he was the one to help her. He could fight his own battles later.

So he smiled at her, and the words came out with a hint of easy laughter. "Have you seen the little mother today? Are her babies safe?"

Hildegarde sparkled. "There are five of them, and I've given the boys strict orders not to dare touch a single one. They can live in the greenhouse all winter—we're troubled with mice anyhow, and the cats will solve that problem. I'll feed them myself."

"Five?" Conrad said. "Then we missed part of the miracle?"

"But only part. How did she know what to do? She looked not much more than a half-grown cat herself. She must not have had babies before. How did she know?"

"Instinct. Animals just know."

She thought of Maria's baby, and her breasts remembered the way they had ached, leaning over the child.

"And people?" she said softly. "Would people know?"

"About babies, you mean?" This conversation wasn't going at all the way he had thought it would. What did she have in her mind?

"Yes. Babies."

"I doubt it. We're too—educated, perhaps. Anyhow, if people knew these things, there would be no need for doctors, and I'd be plowing fields."

They laughed together, and the look they exchanged was a friendly one.

Conrad hazarded a guess. "Why are you thinking of babies? Has Maria been back to the village?"

It never occurred to her that she could not trust him with the secret. She knew he would not tell.

"Yes," she said. And then, "I held him. That was a miracle, too."

"It seems you've had your share of miracles lately," he said, and the teasing note had crept back into his voice. She smiled at him, but his words reminded her that she was here for serious words, not for joy—even if the joy was like food and drink after a lifetime journey of dust.

"Not really, Brother. That's what I want to talk about. We haven't had the miracle Father Rapp has prayed for. The experiment has failed. Over and over and over until I think I can't bear it any more."

"It's sure to be discouraging," he said but added nothing else. He had lost all belief in the Holy Experiment; he considered it a waste of time and, more than that, a misinterpretation of Scripture. This was heresy, and he knew it. He didn't want to infect this girl with his disbelief. She was too vulnerable.

"I think perhaps it's me," she said, her voice so low that he had to stoop toward her to hear. The sweet, light scent of her hair came to him, and he was reminded of the night she had come into the yard with her hair flowing to her waist, the night they had gone to bring Gertrude home. That was when it all began, Conrad thought dazedly, not bothering to define what it was that had begun on that dark, troubled night.

He forced himself to answer her. "Why you?" he said.

"I may not be pure enough for the experiment. I may defile it somehow. Brother Frederick thinks so."

Conrad had to shut his lips tightly to keep sudden words from coming out. "Frederick is jealous" is what he wanted to say, and he was shocked at himself for wanting to say it—and, more for knowing that, in a sense, it was true.

"Do you really think you're impure, Sister?" Conrad said, but the catechism was said in so soft a voice that she could feel no censure.

"I don't know," she said. "I just don't know."

"Can you tell me what troubles you most? Is that what you want to talk about?"

"Oh, yes," she said. She did not understand why she felt no hesitation to talk to this man. She had never really talked to him before, except about impersonal matters. And yet, it seemed to her that she could say anything, anything, and he would not condemn her nor would he fail, as Father Rapp did, to see her clearly with all her faults and weaknesses.

"Well?" he said into her silence.

"I—I have many faults," she said at last. "Everyone—except maybe the Father—has faults. I'm not stupid enough not to know that. But I'm silly sometimes, and I laugh when everyone else is serious, and I—I don't like dressing like everyone else."

The last words were said with more shame than the first ones. Most Harmonists felt a fierce pride in their sameness, and Hildegarde knew it. Her dislike of conformity was a serious flaw and one which could not be lightly dismissed.

Conrad considered what she said. "I don't think laughter is wrong," he said slowly. "I think sometimes it's good to be joyful, but of course others won't agree with me, you know."

He paused and looked at her, but she only nodded. She was waiting for his reaction to the more serious confession.

"As to your wanting to be different from the others in your dress—and in your actions? . . ." (This drew a wry smile of admission from her.) "I'm not sure how I can possibly advise you. I go into the world, you know. Sometimes, I don't dress like a Harmonist."

"Do you like that?" she asked.

"Yes," he said simply.

"Then you feel as I do," she said with a sense of discovery. "I'm not completely alone."

"Have you felt alone, Sister?" His voice was too gentle, but he could not change it.

"I've been alone all my life," she answered honestly. "Oh, not always lonely, you understand. Once, when we were younger, Sister Gertrude and I talked—like friends, you know—and Maria and I could talk. And my mother—my mother is loving and good. Even Father Rapp has made me feel important, but I'm still alone. I guess that sounds foolish."

"Not to me. Some people need another ear to talk to."

She stopped and gazed at him in sheer delight. "Oh," she said impulsively, "I wish you were a girl. We could be friends, couldn't we?"

He felt his blood run warmly up his throat and into his face. Her innocence was genuine.

How could Frederick think her malicious and scheming and wanton?

Seeing his flush, she felt embarrassment touch her. He must think her a fool. "I'm sorry," she said. "That was probably the silliest thing I've ever said."

"Or the wisest," he said dryly, and a small silence stretched out between them.

"Are you sure you've told me all your problems, Sister? Would you worry so much over only what you have told me?"

He was going to force her to be truly honest, to reveal the deepest secrets of her soul. If he were to help her at all, she realized, she had to be totally candid.

"There's more," she said, keeping her voice as expressionless as possible. "I've admitted them only in my prayers, Brother, and I don't know if I dare say them to you. But I'll try."

She was silent a minute and he waited, his mouth feeling dry, wondering what she would say.

"Part of it is Jacob Klein," she said.

Conrad's heart twisted with sudden pain. Was she going to admit actions which would confirm Frederick's accusations?

"I'm not sure I even remember exactly how it was," she went on, her voice breathless and a little frightened. "But I'll try to tell you truly."

She told it all—the small flirtation, the great curiosity, the deliberate touch, the terror of the wine cellar, the greater terror of her capitulation to his kiss which had melted her into the spineless, craven creature who had groveled at

Father Rapp's feet begging for mercy, too cowardly to admit her guilt.

He listened and compassion filled him until he felt he would weep. She had been brought up in an innocence that was unnatural and cruel. How could she be blamed if her body had betrayed her? And Jacob—Jacob had been undisciplined, lusting after her as much as he had loved her.

When she finished, he spoke gently. "Sister, I'm not the one to condemn you or absolve you. I—I understand how you felt. I—myself, that is—think you may have been foolish and not very brave. But I don't know if that is sin."

"And that's not all," she said bravely. "When Gertrude left that night, and when Maria came back with her baby I tortured myself with questions. How could they do what they did if men—if men and women—if all that were like Jacob was?"

"God gave you a mind," he said. "I can't feel it's wrong to use it for thinking, for wondering. All men are not like Jacob Klein, Sister. The tutor—Schmidt—was a gentle, sensitive poet. He appealed to Sister Gertrude's spirit, I think. She followed that and when—when she realized all he wanted, she came running back. It was better, of course. For her, it was."

"And Maria?"

"I know the boy Maria married. He's a good boy. He'll be very kind to her, I think. They probably laugh together. And now they have a baby. You saw him, you say?"

She stopped, clasping her hands together at

the memory. "He was the first tiny baby I ever held. He was—beautiful."

"Yes," Conrad said. "I can imagine."

Again they were silent, and again she broke the silence. "I'm not even sure I believe in the experiment any more. I mean, not just that I might be impure. But that—that Father Rapp might be wrong."

This was the core of the whole confession, Conrad knew. And what could he say? How could he reassure her, shore up her crumbling defenses when his own convictions were fissured by doubt?

"Sister," he began and then stopped. There just weren't any words for him to say.

She looked at him, and her eyes widened. "You wonder, too," she whispered. "You have just as many doubts as I do!"

They stood in complete stillness in the brilliant sunshine, the chill November wind blowing her hair into tumbled gold and touching his face with color. Their eyes looked deeply into the other's eyes, and the silence and sunshine seemed to hold them in a small, secret world of their own.

"Oh, Brother Conrad, what can we do?"

"I don't know," he said helplessly.

Abruptly and absurdly, she was the one who was confident, who was strong. "We can talk to each other," she said. "We can be friends. No one needs to know. But I can ask you things, and you can ask me. I won't know the answers as you will, but I'll listen. I'll really listen, Brother."

Friends, he thought, with an odd, helpless

feeling as though all his moorings had been cut and he had been set adrift upon moving waters with a seaward wind which would permit him no turning back. Not ever a turning back. *Can we be friends? Is her innocence enough to keep her safe? To keep us safe?*

So be it, he thought with recklessness. *I may not believe in the experiment, I may (forgive me) even question the Second Coming, I may flounder in a dozen doubts, but I know God is. I know he loves us and will guide us. We'll trust him. I'll trust him.*

"Yes, friends," he said, smiling down into her earnest face. "You'll be my dearest friend, Sister, and I yours. And when we can, we'll talk. Is that what you want?"

"Oh, yes," she sighed. "More than anything. Will you teach me, Brother? I want to be wise like you."

"I'm not always wise," he warned.

"Good!" she said and laughed. "I'm surrounded by wisdom every day. Shall we be foolish occasionally, Brother?"

"Definitely," he said. "And I'll start. From now on, when we're alone, I'll call you Hildegarde—because we're friends."

She grinned. "I'd like that, Brother."

"You must call me Conrad," he said with a mock frown.

"Dare I?"

"Of course."

"Then I will. When I get brave enough," she added shyly. "Hadn't we better start back toward home?"

"Yes. I wish I could let you ride the horse, but. . . ."

"No, I love to walk. And if you ride on ahead, no one need ever know that we talked. They might think only that you passed me on the road. With a wave."

He swung himself into the saddle and hauled up the horse's head. "To make it true," he said and sketched her a merry salute.

She raised her hand in answer.

He looked down at her. "Auf wiedersehen, Hildegarde. Gott geh mit dir."

"Auf wiedersehen," she answered. "God go with you, too, Conrad."

The last word was almost whispered but it shouted in his ears as he galloped away. God go with us both, he thought soberly, and then gave himself up to joy.

Chapter 20

The next few months were, in spite of continuing failure with the experiment, the happiest time in Hildegarde's life. She and Conrad did not meet often, they had only a few chances to talk, but it was enough for her to know that he was her friend and he could be reached if she had need of him. There was satisfaction and joy in the casual meeting of eyes across the church. It seemed she was warmed and fed by the look he gave her, the look that said, "We are two who no longer are alone in our thoughts and our wonderings." Even when she was alone, she was no longer lonely.

Christmas came, and its ordinary joy was tripled and quadrupled by the serenity in her heart. She piled the fragrant greens in the deep sills of the Great House and the Mutschler house, setting glossy red apples on the massed greens and stepping back to admire the effect. She found some time to make clove-studded oranges from the small bitter fruit which dropped from the miniature orange trees which grew in tubs on the upper floor of the Feast Hall. The scent of the tropical fruit and the heady smell of the spices mingled into a sweetness that delighted her.

On Christmas Eve, the annual concert of carol singing followed the sermon in the church, and the members of the Society stood in the dark, windy churchyard, hands cupped around the flickering flames of their candles while the sweet, solemn words of "Stille Nacht, Heilige Nacht" drifted like crystal into the cold air. Hildegarde stood close to her mother, and she felt love wash through her. It was a little like the feeling she had so many months ago when they had left New Harmony, and she had wanted to gather the whole brotherhood into her arms and hold them. And yet it was entirely different. She had seen the community then as perfect, unflawed, destined for glory. Now, she saw it with older eyes, aware of the divisions that existed in spite of the constant preaching of brotherhood. She wondered, for a minute, why she felt the way she did. Perhaps it was Christmas. Perhaps she was feeling like a child, thrilled with the candles and the singing and the knowledge that sweet cakes and wine waited for them in the Feast Hall.

A movement at her shoulder caught her attention, and she turned her head to see in the dim, flickering light Conrad's face above her. The candles cast a warmth that lit the angles of his cheeks, softened his mouth and made his eyes look bright and excited, as a child's would be. She felt so comfortable with him by now that she did not even miss a note in the song. She only smiled and watched his slow, answering smile. She turned back toward her mother, but she was aware of Conrad's presence, finding his closeness an added pleasure to this special moment.

She never knew whether she stepped back or he stepped forward. She only knew that suddenly her shoulder was against his, and that for the length of two more carols, they stood touching in the flickering dark, and the warmth of his body kept her sheltered from the wind—as the sharing of his mind had kept her sheltered from loneliness these past weeks. She wasn't sure when she was first conscious of the fact that her heart was pounding in hard, slow beats. Or was it her heart? Was it his? Her right shoulder was touching—no, leaning—against his left breast, and it was the beating of his heart that she felt. She was reminded, abruptly, of the way she had felt Jacob's heart pounding in the rash embrace, and she turned with a feeling of fear that jerked in her throat. But Conrad wasn't even looking at her. He was gazing at the star-studded sky, and his singing was as it always was, glad and strong with a sweetness threaded through it.

Hildegarde felt her fear subside. She sang again, and her shoulder remained leaning on the warmth and solidarity of the man who stood so close to her. It was not until later that she realized that even in that momentary little spasm of fear, she had not moved away.

Early in January, Hildegarde went to the laboratory after breakfast, as she always did, and she found Father Rapp already there. He was pale and stern, and he did not even look at her. He was walking from table to cabinet, dismantling equipment, closing books, capping bottles.

"What are you doing?" she asked, feeling a coldness settle in her stomach. This was certainly not his usual manner. He usually read or meditated or gave instructions, and hers were the hands which set up the experiments. What's more, he was not setting up; he was tearing down.

"The experiment is over," he said. "It's finished. We have failed, and it's not God's will that we go on trying and trying and spending money and effort to no avail."

"But, Father," she protested. "The vision . . . what of the vision?"

He didn't answer for a minute, and she watched his actions with a terrible sense of dread and foreboding. There was something being destroyed in this room that was more than an experiment in alchemy. Her faith, her belief were being shaken to their roots.

"Please," she said and her voice frayed and went ragged. "Please, Father, we can't stop. Not now. Let someone else help you. Let. . . ."

He interrupted brusquely. "It's over. I have said it, and there is nothing to be gained in arguing. Here, put these bottles in that box in the corner."

She was crying now. "Oh, Father, please. The vision. . . ."

"It may be that the vision was misinterpreted," he said roughly. "Or perhaps it was only God's way to make me seek you out that night, to save you from that sinner, Klein. He was a greedy one and we're well rid of him—and you're safe."

She stood stricken. This was pure justification. The old man had been misled, he had been mistaken, and he was making excuses. He, the supposed prophet of God, was trying to cover up a mistake.

A year and a half of our lives, Hildegarde thought miserably, just thrown away because he had an idea. Not a vision but an idea. He's just good and great and strong—but he's no holier than any other man. He can be as mistaken as my father—as Maria's father.

She stood staring at the old man, feeling terror fill her. If Father Rapp was wrong, where could she turn for truth?

Conrad. She felt a cold touch of fear that she might have said the word aloud, but Father Rapp did not react in any way. The name had only exploded in her head. Conrad would not be a source of infallible truth, but he would support her, sustain her until she had found something in which she could believe again. She turned, and without a word, ran from the laboratory, knowing that she had to find the one person who would help her.

Father Rapp turned, hearing the sound of her running. He opened his mouth to call her back—didn't the girl know he would need another pair of hands? But he closed his lips before he could make any sound. She was sensitive, and so her disappointment had rendered her helpless for awhile. Let her cry it out, woman fashion, he thought, then she'll be back to help. A sound at the door pulled his head around. Had she returned so soon?

But it was Frederick who stood watching him, his face blank with incredulity.

"What are you doing?" His words were an echo of Hildegarde's, holding the same disbelief.

"The experiment is finished," Father Rapp said. "I've decided that it's wrong to spend any more time on it. There is too much else that needs to be done."

"You have decided?" Frederick was shocked out of his usual submission. "I thought this was God's experiment, God's decision."

"Are you being insolent with me?" The words were barked roughly, as though Frederick were a child to be scolded for a misdemeanor.

"Insolent, my father?" Frederick's voice was very smooth. He was aware of the fact that his heart was jerking unevenly in his breast and that his palms were wet and cold. But this time he would not back away. This time he would face the old man with the truth.

"Perhaps 'insolent' is a strong word," admitted Father Rapp, looking keenly at the face of the man in front of him. "I could use more discretion, I suppose. But it's not like you to question me."

"It's not like you to question God," Frederick replied, his voice quiet, but it seemed to snap in the room.

The old man pulled himself to his full height,

and anger darkened his face. "How dare you?" He spoke heavily, pain as well as anger in his voice. "God speaks to me in many ways. He told me to go to Indiana, but later, he told me to come back to Pennsylvania. He had his reasons for the work on this experiment, but now the reasons are over. I don't know what they were, but I know when I'm led to do what is right."

"Maybe the reason was to give that girl a chance to worm her way into your confidence," Frederick said.

"Watch what you say!" The blazing words were like a slap across Frederick's face and he winced from the blow. But still he did not retract his words.

"She's sly and crafty," Frederick said. "She talks alone to—to men in the Society. She lies to you when she says she's walking alone, thinking of the experiment. She's made a fool of you!"

Father Rapp was breathing heavily. "I don't believe you. What man?"

Frederick hesitated. Conrad Feucht was a good and valuable member of the Brotherhood. Why jeopardize his chances of staying on? He was probably a dupe to the girl's wicked ways, just as Klein had been. No, he wouldn't tell the Father about Conrad.

"I can't say," Frederick replied. "Can't you trust me enough to know that I would not lie to you?"

"She wouldn't lie either, and your accusations are unfounded. You—you're only jealous because I chose her as my assistant instead of you."

The bitter, accusing words hung in the air

between them. Frederick felt the sharp, jagged pain stab through his chest and up into his head. That the beloved Father—for whom the younger man would have died—should say such a cruel thing was unbearable.

Father Rapp was as shocked as Frederick. He hadn't known that such a thought existed in his mind until the words were out, and he knew they could never be recalled.

"The girl has poisoned you," Frederick said at last. "You are as enslaved by her—her wiles as Jacob Klein was."

"Are you accusing me of lust?" The words were whispered, but they stung like a whip.

Frederick stared at his father. A great wave of desolation and grief swept over him until he was drowning in regret. No, of course, he had not meant that. That other people—weaker or less faithful than he—might think such black and evil thoughts was possible. But he, the son, the follower, the disciple, knew better than that. It was only that he thought the old man was fatuous and bewitched.

"Father, Father, no," Frederick said, his voice breaking on a sob. "No, not that. I know you have no desire for her, none—none. I only meant that you—you doted on her like a too fond parent with a spoiled child. Believe me, Father. Forgive me."

Slowly Father Rapp's anger began to lessen. Perhaps he had been hasty. His quick temper had always been his sin, and he knew it. And his accusation of jealousy had been cruel. Frederick was wrong about Hildegarde, of course. But he could not really accuse his father of such a thing. No one could. *I bear the mark of God,* Father Rapp reflected. *I cannot even be touched by all of this.*

With a sense of his own generosity, he put forth a hand to touch Frederick's shoulder.

"I believe you. I misunderstood perhaps. So you must not weep or carry on so. We have exchanged bitter words, and we'll have to pray for forgiveness—both of us. There, does that suit you?"

Frederick heard the words with small comfort. The anger was gone, but nothing would be any different or any better. The experiment would end—because Father Rapp said it would end. Hildegarde would go unaccused and undisciplined.

Someday, Frederick thought, if someone stronger than Hildegarde comes here, someone who will shake the brothers' belief in Father Rapp's goodness, we will be doomed, our oneness scattered down the wind.

"Does it suit you?" Father Rapp asked again, his voice a little sharp. Wasn't the man even listening?

Frederick lifted his face, and the old man was honestly shocked at the ravished anguish in the dark eyes that faced him.

"You have forgiven me, Father?" Frederick said.

"You're forgiven, my son," Father Rapp said.

They knelt together, and their prayers were said. But, although their hands clasped warmly before Frederick finally left the laboratory, the knowledge stayed in both minds that Father Rapp had not asked for forgiveness for the words he had said. Perhaps, Frederick thought desolately, he doesn't even care.

Hildegarde ran through the cold, windy day, trying to find Conrad. Snow drove in stinging gusts from a leaden sky, and the deep snow on the ground covered her ankles, soaking through the leather of her high shoes. The edges of her skirt dragged through several drifts and then hung, wet and cold, against her legs. The falling snow soaked through the heavy woolen shawl, through the cotton dress until her shoulders and arms were wet and cold. But still she could not stop her searching. He had to be somewhere. He had to be there when she needed him. That was part of friendship.

She ran across Grossestrasse to the building which held the apothecary shop and the doctor's treatment room. Conrad was not in either room, and she was starting to leave when Dr. Mueller appeared suddenly at the back door.

"You're looking for me?" he said.

"No—no, I'm not . . ." she faltered. She couldn't admit she was looking for Conrad. Why hadn't she said she was coming for a headache powder?

"Then who?" Dr. Mueller demanded, eyeing her sharply. He was aware of many things, this man who possessed such a variety of talents. He was aware of the fact that the celibate waiting for the Bridegroom was tearing some of the people apart. And instead of greater leniency, instead of some compassion, Father Rapp only grew sterner and stricter. It was all wrong, the doctor had thought a dozen, a hundred times. They had such a beautiful thing here—or it could be—but it was all going wrong. And one of those who is suffering is my boy, Conrad, the doctor thought. I have seen him look at this girl. Will she ruin him or make him whole? Well, God's will be done, he thought heavily. "Who?" he repeated.

"No—no one," she stammered, starting to back out the door.

"Brother Conrad is in Pittsburgh for two days," the doctor said, finding a sour satisfaction in the way her eyes widened, the way quick color stained her face. "He'll be back tomorrow."

She looked as frightened as though he had suddenly admitted to a practice of witchcraft, and without a word, she turned and fled into the dark, bitter day.

She couldn't go directly home. The restlessness, the grief, the terrible lost feeling she was experiencing would be all too plain to her mother. So, for nearly an hour, she wandered through the snow and wind and cold, trying to bring her thoughts into order.

By the time she got home, she was thoroughly soaked and so cold she thought she would never get warm again. Her teeth chattered together, and her body shook with uncontrolled shivering. Her mother seemed to realize at once that the girl was too troubled to be questioned. Briskly, she set about stripping off the wet clothes and rubbing the girl's shivering body dry.

Although it was only midday, Frau Mutschler insisted that Hildegarde put on a warm flannel gown, drink a glass of hot tea and whiskey and climb into her narrow bed. With solicitude that always bordered on fear since she had lost one child in Indiana and nearly lost the other two, the mother filled the warming pan with hot water and, wrapping it in a soft cloth, tucked it against the girl's cold feet.

At last Hildegarde spoke. "The experiment didn't work," she said, and her tears started to fall. "Father Rapp is stopping all the work on it. I don't know if he—if he. . . ."

Christina Mutschler looked into the wet eyes and the flushed face of this beloved child, this girl-woman who had been at the core of every prayer she had ever uttered for twenty-three years. She had watched her changing, her growing, her hardening under the guidance of the Brotherhood. She had tried to believe, as her husband believed, that this was best, that the highest aim for all of them was to be molded in the image of Father Rapp. But sometimes her heart had ached for the laughter and the merriment that had once filled the house. During these past several months, she had watched the joy begin to blossom again, and her heart had had its own suspicions. Now, the miserable little face reflected only a vast unhappiness. *Why can't they let her alone*, the mother thought. *Why do they have to try to make her be what she isn't?*

From long discipline, she pushed the thoughts to the corners of her mind and bent over the bed.

"Don't trouble yourself, meine kleine. You have gotten yourself too cold and wet and you need to rest and get warm. We'll talk when you've slept and have stopped shivering. Just sleep."

Hildegarde looked at her mother and felt another spasm of chill shake her. She wanted to say, "Mother, help me," but she was too cold, too tired, too frightened. So she only nodded and turned her head into the pillow with its clean, sweet-smelling cover. In only a few minutes she was asleep.

She can tell me when she wakes up, Frau Mutschler thought, pulling the covers closer about the slender shoulders. Her hand brushed the flushed cheek, and she drew her fingers back in alarm. The skin was burning hot.

Perhaps she'll be all right when she has rested, the woman thought. *Herr Gott, make her be all right. Don't let it be the fever again. She is too thin from all the working and worrying. She's not strong enough to fight. Please, lieber Gott. . . .*

Hildegarde did not wake until afternoon had darkened into early evening, and then she woke to pain that stabbed deeply into her chest and through to her back, to a cough that wrenched her body, to the certainty that she was on fire and yet she was freezing.

"Mutter," she called. "Mutter."

Her mother came running, and her hands

were cool and steady on the girl's head, her eyes serenely hiding the terror that flared in her.

"It's all right," she said. "Your father will fetch Herr Doktor. Lie still, my child."

"Mutter," Hildegarde gasped.

"No, no talking now. When you're better, we'll talk. Try to rest."

Hildegarde obediently closed her eyes, and the mother ran to the family room. "Hurry," she gasped to her husband. "Get Dr. Mueller. She's terribly sick. The fever again. She has never been so hot before. I fear—oh, hurry."

Gerhard Mutschler put down his work and, without a word, pulled on his heavy jacket and black hat. The look of fear and grief on his wife's face was a greater prod than any of her words had been. The little one must be truly ill. He wondered, with an unfamiliar shake of fear in his heart, if even the doctor could do anything this time. Frau Mutschler was a strong and competent nurse, but her face had held only raw terror. The man did not attempt to comfort her. He ran out into the darkness and the snow, and his thoughts were a prayer as he floundered through the heavy drifts toward Dr. Mueller's house.

Chapter 21

The dark, cold days crawled by, and Hildegarde's fever worsened until it seemed inevitable that the frail spark of life in her body would be blown out by the raging chills and fever that shook her. Her bed was moved into the family room, close to the warmth of the stove, and someone stayed by her bed day and night. Dr. Mueller and Conrad came several times each day, and if anyone noticed the agony on Conrad's face, nothing was said. Hildegarde knew him the first time he came, but after that, all faces blurred before her into crimson blackness, and she tossed and muttered and cried out for water and her mother. In her delirium, she spoke, in her cracked, clogged voice, of the experiment's failure and of Father Rapp's vision that turned out to be no vision at all. Frau Mutschler stood it as long as she could and then, with rare courage, spoke one day to Father Rapp when he came.

"She thinks it's wrong that you stopped work on the experiment," the woman said, twisting her apron in work-hardened hands. "Can't you reach her, Father? Can't you tell her that it was truly God's will? Can't you lift the burden from her heart?"

He looked at Frau Mutschler from under his heavy brow. "That's foolish. Why would she question anything I do?"

The woman said the words with a great effort, "She—she thinks it was wrong. All of it. That you were wrong. This is what is killing her. Maybe if you prayed, Father?"

His pride, that holy pride which bordered on arrogance, drew him up stiffly, and he glared at the mother. No one had any right to tell him that he was at fault or what to pray or how or when. He was on the verge of saying so, of saying that this was something between himself and God, when his eyes fell on the flushed face on the pillow, and his heart twisted with pity and love. Surely, God had not moved him to save this child from Jacob Klein only to lose her to death. And yet, death—reunion with God (because now her soul was pure) would be a beautiful thing, not some sordid end with her purity defiled by man. Perhaps he should not pray for her health, perhaps. . . . But even as the theological part of his mind dredged up these thoughts, his memory brought back snatches of her laughter, her intelligence, the beauty of her face lifted to his in the sanctuary of the church. The old man never knew whether it was piety or selfishness that took him to his knees beside the bed. He bent over his knotted hands.

He did not pray aloud. For once, his thoughts were too chaotic to put into the smooth, easy words that poured from him in church or in the Feast Hall on their feast days. Save her, he thought, wondering honestly at the anguish that daggered through him. Save her.

After long moments, he lifted his head. There was no change in her face. Her head tossed on the pillow and the parched, swollen lips tried to shape the word "water." Frau Mutschler, her hands trembling until she could hardly hold the cup, lifted the golden head and forced several drops of cool liquid between the cracked lips.

"I don't know, Sister," Father Rapp said heavily, a strange humility in his voice. "I don't know if it's God's will that she get better. I don't know. . . ." He bent over the girl and took one of the burning hands in his. It came to him with a sudden astonishment, that this was the first time he had ever touched her except to lay his hands on her head in blessing. How small the hand was, how frail and thin. Gertrude's hands were broad and sturdy, capable and strong. His two children, he thought dazedly, forgetting Johannes who had died so many years before, forgetting Rosina who moved, silent as a shadow through his house, forgetting Frederick who had been his comfort and his stay. Gertrude and Hildegarde—these two were his children. He thought of Gertrude's robust health and wished that he might instill some of it into this frail body.

"Hildegarde," he called, his voice suddenly loud and commanding. "Hildegarde, come back. You are needed, my little one. Come back. . . ."

But this time, unlike the time when she was dying of malaria in Indiana, there was no miracle, this time she failed to hear the strong voice of authority, the voice that dared to send commands into the realm of God.

At last, he put down the hot little hand. He got up stiffly and turned to the mother with a look on his face which she realized with shock was grief. In all the years, she had never seen him look sad, even when his son, Johannes, died. But then, she thought hazily, many had believed that Father Rapp interpreted the accident which ended Johannes's life—the falling of the oak tree which crushed the chest of the young man—as the hand of God, taking the boy from the temptation of a wife who was too lovely.

"Keep hoping, Sister," Father Rapp said with effort. "Keep hoping, and God's will be done."

He left, and the bleak wind slammed the door shut after him.

Christina Mutschler dropped to her knees. "Oh, no," she sobbed, holding the hot hands that seemed to flutter restlessly in hers, "Oh, no, God, not this one. Don't let her die. Don't let her die."

Conrad found her like that, and his heart was wrenched with pity and fear. He lifted the woman to her feet.

"You've been up all night," he said. "I know it. Go and sleep. I'll sit here with the small one, I'll watch out for her. You won't have to worry."

The woman looked into the face of the young man. It was—what was it? Her tired mind fumbled for the explanation. It seemed suddenly necessary that she know. She stared into Conrad's eyes, and he endured the scrutiny, but he did not hide the pain, the fear he was feeling. Or the love. That was it, Frau Mutschler thought with abrupt content. He's not ashamed of *feeling*, he doesn't think it's weak to be afraid or to love.

"Thank you, Brother," she said. "I'll lie down in the small room. But if she calls me. . . ."

"I won't let her fret," he said. "I'll call you at once."

She went into the next room, pushed the door partially shut, then lay down on one of the narrow beds without removing any of her clothes. Then she lay still, completely still, feeling astonishment flood over her. Conrad loved Hildegarde. Not as a member of the Society should love another member, but as she and Gerhard had loved each other back in Germany, when they had first been married, before he had started attending the meetings at the Father's house. The way a man loved a woman. A good love, the woman thought, knowing that her thoughts were wrong. A beautiful love that would be gentle and kind and sweet—that could put a baby in Hildegarde's arms. A grandchild, Christina thought fuzzily, hovering on the verge of exhausted sleep. *Oh, dear God, to have a baby in the house again. Please, God, let her get well. Let her know love. Let her. . . .* The prayer dissolved into oblivion.

For hours, Conrad sat by the bed. Most of the time, there was someone else in the room. Hildegarde's father, brother, and aunt came and went, kneeling in prayer, bringing hot broth from the kitchen or just sitting silently on the wooden settee, looking at the girl. Finally, bedtime came, and Conrad persuaded them all to go to bed.

"I'll sit on for another hour," he said, "and then I'll call her mother. I think tonight—later tonight—there may be a crisis. You'll all need your strength then. Go, now, rest. I'll keep the watch."

The aunt went into the next room where Frau Mutschler lay snoring in exhaustion, and the two men climbed the steps to the upstairs. For awhile, until he was sure that they all slept, Conrad sat in silence, moving only when he needed to replace the cool cloth on the girl's head or to replace the poultices on her chest or to moisten her lips with cold water. When he folded back the high neck of her gown to put a new poultice on her chest, his doctor's skill could not keep his hands from trembling at the sight of the deep hollow at the base of her throat, the sharp bones that angled toward her shoulders, the softness of the skin above her breasts.

When he had finished his ministrations, when he knew that the house was asleep, he sat, not on the chair, but on the edge of the bed. He bent over the girl and gathered her into his arms. *She can't die,* he thought savagely, *not yet, not before she knows that I love her.* He hardly realized that this was the first time he had allowed himself the luxury of the admission.

"Hildegarde," he whispered into her hair, brittle now from the fever and smelling of sickness. "Hildegarde, meine lieble, meine kleine, don't leave me. Come back so I can love you. I'll never hurt you. I'll never touch you unless you want me to. I'll only love you, love you, love you. Oh, my God, don't take her. You don't need her, but I do."

He was not even aware of the words he was saying. This was certainly no Harmonist prayer that he was praying. This was not the prayer he had been taught to say, the prayer of submission, of bowing to the will of God. Nor was he praying, as Father Rapp sometimes prayed, telling God what must be done. He prayed as men pray who are having the heart torn out of their bodies, praying with grief and desperation and fear.

Her fever burned through the heavy material of his coat. "I love you," he wept whispering into her hair. "I love you. Oh, God, I love her, I can't let her go."

He did not hear the outer door open, so intent was he on his own agony. Dr. Mueller's voice came softly through the room.

"Is she dead?"

"No," said Conrad fiercely, not changing his position, not even raising his head. "I won't let her die."

"Put her down," the older man said gently, softly. "She needs medicine as well as love, my boy. Let's work together, shall we?"

Conrad looked dazedly into the eyes of the man who had done more than anyone else in the world to shape him. There was no condemnation on the round, ruddy face. There was only compassion and pity. Was the pity because Hildegarde was dying? No, by God, Conrad raged in his mind. No, she would not die.

He put the inert body back against the pillows and pushed away his own aching fear, so that he was all doctor, not softened and weakened by being part lover. He turned to Dr. Mueller and spoke simply, "What do we do next?"

For an hour the two men worked, and they felt the fever rise, heard the thickening congestion in the chest and knew that within the hour, Hildegarde would die or she would begin to live.

"Call her mother," Dr. Mueller said.

Conrad went softly to the bed of Frau Mutschler. "Sister," he said gently, touching her shoulder. "Sister."

She sat up at once and her voice was thick with sleep and fear.

"Is she . . . is she . . ." The word stuck in her throat.

"She's near the crisis. We need you."

They worked as a team, the three of them, using every bit of skill they knew, surrounding the girl with so much love and prayer that it was like a wall which kept something at bay.

Conrad felt sweat running down his body,

and he felt as though his heart had been drained of all its blood. *If she dies,* he thought, and then made his thoughts affirmative. *If she lives, I'll love her the rest of her life, but I won't make any demands unless she feels the same way.*

The mother's thoughts were too blurred for prayer. She only gave of her strength, her love, as once she had fed this child with her own body.

Dr. Mueller concentrated on using his medical skill. He felt the anguished love of the other two, and it was his own private conviction that if this girl lived, it would be love that saved her.

Suddenly, there was a change in the room. Hildegarde's restless tossing and muttering stopped, and a strange stillness spread out to all of them. For one terrible minute, even the doctor thought that the girl had stopped breathing. Then his trained finger, laid to the base of her throat, felt the frail, racing pulse hesitate, steady itself, and almost imperceptibly begin to slow until it was a steady beating which seemed beautiful. He watched the sweat break out on the small face and the flush began to recede. In only a few minutes, the girl was soaked with sweat, and the three of them, moving skillfully together, stripped off the wet gown (Conrad never even thought of the thin body that touched his hands) and removed the wet covers. Twice more, they did this, and in between, diluted whiskey was forced between the girl's lips. After an hour of constant action, there was a moment in which nothing had to be done. The terrible sweating had stopped, the thin body was cool, the breathing was shallow but regular.

"She's going to make it," Dr. Mueller said with satisfaction. "She's a long way from being all right, but she's going to make it. Who would think that such a little thing had so much fight in her?"

Frau Mutschler was weeping openly, making no attempt to be serene. "Thank God, thank God," she said, bending over the bed. "My child, my baby. Thank God."

Conrad was silent, but he knew that his happiness must be like the sun on his face. He was so tired he felt he would drop where he stood. Never before this had he literally poured his life into someone else. He was drained and hollow, but Hildegarde was alive.

Dr. Mueller looked at his assistant. "You've earned a rest, my son. Go over to my house and sleep so that no one will wake you in the morning. She's going to be all right."

"I hate to leave her," Conrad said, and it was the first time, since he had come into the room, that he had spoken in his normal tone. Until now, he had spoken in a hushed tone or a whisper.

Hildegarde's eyelids fluttered and when they lifted, her eyes were rinsed clean of the fever. She was lucid and aware. She was Hildegarde again. Her eyes saw them all and moved slowly from the older doctor to her mother to Conrad. "Hello," she said in a husky, rough little voice.

"Mutter. Doktor. And—and my dearest—my dearest friend, Conrad."

They stood in silence, shaken by the miracle of her voice. Almost at once, her eyes closed again and she slept, but there was the hint of a smile on the dried, burned lips.

"Good night, my son," the doctor said and looked blandly at Conrad.

"Good night, Brother," Frau Mutschler said, her face still wet with tears. "Thank you. And God bless you my—my son."

Conrad could not trust his voice. He merely nodded his head, looked once more at the dear face on the pillow, and then went out into the night.

"Thank you, God," he said clearly, looking up at the sky. "Thank you."

He was no longer hollow. He was filled up, tamped down and overflowing with joy. He loved her and she was alive. He had held her in his arms. The doctor and the mother had not been shocked. If God willed it, if Hildegarde could learn to love him, too, then dreams would become reality. He lifted his face to the cold night air and breathed with delight. *I'm in love*, he thought, forgetting for that moment that he was a Harmonist, that he was pledged to celibacy. *I'm in love and she's alive*. He ran through the snow, leaping drifts like a boy, feeling his joy shower the night with brightness. All he had promised in his prayer was that he would never touch her unless she wanted it. *God willing*, he thought in his intoxication, *she will want it one day, and soon*.

Hildegarde's convalescence stretched out over many weeks. It seemed as the late winter months moved darkly on that she would never really be strong again. And, at first, she was too weak to even care. It was enough that she was alive, that her mother was there to feed her and prop her up in the large rocking chair, to brush her hair and tie it back with a bit of ribbon that she had saved from her childhood. She knew that she was happiest on the days when Conrad came, but she made no effort to try to understand why. She only let herself hope each morning that Dr. Mueller would be busy that day and send his assistant to check her progress.

But gradually, her strength began to return, and she began to think, to wonder, to ask for something to read. The huge Berleberger Bible was too heavy for her frail hands, so Conrad bought a small English Bible one time when he went to Pittsburgh.

"It will give you good practice with your English," he said, lightly, but he had definite motives. Reading the familiar book in a strange language would sharpen her mind, make her think about what was said, instead of just accepting the familiar cadence of the words. He began to point out parts that he wanted her to read. He stayed clear of Revelation, the backbone of Father Rapp's theology, and asked her to read things like the Book of Ruth, the story of Jacob and Rebecca, the moving story of Christ's first miracle at the wedding of Cana. It was all very subtle, but he knew that Hildegarde would not be unaware of what he was pointing out.

Nor was she. The Scripture was about marriage, about love, about families. This was no worldly book, this was God's holy word, preserved that his children might obey him, might know him, might see him revealed. And yet the things she was reading were not in strict accordance with what Father Rapp said. A year ago, she would have pushed the book aside, thinking herself a sinner for not seeing the truth as Father Rapp saw it. But her faith in the old man had been shattered that day in the laboratory. Oh, she still loved and respected him but she no longer worshiped blindly at his feet. And so she read and she allowed her mind to grow.

She watched her mother. She had never known that so much devotion and unselfishness existed as she found in her mother's constant care. *No one*, thought Hildegarde soberly, *loves me in just that way. But I was born because my mother and father—because they married and succumbed to the flesh. Father Rapp says that's sin. But can sin possibly produce love like this? Her love is almost like the love of God. If it were sin which brought me to life, then—then—* and her thoughts trailed off into confusion. This was something which would take much wisdom to understand.

By early April, she was nearly well. She could be up and dressed for a few hours in the morning and late afternoon, and she was beginning to feel a little of the old energy running through her body. One blue and silver day, her mother decided it was warm enough to let her sit out in the yard. She brought out the big rocker for the girl, tucked her in warmly with coverlets and shawls and then went into the house. Hildegarde felt the sun on her head like a blessing and she let her eyes gaze in delight at the white clouds racing across the clear sky. The sound of voices brought her eyes back to earth, and she felt her heart jerk unexpectedly as she saw that it was Conrad who was coming along Kirkstrasse. He was accompanied by a small boy, one of the children the Society had adopted, and they had fishing poles over their shoulders. Conrad had something in his hand, and it was obvious he was heading for her house.

He pushed open the gate and his eyes widened in surprise at the sight of her. "Look here," he said. "The invalid is no longer an invalid but a healthy girl out in the sun."

She laughed. "It's wonderful to be outside. After awhile, the walls close in on me."

"I brought you something," Conrad said and held out his hand. He was holding a clump of pale pink, trailing arbutus.

With a cry of joy, she reached up to take the flowers. Her fingers were aware of the touch of Conrad's hand, but her mind was even more aware of his kindness. He knew how her heart yearned over flowers. She lifted the small, pale blossoms to her face and inhaled the delicate fragrance.

"They're beautiful," she said.

"To match the one who holds them," he said softly.

Her eyes slid toward the little boy, but the

child was interested in nothing but the promised fishing trip. He tugged at Conrad's sleeve.

"Come on," he said. "You promised. The fish are biting. You said."

"Yes, I'm coming," Conrad said. "Don't sit out too long," he said to Hildegarde, his voice a shade softer. "Don't get chilled."

"I won't," she promised. "Thank you for the flowers, and I hope you have good luck."

"Thank you," Conrad said gravely, "I already have."

She felt the color run into her face, as with a wave, the man and boy turned to leave the yard. Conrad looked back once as he latched the gate, and the look in his eyes was like a touch on her face. Then he turned, and putting his arm across the shoulders of the little boy, started toward the river.

Hildegarde felt something twist in her heart. *What if that were really his child,* she thought. *His child and mine? How gentle he is, how kind. What would it be like to be a wife—really a wife—and to have a child?* But she knew, even as she worded the question in her mind, that that was not what she meant. What she meant was, what would it be like to be Conrad's wife, to bear Conrad's child, to share Conrad's life, to talk to him knowing he cared what she said—to—to (she bent her hot face over the cool blossoms) to feel his arms around her and to rest against him without fear or guilt?

Chapter 22

May came up the Ohio valley with a wash of purple and white blossom, with smells that honeyed the air, with a greening that shook Hildegarde's heart. Her body was drunk with the return of health and strength, and her mind, freed from old confines, soared into dreams and imaginings and questions and hoped-for answers.

Conrad, who had known hours of anguish because of the recognition of the fact that he loved this girl as no Harmonist should, had healed himself with logic and prayer. Hildegarde's survival was living proof to him that God did not damn a man for loving. The prayers of the devout brethren, of the stern and pious old prophet had not broken the fever. But his declaration of love on the terrible night had been heard only by God, and Hildegarde had not died.

He had talked about it to only one person, the

man he respected and loved, Dr. Mueller. They sat up late one night, talking earnestly while the small lamp threw dark, moving shadows on the walls of the examining room.

"You really love her?" the doctor said. "You're no rash boy, you know. You've followed the rules for a long time—during the years when a boy suffers most from the purely biological urge to mate."

Conrad laughed softly. "Yes, I love her. It wasn't hard being a monk when—when I didn't know what it was to love a woman. I have no—how did you say it?—no mere biological urge to mate. I'm no bull bellowing for a female. But I love her and want her to be my wife—really my wife as God intended man and woman to be."

"Strong words, my son. The Father has a different interpretation of God's intent."

"The dual personhood of Adam?" Conrad said. "That in the creation Adam could have procreated himself—by himself? Like splitting in two? And Eve was an afterthought—a condescension of God to satisfy the sinful longing of his child? I may have believed it once—long ago, so long ago that I scarcely remember my gullibility. I've been reading, Brother. I've been reading the Bible in English. I no longer believe."

"Nor I." Dr. Mueller shook his head. "I've lived with celibacy so long that it no longer troubles me, one way or another. But I see what it's doing to the young—to you—to that girl you love."

"She was badly frightened by the business

with Jacob Klein. I'll have—have to win her slowly."

The doctor smiled sadly. "You may find she is warmer than you think, that little one. I've seen her look at you."

Conrad flushed as though he were a boy. He said nothing, and the doctor looked at him keenly.

"Can you leave this town? Are you willing to face the world, to compete with people who are greedy, ruthless, dishonest? You've known very little of that, you know."

"I know. It won't be easy to leave. Even if she'll go, and I don't know that she will. I confess I like the security of the Brotherhood, the warmth, the joint ownership of goods. I still think Christian men should be able to live as we do. But with marriage. With children."

"I agree," Dr. Mueller said. "What's more, I resent the fact that Father Rapp makes all major decisions, and my loyalty to him has been frayed a little at the seams. However, I grant that where ordinary marriage exists, there is also jealousy, infidelity, possessiveness. Celibacy—whether it is natural or not—does away with such dangers."

Conrad looked at the older man. "You neither support me nor condemn me, Brother. You don't even give me answers. You only pose more questions."

When the doctor finally spoke, his voice was very sad. "If I had any answers, my boy, I would apply them to my own life. You think I am old, settled, content. But I, too, wonder if this is truly the place to wait for Christ's coming—if, indeed, he is coming," he added after a very long silence.

There was no shock on Conrad's face. "'I know whom I have believed,'" he quoted softly. "If God condemned my love, she would have died. God listened to me—to me. I don't need any other proof."

"Nor any old man to give you answers," Dr. Mueller said. "Win her, if you can. I'll write a letter to my friend Ludwig Schaffheim in Wheeling, if you decide to leave. He'll find a place for you in his medical office as an assistant. He told me on my last trip that he was looking for a young man."

Conrad's eyes blazed. This removed his last doubt. If he could be sure of having work, if he could earn a living for Hildegarde so that she would not be deprived of the comforts she needed, then nothing could hold him. Nothing. Unless—unless Hildegarde could not leave this place. Or would not. He wouldn't even think of that.

He grasped Dr. Mueller's hand. "Thank you, Brother. All that I am—will ever be—is due to your teaching, your kindness."

"And the Society's discipline," the doctor said with no malice in his voice.

"Agreed," Conrad said soberly. "I'll never stop loving it. Maybe someday—if God wills—or Father Rapp softens his heart—we'll come back. But on our own terms, Brother. On our own terms."

Dr. Mueller laughed. "I may not be here when you do. But, before you come back, you have to leave, my son. You'd better get your rest, so your mind is clear and ready for conquest."

"I have your blessing then?"

The doctor's voice was suddenly heavy with weariness. "For what it's worth, you have my blessing. But I may be the worst sinner of the lot of us."

"Hardly," Conrad said, his face bright, his eyes confident. "I have my own definition of sin, and I'm afraid you don't fit it."

They never talked again, but from that night on, Conrad moved with purpose and conviction toward his goal. He took flowers to Hildegarde and the first wild strawberries that ripened in a sheltered place along the Beaver Road. He was aware of the fact that people were beginning to gossip. Jacob Henrici accused him once to his face of "lusting after that girl."

Conrad only laughed, meeting the eyes of the angry young zealot who accused him. "Be careful what you say, Brother," Conrad said lightly. "You may very well put ideas in my head which had never been there before."

He swung on his heel and walked away swiftly before Henrici could reply, but he was aware of a strange churning of fear and anger in him. If people were beginning to talk, he had to make his move. Nothing must frighten Hildegarde.

The following Wednesday, Conrad managed to be behind the Mutschler family as they left the church after the evening service. The summer twilight had darkened until it was difficult to see the features of faces, but it was still not dark enough to require torches. The lighter color of the streets showed dully against the grass.

Hildegarde's father left his women and walked ahead briskly with his son, eager to get home for a glass of wine and bed. It had been a long day in the fields. Hildegarde, her mother, and aunt walked along more slowly, enjoying the sweetness of the June night. People crowded the sidewalks, so it was not obvious when Conrad fell into step beside Hildegarde. For a few minutes, the other two women did not even notice him.

Hildegarde had been walking along in dreamy silence, thinking of Conrad, wondering what his answer would be to some of the statements that Father Rapp had made in church, knowing that Conrad would have disagreed with a few of the things, and feeling that she would agree with Conrad's interpretation. With the thought of him filling her mind, it was somehow quite natural to look up and see him beside her. They smiled at each other, and she felt only a contented serenity. It was like having her brother or her father beside her.

At that moment, Frau Mutschler looked up and saw Conrad. His eyes met hers over Hildegarde's head, and the older woman knew, in that brief exchange of looks, everything that Conrad wanted to say to her and dared not say. She put her hand under her sister-in-law's arm and spoke clearly, "Sister, let's walk a bit faster. I'm tired and want to get home."

The two women moved ahead, and Hildegarde made no move to follow them. Before she had time to question her instinct to stay beside the man who walked so close to her, she felt her hand taken in a close warm grip. The darkness of the summer night, and the swinging folds of her navy blue dress hid the clasped hands from the sight of anyone who might pass them, and she felt herself being drawn gently to the edge of the road, to the deeper shadows cast by the trees that grew along the street.

There was complete silence between them, but Hildegarde's calm serenity was shattered completely. She remembered the queer shivering that had gone up her arm the night young Lavasseur had kissed her hand at the ball, she remembered the shameful way her body had curved to Jacob's harsh kiss. But this feeling that now burst like an explosion in her was not really like either of those other things. This was not simply because a man was touching her. This was because Conrad was touching her. The excitement of the flesh was there—she could not deny it—but it was both muted and heightened by the knowledge that she was safe with this man, and that when he spoke, his mind would match her mind.

Still they walked in silence, slowly, and more slowly, until they were alone on the road. Fortunately, for Conrad, none of the men in authority came by. No one seemed to notice them as they finally came to a stop, deep in the shadows of a great elm tree.

"Hildegarde, meine leibling, do you know I love you?" he spoke in a breathless whisper. He had planned speeches of persuasion, arguments to defeat any objections she might raise; he had not planned this simple declaration of his heart.

She raised her eyes to him, and he could hardly see the oval blur of her face. "Yes," she said bravely and honestly. "I think I'm beginning to know."

"And?" he asked, not daring to say more. He pulled her hand up to his mouth and then held it hard against his chest, and she felt his heart racing under her palm.

"I don't understand love," she said hesitantly. "But I think about it all the time. If what I feel for you is love, then I love you, too."

"And what do you feel?" he asked softly, longing to kiss her, but holding down hard on his emotions.

"I love to be with you. I like—I love the way you think. I feel safer with you than anyone else. I—I got sick in the winter because I was walking in the snow looking for you. I discovered Father Rapp—well, was wrong, and I needed you."

He stood shaken and stunned. "You might have died," he said.

"But I didn't," she reminded him, and he heard the hint of laughter in her voice.

His voice was ragged. "Listen, my little one, listen to me. When a man loves a woman as I love you, he wants to marry her, he wants her—to have his children. Not like the Brotherhood. Like the world. Only blessed by God. Do you understand me?"

He felt rather than saw her nod. "We would have to leave," she said. "I see that."

"And would you?"

She was silent, but he felt her moving closer to him as though she were straining to see his face. "You would have to teach me," she whispered humbly.

"What I am going to do," he said breathlessly, "is not wrong, my darling. Can you believe me?"

"Yes," she said. "You've never lied to me yet."

He put his arms around her very gently and drew her closer to him until he felt the curved warmth of her body against him. He lowered his head and for the first time in his life, he felt a woman's lips under his. His gentleness, self-control, and great love were enough to keep him from being awkward or inept. His lips pressed warmly against hers, and he felt her split second of instinctive recoil—and then the miraculous softening and response, the pressure of her body against his and the tightening of her arms around his neck. For an eternity, they stood, drowned and oblivious in the shared loveliness of their first kiss. When she finally pulled away, it was only to speak. She stayed close in his arms.

"Is this love, then?" she said, her voice uneven but still holding the soft lilt of joy.

He was hardly able to speak. "This is part of

love," he said. "There are a thousand faces to love. This—the touching and the kissing—and the physical love which comes after kissing—and the talking and the thinking and the children that might be ours—and the praying when we need God."

"He won't desert us," she said, and he marveled that she should be the one who was trying to assure him. "I've tried to be a Harmonist, Conrad. I've tried, but I'm not—Brother Frederick is right. I'm not suitable."

"You're completely lovely," Conrad said fiercely.

She laughed gently, very conscious of the heady wonder of his hard body pressed against hers. "To you, perhaps. I think I was—oh, don't laugh at me—I think I was meant for this. Not just for the gardens and certainly not the laboratory and not for the Society's life with no marriage. But to be here—with you—in your arms. Is that wrong?"

His answer was to bend his mouth to hers, and once again, their kiss held them captive, whirling in a torrent of darkness and stars and the start of a passion that would blossom, with time, into a love that could only be changed by death.

"And you'll go?" he said at last.

"I'll go," she said without hesitation. "But not like Gertrude went—in secret and shame. My mother will know—I think she knows already—and—I'll even tell the Father."

"No, I'll tell him. That's my responsibility. But

what if he comes to you and argues and tells you that we are sinners in the eyes of God?"

She didn't answer glibly. She remembered too well how she had fallen at the old man's feet that bitter night; she knew how much she loved him still.

"I'll probably cry," she said honestly. "And I'll feel terrible, I suppose, but he won't change my mind, Conrad. Nothing—I give my pledge to you—in the sight of God—nothing can ever change my mind."

He knew she told the truth. She was right—she had been meant for him, for love, for human marriage. Great strengths had tried to force her into a pattern which did not fit, but they had not, in the end, been strong enough. She was what she was—lovely and merry and God's human child—free at last.

The Brotherhood would go on, and for some, it would be the answer to everything. But for Hildegarde and him, the lock had to be broken, wrenched from its clasp, and a path spread out before their feet.

"Maybe some day we can come back?" he said.

"Maybe," she said. "But never without each other."

"Never without each other," he agreed and bent once more to the warmth and sweetness of her kiss. After a long time, they walked together down the dark, deserted street, knowing that they need never walk alone or be lonely again.

Afterword

Hildegarde Mutschler and Conrad Feucht left Economy on June 25, 1829. Their first child, Tirzah, was born in Wheeling, West Virginia, in May 1830. Contrary to his usual custom, Father Rapp urged his people to pray that the straying couple might return to the fold. His persistent preference for the girl aroused much bitterness, but sometime before 1832, Conrad and Hildegarde returned to Economy. Whether or not the rigid rules were deliberately broken for them, no one can say, but they had two more children after they returned to the Brotherhood, and Conrad served both as doctor and as a business agent, so evidently he never lost his position of respect and honor.

During the time they were gone from Economy, a schism took place, and at least one-third of the people rejected Father Rapp's stern dictates and left the Society. Dr. Mueller was among those who left. It caused so much pain and bitterness that when Frederick died in 1834, there were many who felt he had died of a broken heart, brought on by the schism and dis-illusionment resulting from Father Rapp's stubborn defense of Hildegarde. In spite of these problems and the failure of the Second Coming to materialize, the Harmonist Society was not dissolved until 1906.

Hildegarde died in 1845, and Conrad lived only two years longer. Whether or not the members of the Divine Economy approved of these two running away to marry, no one doubted that their love was so deep that it was literally impossible for one to live without the other.

Other Living Books Bestsellers

THE BEST CHRISTMAS PAGEANT EVER by Barbara Robinson. A delightfully wild and funny story about what can happen to a Christmas program when the "horrible Herdman" family of brothers and sisters are miscast in the roles of the Christmas story characters from the Bible. 07–0137 $2.50.

ELIJAH by William H. Stephens. He was a rough-hewn farmer who strolled onto the stage of history to deliver warnings to Ahab the king and to defy Jezebel the queen. A powerful biblical novel you will never forget. 07–4023 $3.50.

THE TOTAL MAN by Dan Benson. A practical guide on how to gain confidence and fulfillment. Covering areas such as budgeting of time, money matters, and marital relationships. 07–7289 $3.50.

HOW TO HAVE ALL THE TIME YOU NEED EVERY DAY by Pat King. Drawing from her own and other women's experiences as well as from the Bible and the research of time experts, Pat has written a warm and personal book for every Christian woman. 07–1529 $2.95.

IT'S INCREDIBLE by Ann Kiemel. "It's incredible" is what some people say when a slim young woman says, "Hi, I'm Ann," and starts talking about love and good and beauty. As Ann tells about a Jesus who can make all the difference in their lives, some call that incredible, and turn away. Others become miracles themselves, agreeing with Ann that it's incredible. 07–1818 $2.50.

EVERGREEN CASTLES by Laurie Clifford. A heartwarming story about the growing pains of five children whose hilarious adventures teach them unforgettable lessons about love and forgiveness, life and death. Delightful reading for all ages. 07–0779 $3.50.

JOHN, SON OF THUNDER by Ellen Gunderson Traylor. Travel with John down the desert paths, through the courts of the Holy City, and to the foot of the cross. Journey with him from his luxury as a privileged son of Israel to the bitter hardship of his exile on Patmos. This is a saga of adventure, romance, and discovery — of a man bigger than life — the disciple "whom Jesus loved." 07–1903 $3.95.

WHAT'S IN A NAME? compiled by Linda Francis, John Hartzel, and Al Palmquist. A fascinating name dictionary that features the literal meaning of people's first names, the character quality implied by the name, and an applicable Scripture verse for each name listed. Ideal for expectant parents! 07–7935 $2.95.

Other Living Books Bestsellers

THE MAN WHO COULD DO NO WRONG by Charles E. Blair with John and Elizabeth Sherrill. He built one of the largest churches in America ... then he made a mistake. This is the incredible story of Pastor Charles E. Blair, accused of massive fraud. A book "for error-prone people in search of the Christian's secret for handling mistakes." 07–4002 $3.50.

GIVERS, TAKERS AND OTHER KINDS OF LOVERS by Josh McDowell. This book bypasses vague generalities about love and sex and gets right down to basic questions: Whatever happened to sexual freedom? What's true love like? What is your most important sex organ? Do men respond differently than women? If you're looking for straight answers about God's plan for love and sexuality then this book was written for you. 07–1031 $2.50.

MORE THAN A CARPENTER by Josh McDowell. This best selling author thought Christians must be "out of their minds." He put them down. He argued against their faith. But eventually he saw that his arguments wouldn't stand up. In this book, Josh focuses upon the person who changed his life — Jesus Christ. 07–4552 $2.50.

HIND'S FEET ON HIGH PLACES by Hannah Hurnard. A classic allegory which has sold more than a million copies! 07–1429 $3.50.

THE CATCH ME KILLER by Bob Erler with John Souter. Golden gloves, black belt, green beret, silver badge. Supercop Bob Erler had earned the colors of manhood. Now can he survive prison life? An incredible true story of forgiveness and hope. 07–0214 $3.50.

WHAT WIVES WISH THEIR HUSBANDS KNEW ABOUT WOMEN by Dr. James Dobson. By the best selling author of *DARE TO DISCIPLINE* and *THE STRONG-WILLED CHILD*, here's a vital book that speaks to the unique emotional needs and aspirations of today's woman. An immensely practical, interesting guide. 07–7896 $2.95.

PONTIUS PILATE by Dr. Paul Maier. This fascinating novel is about one of the most famous Romans in history — the man who declared Jesus innocent but who nevertheless sent him to the cross. This powerful biblical novel gives you a unique insight into the life and death of Jesus. 07–4852 $3.95.

BROTHER OF THE BRIDE by Donita Dyer. This exciting sequel to *THE BRIDE'S ESCAPE* tells of the faith of a proud, intelligent Armenian family whose Christian heritage stretched back for centuries. A story of suffering, separation, valor, victory, and reunion. 07–0179 $2.95.

LIFE IS TREMENDOUS by Charlie Jones. Believing that enthusiasm makes the difference, Jones shows how anyone can be happy, involved, relevant, productive, healthy, and secure in the midst of a high-pressure, commercialized, automated society. 07–2184 $2.50.

HOW TO BE HAPPY THOUGH MARRIED by Dr. Tim LaHaye. One of America's most successful marriage counselors gives practical, proven advice for marital happiness. 07–1499 $2.95.

Other Living Books Bestsellers

DAVID AND BATHSHEBA by Roberta Kells Dorr. Was Bathsheba an innocent country girl or a scheming adulteress? What was King David really like? Solomon — the wisest man in the world — was to be king, but could he survive his brothers' intrigues? Here is an epic love story which comes radiantly alive through the art of a fine storyteller. 07–0618 $3.95.

TOO MEAN TO DIE by Nick Pirovolos with William Proctor. In this action-packed story, Nick the Greek tells how he grew from a scrappy immigrant boy to a fearless underworld criminal. Finally caught, he was imprisoned. But something remarkable happened and he was set free — truly set free! 07–7283 $3.50.

FOR WOMEN ONLY. This bestseller gives a balanced, entertaining, diversified treatment of all aspects of womanhood. Edited by Evelyn and J. Allan Petersen, founder of Family Concern. 07–0897 $3.50.

FOR MEN ONLY. Edited by J. Allan Petersen, this book gives solid advice on how men can cope with the tremendous pressures they face every day as fathers, husbands, workers. 07–0892 $3.50.

ROCK. What is rock music really doing to you? Bob Larson presents a well-researched and penetrating look at today's rock music and rock performers. What are lyrics really saying? Who are the top performers and what are their life-styles? 07–5686 $2.95.

THE ALCOHOL TRAP by Fred Foster. A successful film executive was about to lose everything — his family's vacation home, his house in New Jersey, his reputation in the film industry, his wife. This is an emotion-packed story of hope and encouragement, offering valuable insights into the troubled world of high pressure living and alcoholism. 07–0078 $2.95.

LET ME BE A WOMAN. Best selling author Elisabeth Elliot (author of *THROUGH GATES OF SPLENDOR*) presents her profound and unique perspective on womanhood. This is a significant book on a continuing controversial subject. 07–2162 $2.95.

WE'RE IN THE ARMY NOW by Imeldia Morris Eller. Five children become their older brother's "army" as they work together to keep their family intact during a time of crisis for their mother. 07–7862 $2.95.

WILD CHILD by Mari Hanes. A heartrending story of a young boy who was abandoned and struggled alone for survival. You will be moved as you read how one woman's love tames this boy who was more animal than human. 07–8224 $2.95.

THE SURGEON'S FAMILY by David Hernandez with Carole Gift Page. This is an incredible three-generation story of a family that has faced danger and death — and has survived. Walking dead-end streets of violence and poverty, often seemingly without hope, the family of David Hernandez has struggled to find a new kind of life. 07–6684 $2.95.